A Killing Frost

By the same author

Novels

The Wheel
A Portion of the Wilderness
The Long Play
O Stranger the World
The Send Off
The Everything Man
The Pheasant Shoot
Blood Games

Short Stories

Scars and other Ceremonies

Biography

Letter to a Younger Son

The third day comes a frost,
a killing frost.

Shakespeare
King Henry VIII

To Peter

Part One

Sergeant Gordon Mason

1

Trained to be precise in all things, even in the killing of men, he stood behind the closed door of his room, his left arm raised, his watch inches from his face, and waited patiently for the minute-hand to reach the twelve. And then he moved.

He picked up his empty suitcase, stepped out into the corridor, closed the door behind him, and walked quickly towards the stairs. Even with the central-heating at its highest, there were still areas, away from the radiators, where coldness reminded him of what lay outside. But he was not concerned with winter – his purpose made its own season, and it was not cold.

Yet the warmth of his room, and that of the Sergeants' Block, had not prepared him for the intensity of what struck him as he stepped into the white afternoon. The cold seized upon his cheeks and his ears, and he gasped. It struck through the thick weave of his greatcoat and through the thin wool of his gloves. He was momentarily halted, as though under attack. The cold entered his mouth and stung the back of his throat. His eyes watered. The barracks, a patchwork of cleared paths and untouched, thickly-covered paradegrounds, melted. He stood and rubbed his eyelids, until, stronger now and more prepared, he set off for the Company Office.

Under a sky heavy with more snow, his was the only figure that moved. He was aware of the bright windows of the other blocks, the long lines of silent snow-covered trucks, the sharp glitter of coloured lights on the tall dark Christmas tree near the gate, but these were merely customary, a familiar backdrop. He shivered. Only the cold was different, fiercer than yesterday.

By the time he reached the Office, his face was a frozen mask. He kicked his shoes against the step, and the icy doorhandle burned through his glove. Inside, a jungle heat covered him, and he felt himself relax. He put the suitcase down, thumped his hands together and stamped his feet. Ahead of him, crouched over a three-bar electric fire was Lance-Corporal Hill, an old time-server with a ladder of good-conduct stripes on his creased right sleeve.

'He's not back yet, Sarge.'

Obsessional, tied to the plan, Mason swore.

'Where the hell is he?'

'Still over at the Mess, I suppose. It's only just gone three. You know *him*.' He grunted as he stood, folding the paper, the news of distant wars. 'Want a cup of tea? Coffee?'

'I want him here, that's all I want.'

'You're still going, then?' said the old soldier. 'You heard the forecast . . .?'

'Coffee,' said Mason. He pulled a chair from the wall, freed the buttons of his greatcoat, disclosing the blue of his dress uniform, sat down and brought out his cigarettes. 'Expect *us* to keep to the proper times, don't they?' He ducked his forage cap to the flame, shook the match, leaned forward and put it in the ashtray. 'They shout soon enough.'

'Heard the forecast?' said the lance-corporal, bad on his feet, shuffling, soon to leave the warm haven of the service, his hand slightly trembling as it spooned instant-coffee into two mugs decorated with the regimental crest. 'More snow, they say. Blizzards. Warning people not to travel.'

'I'm not going far,' said Mason. He heard the sound of boots outside on the step, a scraping. 'Hold the coffee. This might be him.'

He waited to see who entered, and then stood. He stubbed out his cigarette, and saluted.

Captain Bland, young, fresh-faced, a face blotched now with the cold and the effects of a good lunch and two double-brandies, returned the salute with a carefree wave of his gloved hand. He smiled with clean white teeth, a young smile.

'Needn't have killed your cigarette, Sergeant,' he said. 'Christmas is coming, the goose is getting fat . . . God, it's cold out there. Ah, coffee, Hill. Good man. Anything been happening?'

'No, sir,' said the old soldier.

'Join us, Sergeant?' said Captain Bland, pulling off his gloves.

'No, sir, if you don't mind,' said Mason. 'I've come for my pass and warrant.'

'So you have,' said the captain, the fumes of the brandy making him one with all men, *his* men. 'Didn't I sign them? You should have reminded me, Hill.'

'I did, sir.'

'You probably did. I should have remembered, Sergeant: you're the only madman that's venturing out this weekend. Get them for me, will you, Hill?' The kettle began to sing. 'I'll make the coffee. Sure you won't join us, Mason?'

'I won't, thank you, sir.'

'Petersfield, isn't it?' said the captain, lifting the kettle: 'where you're going?'

'Yes, sir.'

'But your home's in . . . no, don't tell me. I have a memory for these things. Chester. Right?'

'Yes, sir.'

'Two sugars, Hill?' said Captain Bland. He sat on the edge of the table. 'You look very smart, Mason. Not that you ever look anything different, of course. Special occasion?'

'You could say that, sir.'

'Not many trains running, you know that?' said the captain. 'Ah, thank you, Hill.' He put down his coffee. 'Pen, please.' He signed both papers with a flourish, and handed them to Mason. 'You should get yourself a wife, Sergeant. Married accommodation. No Petersfield this weekend, or Chester over Christmas. Living on site isn't too bad, you know. Well, have a good weekend, whatever it is you're doing. I'll see you on Monday, seven on the dot. I'm Orderly Officer.'

'Seven on the dot, sir,' said Mason. 'Thank you.' He closed his wallet on the papers, rebuttoned his pocket and then his greatcoat, picked up his suitcase, and again saluted. 'Goodbye, sir.'

He had wasted five minutes waiting for Bland, and now he almost ran through the darkening afternoon, along black, slippery paths, past piled snow that shone with a blueish light. His breath went before him, into the armoury.

He walked down the chill stone corridor towards the steel door. He pressed the bell and looked up at the lens of the closed-circuit camera. There was a whisper of static, and a voice said:

'Yes?'

'Sergeant Mason,' he said, and gave the day's password: 'Rifleman.'

There was another, softer whisper, and the right-hand division of the steel door swung open. He stepped into a smell of warm metal, and to the sound of a radio. The door closed silently behind him. He walked to the counter, and Corporal Timms. Behind that round, slightly-sweating bespectacled face were ranks of weapons, gleaming, clean and ready.

4

He put his suitcase on the counter.

'Okay,' he said. 'Let's have it.'

There was a pause. The corporal's radio played on: a tinny country-and-western.

'Come on, man,' said Mason. 'I haven't got a lot of time.'

'I don't know, Sarge,' said Timms.

'What don't you know?'

'About letting you have it.'

'We've been all over that,' said Mason. 'It'll be back here, Sunday night. Maybe earlier.'

'They might spring a spot-check . . .'

Mason sighed.

'I'm signing for it, Timms,' he said. '*Signing*. Got that? Any comeback — it's me they're after.'

The pale, anxious eyes behind the glasses considered him.

'If you'd tell me what it's for, Sarge . . .'

'Now look, Timms,' said Mason. 'I'm ordering you now. Not asking. *Ordering*. I want a Sterling and a full magazine. *Now*.' He glanced at the small black transistor. 'And could we have that off?'

The corporal leaned over, and now there was silence. It unnerved Timms: he never liked this duty, sitting alone with black, voiceless weaponry for company.

'All right, Sarge,' he said. 'But you take full responsibility.'

'I said I'd do that from the start.'

Timms stepped away from the counter and went into the maze of grey metal shelving. Mason opened his suitcase. The corporal returned with a Sterling sub-machine gun. He put it alongside the suitcase, together with an empty magazine and a box of .9 mm shells.

'You want the bayonet as well?' he said.

Mason smiled.

'No,' he said. 'I won't need the bayonet.'

He picked up the lightweight, thinly-oiled gun and tested the mechanism. Satisfied, he put it down, opened the box, and filled the magazine with swift, practised movements. He clipped the magazine to the side of the gun, checked that it fitted snugly, and unclipped it. He put both gun and magazine into the suitcase, and closed the lid. Still smiling, he snapped home the locks.

'Thank you,' he said. 'I'll sign now.'

Timms filled in the details, twisted the pad to face the sergeant, and held out the pen. Mason wrote his careful, deliberate signature.

5

He put down the pen and lifted the suitcase.

'Thanks again, Timms,' he said. 'Don't worry. See you Sunday. I'll find you. You can have your radio on again.'

'It'll be Frazer, Sunday,' said Timms.

'I'll find *you*,' said Mason. 'Not Frazer. Let's keep it in the family.'

The corporal inspected the signature.

'You do what you like,' he said.

Mason leaned across the counter and switched on the radio.

'Listen to your music, Timms,' he said. 'Now let me out.'

The door closed silently. No longer able now to hear the radio, he walked swiftly along the corridor, and into that freezing air.

2

Between the Christmas tree and the gate stood a tall mirror. A notice, hung with holly, said: *Are you looking your best?* He saw himself stride past, a lean, cold-pinched figure, making for the hard ice of the street. No one saw him go – the guard reading a paperback in his warm hut. Out there, in west London, store windows blazed with tinsel, the glass patterned with tame snow made of wool. A week to go, and people were everywhere, swirling around him. All the taxis were taken, and he had to walk to Sloane Square to find one. He watched the thin white hand of the fur-coated woman count the fare into the driver's palm, stood aside to let her pass, returned the slight smile, and ducked into a warmth still heavy with her perfume.

'Nice bit of stuff,' said the driver.

'Waterloo Station,' said Mason.

The driver, waiting for the lights to change, craned his head and looked through his steamy window at the sky.

'More to come, pal,' he said.

'Yes,' said Mason, sitting back in almost evening-dark, gloved hands crossed over the suitcase.

The lights changed, and the taxi moved unhindered for a few seconds, then joined the long queue heading for Hyde Park Corner.

'Traffic's murder,' said the driver. 'I'd try the back doubles, but it's just as bad there.'

Mason did not comment.

6

'Going home for Christmas, Sarge?'

'No. Just the weekend, this time.'

'I spent a Christmas in Monte Cassino, you know that?' said the driver. 'Never thought Italy'd be that cold.'

Mason let him go on, half-listening at first, and then not listening, watching the white-blue acres of Green Park come and go; and then St James's, strings of light over black water; and then Westminster Bridge and the whole of London crouched low under an iron sky.

The first flakes began as the taxi took the rise to the black girders of the station.

'Kids'll enjoy themselves,' said the driver, giving Mason his change. 'Got any, Sarge?'

'No,' said Mason. He shivered, out from the warmth of the cab.

'A kids' time, really,' said the driver. 'Right?'

'Right,' said Mason. He handed back a fifty-pence piece, and turned away.

'Thanks, pal,' said the driver. 'All the best.'

Mason walked into the high halls of the station, to notices saying *Due To Severe Weather Conditions* and *Cancellations* and *Restricted Service*. He crossed to the Departures board, and looked up. Few trains were running, the board was almost empty. There was one leaving for Portsmouth at 4:10 from Platform 9, calling at all stations. It would have to do.

He went into the station bar and got himself a lager. He sat down at a red circular table, and put the suitcase beside him on the long seat. He drank some of the lager, put down the glass, took off his cap and unbuttoned his greatcoat.

A drunk offered to buy him a drink, but he refused, sitting there, waiting for his train: a thin, dark man with close-cropped black hair, a sergeant going home on Christmas leave, that suitcase on which his left hand rested so protectively, full of presents for his wife and children, travelling to preside over turkey and the needs of flushed-faced relatives . . .

Outside, in high loudspeakers, taped carols began: echoing in the curving, darkening roof, the voices hollowed and made strangely inhuman, singing of peace and goodwill to all men.

Simon and Anita Silverman

1

He had told them to make a giant sun, and they made it with
contrasting materials: polystyrene, lino offcuts, balsa wood, clay,
drinking-straws, beads, perspex and broken ceramic tiles. Then
they sprayed it with gold paint. But what it lost in texture, it gained
in fire and awesomeness. Now it hung there, at the far end of the
studio, its rays spanning the wall and almost touching the ceiling
and the floor. It was magnificent, it glowed, it warmed the long,
white-walled room, and, as he finished the letter, folding the single
sheet into the envelope and sealing the flap, he acknowledged the
golden disc as a symbol of wholeness, completeness, a spur to this
final, irrevocable decision.

He turned the envelope over, and wrote: *The Principal.* Standing
now from his desk, holding the letter in both hands, he acknowledged another sun: that which burned in the flesh of the
West Indian model, who, naked on the dais, met his eyes and raised
her dark brows. He looked at the clock above the door: 12:50.

'Okay,' he said. 'That's it. Rest, please, Miss Jones.'

As the girl began slowly to unlock her limbs, the students sat
back from their boards or stepped away from their easels. Still
holding the envelope, he moved among them, commenting on what
they had done, until the last had gone, and the studio was empty,
save for himself and the girl dressing behind the screen; and the
glowing, giant sun.

She came out, ready for the street. And, dressed, she was almost
commonplace: all that beauty hidden.

'Will you do my timetable, Simon?' she said, her voice a mixture
of Freetown and Brixton.

'I have already, Gloria,' he said. 'It's on the shelf, there.'

'Thank you.'

He went back to his desk.

'Oh, and, Gloria . . .' he said.

The edges of her long red scarf drifted as she turned. He took the
chocolates from the drawer, and held them out.

'You never forget, do you, Simon?' she said, and smiled. 'And I
never get you anything.'

He wanted to tell her that this was the last time, that it would never happen again. But he said:

'Your beauty is gift enough . . .'

She leaned forward and kissed his cheek.

'Thank you,' she said. 'Merry Christmas.'

'You, too.'

He followed her out, and switched off the lights. They walked together to the stairs, where they parted: she to the Bursar, he to the Staffroom. He had cleared his pigeon-hole the previous day – now there was only his briefcase and coat to collect. As he opened the door to leave, he brushed against Tom Stafford, the potter, who was entering.

'Off sharpish, aren't you, Simon?' said Stafford, hands and smock white with dried clay. 'You'll be at the *Drovers*'?'

'Not this time, Tom.'

'Come on, we always . . .'

'I can't, this time: I'm going down to my daughter's today.'

'You can spare . . .'

'I can't, Tom. Sorry. Give my apologies to the others. I'll see you around.'

He fought against a tide of students, and reached the Principal's office.

The secretary's chair was vacant. He leaned across her desk and rested the envelope on her typewriter. He heard voices and laughter from the inner room, and began to make his escape. But he was not quick enough. The door opened and Miss Bothwell appeared, carrying the first of her seasonal sherries. Behind her was a smiling Derek Fielder, grey suit, grey bow-tie, grey hair, red glistening face: the Principal. He, too, carried a full glass.

'Just in time, Simon,' said Fielder. 'Go in and help yourself.'

'No thank you,' said Silverman. 'I was just leaving . . .'

'Did you want me?'

'No . . .'

'Skulking off and leaving this, were you, Mr Silverman?' she said, holding up the envelope.

'Oh God,' said Fielder: 'not another requisition, Simon. Don't spoil my Christmas, there's a good chap.'

'It's not a requisition,' said Silverman. 'Do you mind if I go now? I . . .'

'Hang on, hang on,' said the Principal. He put down his glass

9

and reached for the letter. 'What's the rush? Another plea for Headly, is it?' Silverman watched him open the envelope. Silence. Miss Bothwell, straight and thin behind her desk, sipped her sherry. He wondered, not for the first time, what *she* was like under her clothes; if anyone had ever cupped those small, puritan breasts: strange woman for the liberty-hall of an art school . . . The Principal finished reading, and looked up. He was no longer smiling. 'Would you care to step into my office for a moment, Simon?'

Silverman was tempted to say no. He had hoped to be away and clear by now, spared this confrontation. But he followed the grey suit and the red neck and the grey curling hair into that panelled quietness.

'Close the door, Simon. I insist you have a drink.'

'If you insist.'

'Sit down, Simon . . .'

Silverman took the armchair by the window. The sky over the leafless trees of the courtyard was several shades darker than the suit. He put his briefcase on the floor, and draped his coat over his thighs. Waited, hands resting lightly on the thick tweed. He took the cold glass.

'Thank you,' he said. 'Cheers.'

'Cheers to you,' said the Principal. He sat down behind his desk and put the letter on his blotter. He drank some of his sherry. 'Now, what's all this about?'

'I think it's pretty straightforward,' said Silverman. 'This is my last day.'

'It can't be your last day,' said Fielder. 'You have a contract: a term's notice. Not to mention your responsibility to your students. Look, I'm sorry about the Headly business, Simon. Perhaps I acted too . . . hastily. He can come back after Christmas. The suspension might have done some good.'

'It's not Headly, Derek. Nothing to do with you, or the school. I'm getting out.'

'Just like that?'

'Just like that.'

'Why?'

'I've had enough, that's all. I'm finished with teaching. Thirty years is a long time.'

'And you'll do what?'

'I'll paint.'

10

'Paint? You'll *paint*?'

'All the time.'

The Principal finished his sherry, half-rose to get another, but changed his mind.

'Does Anita agree with this?' he said.

'She doesn't know. Yet.'

'You haven't discussed it with her?'

'No.'

Fielder thought of that small, constrained, respectable, convention-loving woman. He made a steeple of his fingers and rested his chin on the point.

'You're going to have yourself a time, aren't you?'

'She'll come around.'

'And if she doesn't?'

A silence. In the pause they both heard singing from the courtyard: students celebrating early.

'Then I'll leave her,' said Silverman, and was surprised at his own calmness; then by a sudden surge of happiness. 'Yes, I'll leave her.'

Fielder looked over his steeple at a good teacher, but a romantic fool. He saw a big man in clothes that always seemed too small for that wrestler's body. He saw a dark-bearded Jew, with fine eyes; thinning, grizzled hair, big hands, capable. A man too involved with the private lives of his students – witness the Headly affair, the boy arriving drunk, destroying the peace of the Life Room. A loss, if he went. Not that it would be hard to replace him: London was full of artists crying out for part-time teaching.

'How old are you, Simon?' he said.

Silverman drained his glass.

'I'll have another, if I may.'

'Help yourself.'

Silverman let his coat drop to the carpet, stepped over it, and crossed to the sideboard.

'You know damn well how old I am,' he said, lifting the decanter.

'I know you're in your fifties, but I . . .'

'Fifty-nine,' said Silverman.

'Gauguin was younger,' said Fielder.

Silverman laughed. He turned and leaned against the sideboard.

'I'm not doing a Gauguin,' he said. 'Paddington's not the South Seas.'

'You couldn't make a living as a painter,' said Fielder. 'Who does, these days? Christ, look around you . . .'

'Who's talking about making a living?' said Silverman. He drank the sherry in one long swallow. 'I don't want to discuss it, Derek. I'm sorry, but I . . .'

'Have you told any of your students?'

'No. You're the only one who knows, at the moment.' He went back to his coat and picked it up. 'Merry Christmas.'

'Give me a ring after the holiday, Simon,' said Fielder. 'Say the twenty-seventh. At home. Or, better, come over and have dinner.'

'I can't,' said Silverman. 'Carol, my daughter, is having a baby. We're going down there today. I don't expect to be back until the New Year. Then I'll tell Anita.'

'I don't envy you.'

'You should,' said Silverman. He picked up his briefcase, stepped to the table, and held out his hand. 'No hard feelings?'

'Of course there are hard feelings — leaving it this late.'

'I wasn't completely certain myself, until this morning.'

Fielder stood up. Behind him the sky was almost black. He took Silverman's hand, and released it.

'I'll contact you before term starts, Simon.

'You know you can't leave it that late. You'd better start thinking of someone else.'

'I will contact you, anyway. Anita may convince you otherwise.'

'Not any more,' said Silverman. 'Goodbye, Derek. What must be done, must be done.'

'Have you thought of what this will do to your pension rights?' said Fielder.

Silverman, his hand on the doorknob, looked back. He laughed again.

'Did Gauguin?' he said, and opened the door.

2

Anita Silverman switched off the antique vacuum-cleaner. It coughed and whirred to silence. She rested against the wall, and looked at the tidy living-room. Nothing she did ever made the place look anything other than temporary. Nothing here reflected her personality. The compromises: they alone were hers. She realised that now. But with the realisation came not a loss of hope, but a sudden bitter rebellion. Things would change in the New Year: a fresh start. New furniture, even if it had to be bought on hire-purchase. A new bed. The whole place decorated for Spring. White and yellow. Yes.

She picked up the vacuum-cleaner and carried it to the kitchen. *Kitchen*? A box overlooking the skein of tracks leading into Paddington Station. How dark everything was. Oh for some sun, an end to winter. She shut the cupboard door and took off her apron. The telephone rang in the small hall.

Looking into the square mirror above the hall table, she saw again the deep lines about her mouth, sighed, and lifted the receiver.

'Four seven three,' she said.

'It's Carol.'

'Hallo, dear. How are you?'

'Fine. Look, Mum, you don't have to come.'

'We're coming. It's all arranged. I'm just waiting for your father.'

'But the weather . . . Things look awful here. Have you heard the forecast?'

'When are they ever right?' said her mother. 'No, don't you worry. We'll get a taxi from the station. See you about five.'

'Are you sure?'

'Yes, of course. You want us, don't you? Both of you?'

'Yes, you know we do. But you could leave it till next week. The weather may . . .'

'No, let's stick to what we said, Carol. I'm looking forward to seeing you. It seems ages. Around five.'

A silence.

'All right, Mum. But take care.'

'I will, dear. Bye-bye.'

She put the phone down, reached out a hand, and switched on the hall light. In that hard white glare she looked again at her face. Where had the fresh girl that was herself at Carol's age, where had she gone? Who was this lined, worried-looking stranger? Where was the fire and hope of those early years, the . . .

A key turned in the lock, and he entered. He looked cold but cheerful, and he carried his briefcase and a bottle-shaped parcel.

'Free, free at last!' he cried. He kissed her cheek with cold lips.

13

She sniffed. 'No, I didn't go to the *Drovers'*. I came straight home.'

'What's that?' she said, tapping the parcel with one finger.

'Champagne,' he said.

She turned away from him.

'You're mad,' she said. 'Absolutely mad.'

He followed her into the living-room. It was too tidy, straight lines everywhere, ordered.

'You won't begrudge your daughter champagne for her first-born?' he said.

'I begrudge your extravagance, Simon,' she said. 'But let's not start that again. Carol's just phoned. She's worried about the weather. I've done some sandwiches and a flask of coffee. We can eat in the train.'

'Anything you say, my love,' he said. 'I'll just go and get changed.'

He put the briefcase and the parcel on the table, took off his coat and jacket, and went into the bedroom. She stood there, her finger-tips resting on the table. She reached out and unwrapped the bottle. She looked from its richness to the battered furniture, and on to the bedroom.

'Absolutely mad,' she said softly. She raised her voice. 'Did you see Derek about doing extra lessons after Christmas, Simon?'

'He wasn't available,' he said, coming bare-chested, passing through to the bathroom. He smiled. 'Let's not talk about that now. Let's enjoy our daughter. Right? I won't be long.'

Half an hour later they were riding in the bus to Waterloo Station, the single suitcase stowed in the luggage-space under the stairs; the champagne, in its tissue and festive wrapping, cradled in his gloved hands: promise of celebration, birth of another life, a new beginning.

Ambrose Calvin alias Jake Barnes

His back to the snowy wastes of Hyde Park, the dark leafless trees, he rested against the hard iron rail of the fence and looked across swift-flowing traffic to the tall hotel. How it had glowed in the past, on those long lonely night-walks, the day's writing done, the city opening like a jungle or a paradise, the hotel a giant liner beached at the end of Park Lane, alive with lights! And he had passed it then, and hungered for what lay behind the elegant doorman: the bars, the restaurants, the suites, the penthouse from whose wide windows you could see the Serpentine, even the Round Pond in Kensington Gardens, a wink of light before the hazy end of the capital. A prize to be won – and today was the day.

As he watched, he saw a taxi swing towards the entrance. He saw the doorman step forward. And when the taxi pulled away, Mark Weaver, his agent, stood waiting before the tall golden doors.

Calvin, in the past, would have called, shouted a greeting. The young, untried Calvin would have done so, loping through the traffic, waving. Not any more. Too much had been done, too many bad times weathered. Too many promises, broken. Instead, now, he went circumspectly, as befitted a man heading for perhaps the biggest moment of his life. Walked slowly, as cars swirled around him, so calmly that Weaver had time to watch him coming, and to marvel at the man's restraint, remembering other times, other enthusiasms.

'Ambrose!' he said. 'Good to see you.'

'Hallo, Mark,' said Calvin. How direct were the agent's eyes now! How firm and confident and almost loving the handshake! 'Long time.'

'We always knew it would happen, one day,' said Weaver, leading the way.

The doorman pulled at the great golden handle. Warm perfumed air took away winter's reality. So this was how it looked inside: the spacious lobby, the discreet amber lights, carpets to drown in.

'*I* always knew it would happen,' said Calvin.

Weaver patted his arm. Smiled.

'Agents have to be cautious, Ambrose. So many come and go, promising riches.'

'True,' said Calvin.

He followed the agent to the reception-desk. The girl's make-up was perfect. As was the smile: a light to Arab princes and movie stars and the oppressed rich.

'Mr Brady, please,' said Weaver. 'I have an appointment.'

'Your name, sir?' The voice was colourless, smoothed, ironed, with a touch of starch.

'Mark Weaver.'

'Will you take the lift, sir? Suite 42. Fourth floor.'

The liftman was small and old, in a green uniform that was just a shade too big. Calvin looked at the white hair, the slightly bowed shoulders. The small hands in white gloves. The floors ticked by. He thought of the restroom in the bowels of the hotel: cheese sandwiches, a nap taken over the daily paper; home to a high-rise flat in Battersea.

'Fourth,' said the man, turning that white head and smiling.

'Thank you,' said Calvin. Did the arrogantly successful tip?

The two men walked along the wide, green, silent corridor.

'No wise words?' said Calvin.

'Let me handle him,' said the agent.

'Met him before, have you?'

'No. But I know the type.'

'Do I play the shy, untried boy . . .?'

'Just be your usual charming self.'

He tapped on the door of Suite 42. They waited. Complete silence. The door opened. A young man in casual blues smiled.

'Ray Dexter,' he said. 'Irwin's runaround.' He stepped back. 'Come in.'

Envy burned in Calvin. He had seen the room in many a movie, he was aware of the lead behind the gold; but still he burned.

The young man in blue went before them noiselessly into the living-room. Flowers were everywhere, masking the hard city glimpsed through tall, thin white curtains.

'Mr Weaver and Mr Calvin,' he said.

2

Irwin Brady stayed in the armchair. He held out a pale, speckled hand.

'Little back trouble here,' he said. 'Forgive me. It'll pass.' The hand was withdrawn, to return to rest on clean, sharply-creased, grey slacks. 'Make yourselves at home.'

The armchair seemed to swallow Calvin, and to go on swallowing. He clutched at the flowered arms, and braced his legs. He was very conscious of the newness of his shoes: that bright, shining chestnut-brown against the dark green.

'I've taken the liberty of ordering lunch up here,' said Brady. 'Just cold cuts and salad. I hope that's okay. I don't eat much in the middle of the day.'

'You don't each much, period,' said Dexter.

The man in the grey shirt, shining bald head, large frog-eyes, speckled face and hands, grunted.

'Get the people some drinks,' he said. 'You want a drink, Calvin?'

'Whisky,' said Calvin. 'A large one. Ice, a touch of soda.'

The liquid frog-eyes considered him. The full lips pursed, the hands twitched.

'You a real drinker?' said Brady. 'Put much away?'

'No,' said Calvin. 'I just felt like . . .'

'Do nothing to excess,' said Brady. 'Your body's a temple, remember that.' He grinned suddenly, and was human. 'Mine's a mite rickety at this moment, but don't let it fool you. Weaver?'

'The same,' said the agent from the depths of his own chair.

'The big drinkers,' said Brady. He shifted his head to look at Dexter. 'Give them what they want; then check on the food, right?'

'Right,' said the youth.

When Dexter had gone, Brady watched them drink.

'Nothing for you?' said Weaver.

Brady tapped that wide brow.

'Mind as sharp as a razor. I don't dull it. I leave that to the men I'm dealing with. Ha.' He swung his head at Calvin, and eased his back deeper into his chair. Still not comfortable, he heaved himself to a more upright position. 'Liked your book, Calvin.'

'Thank you.'

'Fine imagination working there,' said Brady. He winced, and cursed softly. 'Experienced any of what you wrote?'

17

'No.'

Brady laughed.

'Not even the sex?'

'Not that kind,' said Calvin.

'Ha.' He glanced at Weaver, and back again. 'What's this guy told you, Calvin?'

'I've told him . . .' began the agent.

'I'm asking the creator, not the opportunist,' said Brady. 'What's he told you?'

Dexter peered around the door.

'Food's on its way, Irwin.'

'Fine, fine,' said Brady. 'Well, Calvin?'

'Only that you're interested in buying the film rights. That's all.'

'I did intend . . .' began the agent again.

'Leave it be, Weaver,' said Brady. 'He tell you we want a few changes?'

Calvin looked across at Weaver. The agent gave a wide, over-friendly smile, and lifted his glass.

'No,' said Calvin. 'He didn't tell me that.'

'Would you object?' said Brady. 'Some writers think they're God Almighty.'

'It depends on what you want changing,' said Calvin. The whisky was getting to him, working on an empty stomach, and he told himself to keep clear-headed.

'We want Stanhope to be a three-foot black dwarf,' said Brady. A great roar of laughter shook that heavy frame. 'Okay, okay, a little joke there . . .'

'A little one for sure,' said Dexter, lounging against the doorframe.

'Earn your money, Ray,' said Brady. 'Go meet the food.'

'Yes, Master,' said the youth, and went away.

'We want to change the location to the States,' said Brady. 'Alabama . . . Georgia – some such.'

Calvin looked at his agent. Weaver still had that fixed, sunny smile.

'I'd have thought the situation particularly English,' said Calvin, seeing that hard Northern coast dissolve, the gaunt house he had created and lived in for two years, filling with white-suited Southerners . . .

'Hell, no!' said Brady. 'Humanity ain't that different. People are the same all over. The same terrors, the same alarms. If you prick us, do we not bleed? The world's a bus-stop.' He smiled. 'How's that for a title?'

'But the customs of the country . . .' began Calvin.

'No, Ambrose, I can see it,' said Weaver, trying to make a frame with his hands, encumbered by his drink. 'After all, it's a universal theme . . .'

'Sure,' said Brady. 'Yorkshire or Georgia . . .'

'It was Northumberland,' said Calvin.

'Names, names,' said Brady, dismissing the correction. 'They don't matter a damn. It's the people.'

'Then why not England?' said Calvin.

'We going to have trouble with you?' said Brady.

'Of course not, Mr Brady,' said Weaver, giving his client a swift, warning look, which was not lost on the producer. 'Too much is at stake. Right, Ambrose?'

Calvin was silent. He looked into his glass, and finished his drink.

'Another?' said Brady.

'Why not?' said Calvin.

The producer nodded and smiled.

'Go to it.'

As Calvin fought to free himself from the armchair, Dexter entered, pushing a loaded, gleaming trolley which moved silently to the table near the window, and stopped. The youth turned, took a stiff white cloth from the lower shelf of the trolley, and said:

'Gentlemen?'

'Sure, let's eat,' said Brady, and began to heave himself painfully from his chair.

'Here, let me help you,' said Weaver, putting down his drink.

Brady looked up.

'No, Calvin's on his feet. Give a hand here, will you?'

Calvin looked down at that fleshy, shining face. There was a pause. Then he grasped the warm, shirt-sleeved arm, and pulled.

'Goddam back,' said Brady. He arched his body, and patted Calvin's shoulder. 'Thanks, friend.' He nodded at Dexter. 'You may begin, slave.'

The youth served them, poured the chilled white wine, and left for a more substantial lunch in the Steak Room. Calvin ate hungrily. The food was excellent: crisp and fresh, more than enough for three.

They ate in silence for a while. Facing the window, Calvin looked out at a city that was now his own.

'A happy man?' said Brady.

'What?' said Calvin.

'You were smiling.'

Calvin moistened his dry lips. Made at ease by the drink, he was still cautious.

'A new experience,' he said.

'Eating?' said Brady.

'Bartering.'

'Hell, who's bartering?' said Brady. 'The price has been fixed. Right, Weaver?'

Calvin waited in the silence. A shred of beef had lodged between his teeth, and he probed at it with his tongue, mouth closed, looking out at the park, but not seeing it.

'Eighty thousand,' said the agent.

Calvin was surprised at his own calmness. The shred was free now, and he washed it down with some wine.

'Pounds?' he said.

'Dollars,' said Brady. 'It ain't *Gone With The Wind*.'

'So why are we here?' said Calvin.

'I was going to tell you how much, Ambrose,' said Weaver. 'Don't be difficult.'

'Who's difficult?' said Calvin.

'So you're happy?' said Brady. He pushed his hand across the table. 'A deal?'

'Do I have any say in the script?' said Calvin.

'No,' said Brady, patiently, withdrawing his hand, picking up his fork and spearing a small potato. 'Leave it to the boys who know.'

'Northumberland to Georgia,' said Calvin, leaning back, relaxed, a man with forty thousand pounds, all horizons gone. 'I can live with that.'

'Sure,' said Brady. The smile was thin, the eyes knowing. He speared another potato.

'Anything else?' said Calvin.

'Just the signing.'

'I mean – any other changes?'

'You can buy a lot of time with eighty thousand dollars, Ambrose,' said Weaver.

'Less commission,' said Calvin. 'Less tax.' He helped himself to more wine. 'Well?'

Brady put down his fork, eased his back, and rested his hands in his lap.

'It's a great book, Calvin,' he said. 'But we don't like Stanhope going off his rocker.'

Calvin gave a short laugh. The room was suddenly very warm, his mouth drying.

'You see any other way?' he said.

'Sure,' said Brady. 'I got a very capable man working on it at the moment, back home. We see Stanhope surviving. To fight another day, as it were. We see him handing over the house and the land, and letting the others squabble over it. He's free, he's kept his integrity, he can look at them from afar – he's a whole man.'

'But the whole book's a charting of his collapse,' said Calvin. 'It's built up, chapter by chapter. It's a tragedy: a man broken by his own apartness, his own . . . inhumanity.'

'Maybe so,' said Brady. He cut into some meat, ate it, and pointed his fork. 'Listen, Calvin, we're buying an idea. A framework. The book's still yours – nothing can change that. And, like the man said: you can buy a lot of time with eighty grand.'

'Yes, I know, but . . .'

'For Christ's sake, don't give me the enraged creator bit,' said Brady.

'They're still using your title, Ambrose,' said Weaver. 'I can tie in a very lucrative paperback deal, once this is settled. The good times are beginning, believe me.'

Down there, in the park, in the winter cold, a younger Ambrose Calvin was looking across at the bright hotel. The older Calvin raised his full glass.

'Okay,' he said. 'To the book of the film.'

And everyone smiled.

3

At the station he opened the door of a phone-booth, and stepped inside. There was a smell of dead air, and the floor was littered with empty packs and the ends of burned matches. He had known a niggling dissatisfaction since leaving the hotel, but now, as he dialled, he was aware of a growing excitement. Her voice, when she answered, was tired, and he could hear the noise of his children. And then she came alive.

'How much?' she said.

'Tell you when I see you,' he said. 'I want to see your face.'

'Oh, tell me now.'

'No, later. I'm at Waterloo. I'm catching the 4:10. It's a slow: calling at all stations. I'll be late . . .'

'Isn't the weather awful?' she said.

He smiled at himself in the dusty mirror.

'Not any more,' he said.

Laura Stone

1

She stood there, helping, her left hand cupped over the girl's forehead, looking away, and trying not to listen. But at last it was over, and that white, drained face, that callow, inexperienced face, moved out of her hand, and looked up.

'I'm sorry, Miss Stone.'

'It doesn't matter, Janet,' she said. 'It happens to all of us.' She pulled two paper towels from the wall. 'Here.'

The girl wiped her mouth, and then her eyes.

'I can't imagine it happening to you,' she said. 'Ever.'

'Oh, it did, believe me,' said Laura. 'Once. Feel better?'

'Yes. Yes, thank you.'

'Rinse your mouth out. And I think I have a peppermint in my bag.'

The girl spat out the water, wiped her mouth once again, and straightened.

'Ready for all emergencies,' she said.

'I always am,' said Laura.

'Ugh,' said the girl. 'I've got some on me.' She dabbed at her skirt. 'My mother will kill me. And I was so looking forward to this. Now look at me. Everyone will know.'

'They don't need to,' said Laura. 'And what if they do? You conducted yourself very well.'

'Yes, I did, didn't I,' said the girl. 'Managed to get in here in time: just.' She unwrapped the peppermint and put it in her mouth. 'Thanks again, Miss Stone. Sorry for the bother.'

'I don't think you should have any more to drink.'

'Oh, I won't. You can bet on that. I'm going home.'

'The best thing you can do,' said Laura. 'And a little tip, Janet: another time, get some milk into you before you start. Half a pint, or more. It lines the stomach. A tip from an old AA member.'

The girl smiled in that white face.

'I will, don't you worry.'

Laura turned to go.

'And clean out the basin, Janet,' she said. 'You'll do that, won't you? Ready for the next.'

23

A tall woman, too heavy in the beam to be called graceful, dressed in a slimming black and white costume, with an open-necked white blouse, she moved from the blue-tiled chill of the toilet, and into the over-heated, smoke-hazed din of the restaurant's private room. There was laughter and screams and shouts, the juke-box punished the air, and men and women with damp faces, wet open mouths and glazed eyes, crossed and recrossed her path. Fingers plucked at her arms, bodies thudded against her; a junior clerk stumbled and fell at her feet, to wilder laughter.

He grasped her ankles and looked up.

'Hallo, beautiful,' he said.

Freeing herself, she found Holden in the way, tie loosened, collar awry, hand holding an empty glass.

'Refill,' he said. 'Going for a refill. And one for you, too, my dear Laura.'

'No, thank you,' she said. 'I have to go now.'

'Oh, come on,' he said. 'Unbend a little. The night is yet young.'

'It's old enough for me,' she said. 'Have you seen Mr James in your travels?'

'I never look for my superiors at a time like this,' he said. He took her arm. 'Come on, Laura. Be human for a change.'

She wrenched herself away, so strongly that even he felt the strength of her rejection. He waved the empty glass.

'Okay, okay,' he said. 'Have it your way, love. And a happy New Year.'

She moved through the heat and the fug, but James had gone, sensible man. She said a few goodbyes, got her coat, threaded her way through couples sitting on the stairs, and made her way to the street.

She snuggled deeper into the thick fur of her collar as she walked quickly through the strangely quiet streets of the city. It was office-party time, and commerce was at a standstill: the giant buildings lining the riverside empty; fluorescent-tubes blazing in rooms where cards were ranged, decorations looped and shone, and typewriters were covered. Outside, on the quays, the tall cranes were motionless. Only the icy green river moved, and cold seagulls cried.

She pushed open one of the great glass doors of Morgan Enterprises. The commissionaire looked up from his crossword.

'You're back early, Miss Stone.'

'Not quite my scene, as they say, George,' she said. 'Has Mr James been by?'

'No,' he said. 'But I've only just taken over from Reg.'

'Thank you,' she said.

She took the lift to the third floor, and her own office. The door was locked, which surprised her. She used her key, and entered. Once inside, her shoulders sagged, and she let out a slow deep breath. She stood for a few seconds, looking out at the river, the lights on the other side emphasising the unnatural dark of the afternoon. Then she began to collect her presents, her cards, her own shopping: clearing her desk. When she had finished, she went on into the director's office. It was empty.

She went around his desk, took a sheet of notepaper from the rack, and prepared to write a message. It was then that she heard a slight noise from the Boardroom: a gentle bump, a rustling.

She left the message unwritten, and opened the door.

2

On the deep pile of the brown carpet, between the long table and the wall heater, two people were copulating. The girl's legs were wide, her grimacing face turned away from the glow of the heater, her hands gripping his shoulders, and her breath coming strongly through a red open mouth. His head was pressed against hers, his hands lost in her hair, his white naked legs reared, and pumping. There was no sound, save that of fierce, excited breathing. They were lost in each other, and had not heard her enter.

She stayed watching for no longer than six seconds, yet it seemed hours. And then the girl on the floor opened her large ecstatic eyes. Body arching, she focused, and saw Laura. And into her face came a look of utter triumph. The man was deep inside her, pressing hard and furious, yet she was captor and lover and victor; and she knew her power. Still looking at Laura, she gripped the director's shoulders tighter, and made a swift, convulsive movement with her legs. He groaned, and pumped harder. Over his straining shoulders, the girl smiled on.

Laura stepped back, closed the door, lifted the two large paper bags from her own desk, and left the office.

Down in the entrance hall, the commissionaire was still working at his crossword.

'Is Mr James there?' he said.

'Yes,' she said. 'He's there.'

'Well, have a good Christmas, Miss Stone,' he said. 'And thanks for the card, and everything.'

'That's all right, George,' she said. 'You have a good time, too.'

'Want me to get you a taxi?' he said.

'No, I'll manage,' she said. 'Goodbye.'

In a small café near St Paul's, she finished her second coffee, her mind made up. She took the bill to the cashier and waited for her change.

'Is there a phone I could use?' she said, putting the coins into her purse.

'At the back, madam: behind that door.'

'Thank you.'

She stood under the curving plastic dome, her bags at her feet. Recovering now, she felt only a chilling anger. Then, as she dialled the number, she found herself laughing. Little Sheila Rogers! My *God*!

A voice said:

'Hallo?' Always that soft quaver.

'Mother? It's Laura.'

Silence, but for the steady hum of the wires.

'Laura? Is it you? Are you all right?'

'Yes, I'm fine. Look, Mother, can I come down?'

'Come down? Now? *Today?*'

'Yes. Can I come down for Christmas?'

'Well, I don't know . . . Why do you want to come?'

'I haven't seen you in years.'

'And whose fault is that?'

'Can I come?'

'My dear, the weather is too . . . We haven't got a lot in, Laura.'

'We'll go shopping tomorrow. Like . . . old times.'

'I don't want the old times, Laura. I don't want all that again: the days before you left . . .'

'I've changed, Mother. Cross my heart.'

'Why are you laughing?'

'Private joke, Mother. May I come?'

'Yes, I suppose so. We had nothing planned. Is that man still . . . supporting you? Your friend?'

'All news when I see you.'

'I'll believe that when I hear it, Laura. You've told me nothing. Your father . . .'

'Is Dad there?'

'He's . . . in his room.'

'I'll catch the next train out of Waterloo.'

'All right.' A pause. 'Forgive me, dear, for sounding . . . cautious. Unwelcoming. It'll be nice to see you, Laura. If . . .'

'I'll see you soon. 'Bye.'

She picked up her bags, and left the café. As she walked down Ludgate Hill, snow began falling out of a black sky. But, as it touched the hairs of her coat and stayed, she did not care what season had come to the world: she was free of Warren James; a weight had been lifted from her heart; and the glitter and sparkle that was Christmas, a brightness however temporary, was reflected in her face.

Clive Parsons

1

When he discovered that she had locked the door, he began a systematic destruction of his room. He was amazed how much havoc could be caused in almost total silence. He ripped his bed to shreds, plunging the old scout knife deep into the mattress. He tore down the pictures of Christ and Mary: the sentimental shepherd with the upraised finger and the bleeding red-plush heart; the frosty smile of the lady in blue. He broke the crucifix. He took out every drawer and scattered their contents. He found every item of clothing that she had ever bought him, and tore them apart. He split open what remained of his school books – *St Benedict's R.C.* on every cover – and destroyed the parchment of his altar-boy certificate. He ground into the flowered carpet, in slow silence, every glass and china ornament. He went to work on the curtains with his knife, leaving them in tatters. He took a bottle of ink and scattered three blue trails on the white walls. And when he had finished, breathing heavily, he put on his parka and then his raincoat, picked up his suitcase, and pressed his ear to the door.

There was no sound in the house. He looked at his watch: 2:35 pm. He sat on the edge of the wrecked bed, put the suitcase near his shoes, and linked his hands. The last day in this house, this room. Never again. Never again that uplifted finger, the smell of incense, the daily eating of a god. Never.

Outside, framed by white tower-blocks, the dark sky grew darker.

'Strike me down, then,' he said to the silence.

Nothing struck him down. He smiled, stood up, lifted his suitcase, and once again went to the door. As he stood there, he heard a car stop outside the house.

'I'm going to count ten!' he shouted. 'If this door isn't open by then, I'm going to kick it down! You hear me?'

The front door bell rang.

'You hear me?' he cried. He heard the front door open, and then a murmur of voices. 'I'm starting!' he shouted. 'One, two . . .'

Footsteps hurried up the stairs.

'Clive?' said a man's voice outside the door. 'Clive, my son.' She had called Father Joseph.

'. . . seven, eight . . .'

'I think you'd better open the door, Mrs Parsons,' said the priest.

'. . . nine . . .'

The key turned in the lock, and the door was pushed open. His mother looked in at the room.

'Oh my God!' she said, a hand to her mouth. 'Oh, sweet Jesus.'

The priest, an old man with a wide body, blocked the doorway.

'What's all this now, Clive?' he said. 'What are you doing to your poor mother, you fool?'

The boy looked at the priest. There was no longer any terror for him, any fear or guilt, in that black shiny coat, the white collar brilliant against the black, those always unnaturally clean hands with their pink, trimmed nails.

'You'd better ask her,' he said. 'I'm going now. Out of the way, please.'

The priest put his hand on the boy's chest.

'You're going nowhere until we have a little chat, my son,' he said. 'And until you've done something about that room. You have no father: I'll be your father.'

'I thought you were celibate,' said Clive.

The priest's mouth thinned.

'Oh, Father,' said Mrs Parsons: 'will you listen to what he's saying?' Fierce with rage, she looked at her son. 'You're going nowhere, like the Father says.'

He looked at her. He had come from that thin body, into this world. And she and the Church had robbed him of life, even in the pretence of giving it. And it was over, didn't they understand? There was no going back. The ruined room belonged to a scared child.

'Take your hand off me,' he said to the priest.

Father Joseph took his hand away. It was nothing unusual, this rebellion. Had he not felt the same, once, a stranger in his own holy family, when the flesh beckoned at every corner, until the Lord had tamed desire with prayer and promise? It was natural, this humanity, before one was cleansed, made over. He stood aside.

'Then go,' he said.

'How can he go, Father?' said Mrs Parsons. 'How can you let him go? It's the girl, don't you see?'

They stood on the landing: the priest, the mother and the son, and around all of them was a sense of flight, an invisible whirring of wings.

'You want to go?' said the priest.

'Of course,' said Clive. Yet he stood still, momentarily unsure before an open cell. 'Of course I do.'

'Your mother has given you eighteen years of care and attention,' said Father Joseph. 'You can spare a few moments of your time.'

'I've given her eighteen years of my time,' said the boy. 'And the Church.'

'And you served it well,' said the priest. 'Until now. Come downstairs, have a cup of tea . . .'

'I haven't got the time.'

'Five minutes . . .' said Father Joseph. He reached out a hand, but dropped it. 'Yes?'

2

They sat in the living-room, watched by Christ and Mary, in a smell of furniture polish; the silence laced by the flutter and trills of the canary in its cage by the window.

'Where did you meet her?' said the priest.

'We having some tea, or not?' said the boy.

'You deserve nothing,' said his mother. 'My God, that room . . .'

The priest waved a clean white hand.

'Make some tea, Mrs Parsons. Please.'

'He deserves nothing,' she said. But she went out of the room, and along the hall into the kitchen.

The priest waited until he heard the drumming of water in the kettle, then he leaned forward and slapped the boy hard across the mouth.

'That's what your father would've done,' he said. 'You want another?'

Clive touched the corner of his mouth, and looked at his finger. There was no blood.

'You can try,' he said. 'You can try it again.' He sat back in his chair, and laughed.

'That's better,' said the priest. He patted the pockets of his coat, and brought out his cigarettes. 'You don't, do you?'

'Yes, I do.'

'The sins you've hidden, Clive,' said the priest, and held out the packet.

'You can't buy me with this, you know,' said the boy, accepting the light. 'I'm off out of it.'

'Is she a local girl?' said the priest.

'I don't have to tell you anything. Christ, why am I sitting here? I don't want any tea.'

'You can't leave your mother over Christmas . . .'

'I met this girl at work . . .'

'A Catholic girl . . .?'

'You must be joking,' said Clive. 'Don't you understand? I'm out of it.'

Behind a cloud of smoke, in that dark winter room, the priest said:

'You're never out of it, Clive. You know that.'

The boy stood and picked up his suitcase.

'Okay, I'm sorry about the room. She shouldn't have locked the door. She asked for it. I can't stay here over Christmas. I've been invited . . . elsewhere. I'll come back, after, and collect the rest of my things. You remember my sister?'

'Of course.'

'Then you know why I'm leaving.' He went to the door. The priest moved swiftly, and barred his way.

'I never hit my father,' said the boy, 'but there's always a first time.'

'Mrs Parsons!' called the priest.

She came, equally swiftly.

'Yes?'

'You'll have to let him go,' said the priest. 'You'll do no good, holding him here. You won't be lonely: we'll look after you. Give yourselves a breathing-space. He'll realise . . .'

'And he's *smoking* . . .!' she said.

The boy sighed.

'And I run a drug chain; I'm a pimp; and Christmas will be one big orgy,' he said. 'Satisfied?'

'I lost my Margaret, Father,' she said. The boy made a sound in his throat. 'I . . . I don't want to lose him.'

'I'm sorry about the room,' said Clive. 'You shouldn't have locked the door.'

31

He moved past the priest and made his way down the hall.

'Where are you going?' said Father Joseph.

'Waterloo Station.'

'If you wait a moment, I'll run you there.'

'No thanks,' said the boy. 'Just leave me alone, okay?'

He opened the front door. The cold leapt and fixed itself on his face, ached on his swelling lips.

She called something, back there in the warm, shadowed hall, but he did not hear: running across the road and past the pub where men were singing.

3

There was only one train running to Witley: the 4:10, calling at all stations. He wandered into the station bookstore: a stocky, fair-haired youth in a short brown raincoat, scarf, jeans, and unpolished black shoes. He looked at the paperbacks, all the bright covers. He finally chose *The Third Assassin*, by Jake Barnes, the title centered in a golden telescopic-sight. It was then, looking out at the flurry of snow at the ends of the platforms, that he discovered he was hungry, very hungry. He walked out of the bookstore, across the cold grey concourse with its echoing carols, and into the crowded bar. He bought two sandwiches and a beer and took them over to a table.

'Okay if I sit here?' he said.

The sergeant shifted himself and his suitcase along the red seat.

'Help yourself,' he said.

Part Two

1

High in that black framework, in the chilling girders, among rebounding, echoing carols, two ragged pigeons huddled together for warmth, having no knowledge of the human hope that surrounded them in the music. Shifting frozen claws, they opened and closed golden eyes; and then dropped like grey stones that grew wings, to land among crumbs scattered by the woman who tended the tea-trolley.

The 4:10 to Portsmouth had been announced, and people moved from the bookstore and the bar, forming a queue at Platform 9. Beyond the drumming train, out there in a dark that was now almost night, the snow fell steadily. Another train came out of that night, heading for Platform 7, points fizzing and flashing: a white hood with a single cold eye, hinting, and then saying what lay outside.

'Huskies in the guard's-van,' said the ticket-collector at the gate, his day finished at six, and home, a fire and TV beckoning. 'Hurry along, please. Moscow, first stop.'

The train was no crack express. It was suburban and shabby, an old familiar, four carriages long, without connecting-corridor or toilet, the interior uncleaned. But it was warm, and that was all its passengers demanded. Commuters and shoppers and Christmas travellers, they moved their briefcases and their bags bearing the names of famous stores, their gift-laden suitcases, along the aisles, reaching to the racks, grunting, removing their coats, then sitting, watching other faces passing, the other strangers. Doors slammed, cigarettes were lit, drunks prepared to sleep, the train drummed and sang.

In the third carriage, Anita Silverman looked at the champagne in her husband's arms.

'It'll be safer up there,' she said.

'I'll hang on to it.'

'You'll have a long wait,' she said. 'It's stopping at every station.'

'That's what I'm afraid of,' said Silverman: 'the stopping and starting, the jerking . . .' He looked across at the woman sitting opposite, by the window. 'You wouldn't like to be showered with champagne, would you?'

Laura, still seeing the naked legs, the pumping, the girl's triumphant face, said:

34

'I'm sorry . . .?'

'I said you wouldn't like to be showered with champagne, would you? My wife thinks I ought to trust the rack.'

She looked from the large rock-like head to the bottle-shaped parcel in the large hands.

'I can think of worse things,' she said. 'I can't see this train racing.'

'Fair enough,' said Silverman. 'Two against one.' He stood up and put the bottle in the centre of the rack, rolled it back and forth, and sat down again.

The carriage door opened. The guard looked in, bringing bitter air.

'Just warning you all,' he said: 'weather's getting worse. We'll do the best we can, but we're bound to be late.'

'Good old British Rail,' said a drunk who was drowsy, but not yet asleep. 'Press on, pal.'

The door slammed shut, and the guard moved on to the next carriage.

2

Inside his warm cab the driver looked at his watch. He opened his window and looked down the platform, pooled with yellow light, the distant neon-glitter of the station. A late passenger was running for the train. A door opened and closed. A whistle sounded, an arm was raised. The driver closed his door, shivered, checked the signals, set the windscreen-wipers ticking, and moved his right hand, slowly. Power surged through the train. Lights flickered in the carriages, then steadied. The steady humming became a whine. The driver released the brake, and the engine jerked forward. Power increasing every second under his hand, the driver took the train, slowly and smoothly, out of the station, out from under that latchwork of steel hung with small lights like stars; and into the dark.

And as it appeared, out from that metal, man-made shelter, coming slowly as though apprehensive, so another power that prowled the city, leapt. A fierce snow-laden wind struck the cab, and within a second the windscreen and the train was blinded, until the wipers recovered and began their work. Southwards moved the slow train, down between the high, shining office-blocks, along a stone canyon marked with promises of Christmas that shivered and struggled in the wind, threatening to fall deeper to where lines of cars fought to find their homes. The wind seemed to come from all directions, but the east side of the train took most of its fury: snow began to build up on the windows, and did not melt.

Calvin, sitting on the other side, where the windows were relatively clear, looked into offices where men and women still worked on; saw the pale orange moon of Big Ben come and go; glimpsed other lives in uncurtained tenement rooms: a man stretching his arms before the storm, safe; figures huddled before the blue ice of TV screens. And then the river curved away, and all was suddenly blackness, strung with dipping cords of light. The train picked up speed, and sharp, crackling bursts of white fire came from the frozen points, illuminating, like a giant photoflash, the sides of windowless warehouses, a solitary cyclist battling on, wrapped in snow.

At the other end of the carriage, by a blinded window, the boy opened his paperback and began reading. To his right, one row back, his left hand resting on the suitcase, Sergeant Mason looked out as the last towers of the city fell back, but saw nothing: his mind rehearsing yet again what he had to do.

3

The first stop was Wimbledon. The train dragged its white face into the station, and passengers for whom this was home, gathered their possessions thankfully, so slow had been the journey; only to find, on opening the doors, that the Arctic had moved south, and that a blizzard was roaring along platforms that before had been so tamely predictable. Those few travellers who boarded the train showed shocked faces as they beat the snow from their coats, and as they sat, told stories of stranded cars and thickening drifts and the first casualties. But, as the warmth got to them, and the train moved forward, and the snow melted in their hair, they began to relax, seeing adventure where there had lately been fear. Until the next station, and the open doors, and the blizzard stronger than ever, and the entry of more shaken men and women, and the bruising cold . . .

36

But the train pushed on. And Anita remembered the coffee and the sandwiches.

She stood up from her seat, and brought the bag down from the rack. She took out the flask and the greaseproof pack, and put the bag between herself and Simon.

'Hungry?' she said.

'Starving'.

She gave him a sandwich and spun the top of the flask. And the smell of the coffee moved through the carriage, and people lifted their heads. It spoke of so many things: it spoke of home and the breakfast-table, of normality and fellowship and humanity, of a sharing, and in spite of themselves the passengers smiled, remembering; while, outside, that which was not normal, not a sharing, swung cold and mindless across the land, going its own unchartered way, oblivious of what it covered, obliterated, suffocated.

She held out the steaming, plastic cup.

Chewing, he shook his head; swallowed.

'No,' he said. 'You first.'

'Such manners,' she said. She smiled at the girl. 'And in company.' She sipped the coffee. 'Going far?'

'Liphook,' said Laura.

'You live there?' said Anita.

'My parents do.'

'Going home for the holiday?'

'Yes.'

'Nice,' said Anita. 'Nice to be going back, at Christmas. Nothing like the family, is there?'

'Nothing,' said Laura, and looked at her window, through which she could see only a thickening blue-whiteness which bleached her own reflection to that of a negative.

Back a little, Calvin watched a land and a route he had known since childhood, change before his eyes. Full night had not yet come, but the snow made another kind of light: a chilling ghostly glow that covered everything. All the landmarks had gone, or been transformed to that which was no longer recognisable; and the intermittent flashes from the track reminded him of shellfire over a wintry battlefield. It was only the names of the stations, glimpsed between wildly dancing lamps and large, swirling flakes: Esher, Hersham, Walton-on-Thames, Weybridge − only these brought reassurance, yet were like outposts before a final, empty continent.

37

After Woking the train crawled, and he grew impatient, the fingers of his right hand tapping his knee, his mind urging the engine on, wanting to be home, to tell the news, to see her face, the widening eyes of his children . . .

By the time the train pulled slowly out of Guildford, most of the commuters and the shoppers had left. It pulled away from a town whose minor roads were now impassable, a town lashed by a blizzard so severe that traffic was coming to a halt, and whose streets were emptying. Yet still the train battled on, as though it trusted that further south it might break through to different weather, perhaps even a glint of the day's last sun: a sun which burned, unperturbed, miles high in a clearer sky.

To the boy the story was all. He had not lifted his eyes once from the pages: the carriage was warm, people came and went, but he was elsewhere:

Beyond the clear circle of the telescopic-sight he saw the sun flash on the General's decorations, those useless symbols of a nation's hypocrisy, whilst behind those gold and silver discs lay the piled bodies of Everett's companions, those sacrificed infantrymen, those bloodied boys, who had died for nothing but this spread meal on a balcony, this ignoble celebration.

Everett settled the barrel of the gun more securely on the coping, looked again through the sight, and began to slowly press the trigger . . .

The boy turned the page.

From where he sat, Mason watched the boy reading. He marked the fair hair, the preoccupation. He himself had never been a reader. Even newspapers were a waste of time, like TV: everything slanted. To be moving, to be active: that was the secret. He looked away, hearing only the whisper of snow on the window.

*   *   *

At Farncombe the long white platforms were empty. The train stayed longest here, as though summoning enough strength for the rest of the journey.

'Wake him up,' said Anita.

Silverman, who had crossed the carriage to look through a clearer window at a turbulent world, turned from the white stare of what remained of the fences.

38

'What?'

'Wake him up,' she said, nodding at the drunk slumped in the corner. 'Find out where he's going.'

Silverman looked down at the closed face. He hated any lack of control, the going over the top, the unmanliness. Reluctantly, he shook the drunk's shoulder. The man's eyelids twitched, a hand came up, fell back. The eyes opened, blearily, and focused.

'Wha . . .?'

'Where are you going?' said Silverman, looking away from the brown teeth.

'What?'

'This is Farncombe. Where are you going?'

The man raised himself, moistened his lips.

'It's all right, chief,' he said. 'Next stop, me. Godalming, right?' He squinted at the window. 'Still snowing, is it?'

Silverman grunted, but said nothing. He was about to move back to his own seat, when the drunk held his sleeve.

'Where you making for, chief?'

'Haslemere.'

Still holding Silverman's sleeve, the man looked out of the window as the train lurched forward.

'I hope you make it,' he said. He grinned with those brown teeth. 'I hope *I* make it.'

Silverman pulled away, and sat beside his wife.

'You want another sandwich?' she said.

'No, thanks,' he said. He rubbed his chest. 'I've got a touch of indigestion.'

'You ate it too quickly,' said Anita. She took out a sandwich. There was one left in the pack. She held it out to the girl. 'Would you like this?'

'No, thank you,' said Laura. The wind, coming unhampered now across a clear stretch of country, struck the train with such force that it shuddered from end to end, and tipped slightly, before righting itself and moving on. 'Do you think we'll make it?' Her smile was no disguise.

'We'll struggle through,' said Anita. 'We'll get there.' She looked across at the drunk. 'He's asleep again, Simon.'

The drunk opened one eye.

'No, I'm not,' he said. He sat up and rubbed the window with his sleeve. 'It looks like Siberia out there. I've got to get a bus after this.'

'You'll be lucky,' said Silverman.

The man grinned.

'The pubs'll be open, though, won't they? I can wait in there till it's all over.' He watched the woman begin to wrap the last sandwich. 'I'll have that, if no one wants it. I feel a bit peckish.'

'You get yourself something in the pub,' said Anita. 'You'll be all right there.' She finished folding the greaseproof, and put the sandwich in the bag.

The drunk turned back to the window, watching the first lights of Godalming move through the snow.

When the train stopped, he fastened the buttons of his overcoat, put on his cap, pulled at the peak, and came across the carriage.

'Excuse me, folks,' he said, and bent to open the door. He had trouble with the stiff catch, and Silverman had to help him. The door swung open and crashed back against the side of the train. The snow entered, hitting the drunk full in the face, and flew in a wild storm about the carriage. He took a step back, blinded now, icy flakes melting in his open mouth. Then he pushed himself forward, and stepped out on to the platform. The wind circled him, tearing at the edges of his coat, and as he fought to close the door, he feared he might be thrown under the train, and he gasped and swore as his boots slipped in the deep drifts of the platform. Finally he made it, helped by the wind. The door slammed shut, and he turned away from the long, caked whiteness of the carriages, and bent his head to where he thought the exit might be, buffeted and shaken, coated in seconds, the snow like a frozen hand thrust down the back of his neck. Behind him, the train drummed steadily; and then inched forward, the red tail-light fading as he joined other white figures jostling to enter a hall bright with summer posters of France and Greece, coming like creatures from another world, a world that knew nothing of surfboards or swimsuits, of heat-hazed broken temples.

Unprotected, facing miles of open fields, Milford station had suffered the full force of the blizzard for over an hour, and the train pushed through a continuously moving wall of snow that had crushed fences and snapped tall poplars so that they lay beyond the station forecourt, and were slowly being made part of another, stranger parking-lot. One man got off the train, and was immediately knee-deep and captured. A light swung crazily above the now faceless clock as he blundered towards a door which had lost all its glass panels.

With a sound that was almost a sigh, the train pressed against the wall, was allowed entry; and then the wall closed around it; and it was as if nothing had come, or gone. The wind roared on, and another tree snapped, and was carried fifty yards to lodge in an upended trailer.

Midway between Milford and Witley, in the heart of the storm, on an open section of track between farmland which had lost its hedges, fences and gates – all its divisions – the track itself under a six-mile long thickening drift, the train gave a sudden, sharp forward lurch. The lights flickered; the engine made one last full-powered lunge. And then was still.

4

Six people sat in the third carriage. All were silent. The lights burned steadily, heat still came from under the seats, the racks bore evidences of Christmas. All appeared normal, except that, outside, a different night had come; and the train had stopped.

At the far end of the carriage, towards the engine, the boy no longer read. He closed the paperback, shifted along the seat, and rubbed the window. Nothing but a shelf of white, stretching into the dark. Two rows back, Mason felt no disquiet: machines obeyed, and would obey – steel was stronger than snow – the train would soon recover. Silverman, behind Mason, and to the left, was not so confident. He knew, and respected, forces stronger than himself, and he felt the first stirrings of fear. Anita, like Mason, was not unduly worried: a signal at red, perhaps; a temporary loss of power. She reached for the bag.

'Shall we finish the coffee?' she said.

'No, I don't think so,' said Silverman.

'Why not?'

He looked at her placid, suddenly all-too-familiar face, and did not wish to say the waiting might be long, and that it would be wiser to see what happened, to conserve what they had. Instead, he said:

'I don't feel like any, thanks.'

'I do,' she said.

'Well, go ahead,' he said, and looked at the white window.

'You'll join me, won't you?' said Anita to the girl, holding up the flask.

'I will, this time, thank you,' said Laura. She gave a sudden, uncertain laugh. 'What awful weather!'

Anita poured the coffee into the cup. Simon looked back from the window.

'Don't you think you ought to save some of that?' he said. 'Not use it all?'

'Oh, come on, Simon,' she said. 'It's only two more stations. We'll be there in a few minutes.' The engine began drumming again, and a healthy surge of power made the carriage tremble. 'There, you see? We're starting again.'

The engine seemed to bound forward. The coffee swayed in the cup, and coated Anita's fingers.

'Here,' she said. 'Take it.'

Laura took the cup. The engine travelled a yard; and then stopped. The power began to die; the lights paled.

'So much for your starting,' said Silverman.

'Oh, don't be so defeatist, Simon,' she said. She finished wiping her hand. 'It's sugared – is that all right?'

'Yes,' said Laura. The coffee was strong and over-sweet, but welcome, her throat no longer dry. 'Fine, thank you.'

Although the lights had brightened, there was no sound at all now from the engine. Once talking stopped, there was only the vicious whipping of the wind, and the slithery building, inch by inch, of snowdrifts.

At the other end of the carriage, Calvin could no longer see out of his window. The wind seemed to be coming from all quarters now, and the west-facing side of the train was now as blind as the east. Had he not been the carrier of exceptional news, he told himself he might have enjoyed this delay – every experience was profitable – but his imagination was such that, given the impetus, no situation had to be endured to the end. It was part of the continuing nature of his life that, richer today than he had ever been, everything now conspired to shrivel his elation, and to fill this waiting time with thoughts he would rather avoid. He looked above his head at the presents he had bought his family, and saw his home, and three faces peering out as snow fell steadily on an empty road.

Twenty minutes passed. The engine had not moved. The wind was as powerful as ever, and so thickly white were the windows that it was not impossible to believe that the train was slowly being buried.

The English are not reserved. What passes for reserve is an unspoken acknowledgement of an individual's right to privacy, a refusal to interfere. In other countries, perhaps, the carriage would be loud with talk as travellers discussed the situation. But here there was complete silence, except for the whisper of pages being turned as the boy read his paperback: a sound only he heard. But the silence eventually broke through the story: he closed the book, and, finger marking the place, he moved to sit opposite the sergeant he had seen in the bar.

'What do you think?' he said.

Mason, his hand draped over his suitcase, looked at the boy, the fresh openness, the unformed features.

'About what?' he said.

Stung, the boy waved a hand.

'Well, this . . .'

'What do you suggest?' said Mason.

'Well, I mean, what do you think's happened?'

'We know what's happened, don't we?' said Mason, patiently, as though to a new recruit: 'we're in the middle of a snowstorm. It's clogged up the lines. We'll move soon, or we won't move. It'll happen, sooner or later. Got any other ideas?'

'No,' said the boy. 'I suppose not.' He sat back against the seat. 'You like the army?'

Mason looked at the paperback in the boy's linked hands.

'Good book?' he said.

'Not bad.'

'Let's have a look,' said Mason. He glanced at the cover and flipped through the pages. He handed it back.

'I thought about joining the army, once,' said the boy.

'How old are you?' said Mason.

'Eighteen.'

Mason nodded, and was silent. The boy felt an indifference, and looked away from that dark, closed face, down to the end of the carriage.

The sound of voices behind her had brought to Anita a sense of normality, the warmth of human contact. She stood up.

'What are you doing now?' said Silverman.

She looked down the carriage to a man who was sitting alone; and then behind her to the raised face of a youth, and the dark head of another man.

'There's only six of us,' she called. 'Shall we all sit together?

43

Heaven knows how long we're going to wait.'

Embarrassed, Silverman looked at the girl.

'Sorry,' he said.

Laura smiled.

'I don't mind,' she said.

Calvin looked down the carriage at the woman. He was always the observer, never the participant: it was part of his craft. But he was tired of his circling thoughts, and he stood up and joined her, sitting next to Laura. He looked across at the big man near the window.

'Going far?' he said.

'Jesus!' said Silverman, appalled at the cliché, and tugged at his wife's coat. 'Sit down, Anita, please.'

She continued to look to her left.

'Coming?' she said.

The boy looked at the sergeant.

'Shall we?' he said.

'You go,' said Mason. 'I'm okay here, son.'

Still holding his book, the boy joined the group, sitting alone to the right of Calvin, across the aisle. He reached up a hand and put the book in the rack. Still standing, Anita looked at the back of Mason's head.

'Yes?' she called.

'He says he's okay there,' said the boy.

'Sensible man,' said Silverman.

Anita sat down and prodded him with her elbow.

'Don't be so grumpy, you,' she said.

He spread his hands.

'Why not leave people alone?' he said. 'Perhaps they aren't so gregarious as you.'

'Or as cold as you,' she said.

There was an awkward silence.

'There you are, you see,' said Silverman: 'the secrets of the bedchamber out already.'

Laura and Calvin laughed, and the group relaxed.

'Sorry about my wife,' said Silverman. 'And she's finished all the coffee, too.'

'What do you think has happened?' said Laura.

The boy leaned forward his fair head, and linked his fingers.

'The snowstorm's clogged up the lines, I think,' he said. 'They'll send a snowplough, or something.'

His words hung in the air.

'At least we have light and heat,' said Calvin.

'I wish we had a toilet,' said Laura, in spite of herself, and again gave that short nervous laugh.

'You, too, eh?' said Silverman. 'All friends together. If this goes on much longer, we'll have to be.'

Alone in his seat, Mason lifted the suitcase on to his knees, and sprang the locks. He opened the lid a fraction, and looked in at the dull shine of the gun and the magazine. He put in his right hand and ran his fingers along the barrel. When he took out his hand, there was a slight blur of oil on his fingertips. He sniffed it, and it was like smelling home. He closed the lid, pressed the catches, and put the suitcase to his left. He put his feet on the opposite seat and closed his eyes. He could hear the wind and the snow, and their voices, back down the carriage. He granted that what he had to do set him apart. He was in no mood for conversation. He had fretted at having to wait for Bland, but that was human weakness on the officer's part. This waiting was different. There was nothing he could do. Nature had stepped in, and he would have to wait until Nature relented, or was forced to retreat. He felt no fear. That which was in the wind — the strength that threw all before it — that was part of his nature also, and was no enemy. There were always things that had to be destroyed, cleared away, so that life could begin again, new, uncorrupted. He folded his arms and settled himself for sleep. Or so he told himself.

*   *   *

They had told each other their destinations, but nothing more, and now there was silence. The wind seemed to have found every crack, and there was a continuous shrill skirling, as though from a hundred narrow pipes. At times the carriage shuddered, as though trying to dislodge what covered it.

'At least we'll have a white Christmas,' said Laura, pressing her thighs together and leaning back.

Silverman sighed, and looked away from her strained face.

'Isn't it amazing,' he said: 'all creation to discuss, and yet it's always the weather.'

'Start us off, then,' she said, her hands coming forward and gripping her knees.

He smiled.

'I'm sorry,' he said; 'don't mind me.'

'No, go on,' she said, her mouth tightening. 'We've got all the time in the world.'

'You don't look as though *you* have,' he said.

'Oh, isn't it *awful*?' she said. 'It was an office party: you know the sort of thing. I don't like a lot to drink: mine was mostly soda water. Oh dear, I'm sorry.'

'Why apologise for a natural function?' said Silverman. 'Christ, we all piss, we all shit . . .'

'Simon!' said Anita.

He spread his hands again.

'Well, don't we? Do you have another arrangement? Girl here, busting a gut, and holding it all back because of some stupid . . . deference. To whom? To others like herself. Us.' He shook his head. 'I can never understand it.'

'Use the end of the carriage,' said Calvin.

White-faced now, alternating between embarrassment and need, she turned her head towards him.

'What?'

'Look,' he said: 'the man's right. We're all human. There are plenty of newspapers on my seat. Spread some on the floor, do what you have to do, fold the paper, and throw it out of the window.'

Hands tight in her lap, she looked at their faces. The boy looked at the floor.

'Go on, girl,' said Silverman. 'Don't mind us. It could happen to anyone. God, what it is to be civilised!'

'I think I must,' she said, standing up. 'Talk as loud as you can, won't you?'

'That's the spirit,' said Silverman. 'Now, people, what do you think of this current recession . . .?'

Hurrying to the rear of the carriage, the humour of the situation struck her, and she stifled a giggle. On his seat were a pile of papers and magazines. She spread two of the larger newspapers on the floor between the seats, glanced along to where the others were talking, pulled down her tights and her pants, and squatted. When she had finished, she stood up, pulled on her pants and tights, smoothed her skirt, and folded the papers. Almost faint with relief, she rested her left hand on the rack, her fingers brushing a number of parcels, closed her eyes, and let her shoulders drop. Then she moved to the window and pulled at the cold, silver bar. It did not move. She put

46

the square of moist paper under her right shoe, and used both hands. The bar stayed firm. She gave one more tug, and then lifted her head.

'I'm sorry,' she called: 'I can't open this window.'

The talking stopped. Calvin came along the carriage and stood beside her. He gave the bar two hard thumps with his fist, and said:

'Together, right?'

She nodded, and placed her fingers next to his.

'Now,' he said.

They pulled downward, hard. The window creaked, and then shot down, to halt halfway. Framed in that space was a smooth wall of snow with six inches of night above it, a night full of snowflakes hastening wildly to complete the task. The smoothness of the wall was its most terrifying feature. It was as if it *stared* into the carriage, as a blind man seems to stare with his milky, blue-white orbs. And then the wall, robbed of its support, the glass, began to slowly topple into the carriage.

'Get rid of the paper!' said Calvin.

She reached down, grabbed the square, and thrust it into the crumbling, widening gap. Then, together, they began to lift the bar. It was hard work. She had to push back the wall as he brought up the window, inch by squeaking inch, and the bone-numbing cold chilled her heart. At last they made it. They stood by the closed window, their shoes coated with snow, and looked at each other. And in their faces, under the blown and whitened hair, they read the same realisation: that, unless the snow stopped, the wall would grow, and the train become entombed.

Calvin pressed his ear to the panelling above the back seats.

'What are you doing?' she said, and shivered.

'I had a crazy idea I might hear something from the next carriage,' he said. He banged hard on the panelling, and listened again.

'Nothing,' he said.

'There's a gap between . . .' she said.

'I know.'

'All right down there?' shouted Silverman.

'Yes,' said Calvin. He dusted the snow from his hair, and then leaned forward and did the same for Laura. It was an instinctive, human response, and they smiled at each other, however wanly.

'Do we tell them?' he said, quietly.

'What good would it do?' she said. 'Someone must know we're here.'

'I think we'd better get back,' he said.

They returned, and took the same places.

'Better?' said Silverman.

'Yes, thank you,' she said. 'Much.'

'There, you see?' he said: 'a civilised solving of a natural problem. No fuss: the actions of reasonable people.'

'Give the man a coconut,' said his wife.

The acknowledgement of so basic a need, of their own vulnerable humanity: this had melted the barriers, and they were easier with each other.

'If I'd brought my cards,' said the boy: 'we could have had a game of solo. Best card game, solo. No one got any cards, have they?'

The wind roared on, the pipes skirled, the carriage shifted.

'I think you'd better tell them,' said Laura to Calvin. 'Perhaps reasonable people could do something about that, too.'

'I doubt it,' he said. An imaginative man, a creator of extreme situations in which he physically had no part, yet controlled, he was faced now with lives which were separate and uncontrollable, not confined to a page; and a dilemma which could not be left until the next day, when he carried coffee to his study, and his cleared, waiting desk.

'Tell us what?' said Anita.

'I think you might know, anyway,' said Calvin. He paused. 'The snow's over the window, back there.'

'How far?' said Silverman.

'About half way.'

'And it's still coming down?' said the boy.

Calvin nodded. They were silent.

'I think you'd better get that other chap over here,' said Silverman. 'He ought to know.'

'I think he's asleep,' said the boy.

'Well, wake him up,' said Silverman. He gave almost an echo of Laura's nervous laugh. 'He can't die asleep.'

'Who's talking about dying?' said the boy.

'Only kidding, son,' said Silverman.

'Well, don't kid,' said Anita. She looked at Calvin. 'I want to see.'

'What?'

'I want to see what it's like.' She stood. 'Show me.'

'It's better we keep . . .'

'Please show me,' she said.

The whole group were now standing. They followed Calvin down to the end of the carriage.

'I don't want to take it as far as last time,' he said. 'Just give me a hand here, please.'

Silverman stood beside him. They pulled together, until the rim of the wall appeared. Snowflakes spun in out of blackness. Anita stepped between the two men and touched the ledge. She tried to peer in both directions, but she was not tall enough.

'All right,' she said. 'Thank you. Close it.'

They did so, lifting hard.

'Satisfied?' said Silverman.

'We could be . . . covered,' said the boy.

'True,' said Anita. 'But we'll have been found by then. Or we'll have thought of something. Don't get worried.'

'Ha!' said Silverman.

She shot him a glance.

'Let's get back to our seats,' she said. 'What's your name?'

'Clive,' he said.

'Well, Clive, you go ahead and wake that man up, will you? We ought to be together.'

'Yes,' he said.

He went before them, down the carriage.

And then the lights went out.

Part Three

1

They stood motionless, each in their separate darknesses, but feeling precisely the same emotion: sudden, engulfing fear. They gasped, and it sounded like one giant breath, there in the blackness. At the other end of the carriage, Mason, who had not slept, but had simply kept himself apart, saw his eyelids darken, lifted them, and, blinded like the others, sat rigidly in his seat, as if waiting for the next second to give him sight. But there was no light. Only a wind-haunted blackness, and a stinging of snow.

'Oh my Jesus,' said Silverman, into the dark. 'Everyone okay?'

'Just stand still where you are,' said Anita, swallowing the sourness in her throat, her heartbeat slowing. 'Light a match, Simon.'

There was a rustle of clothing, the sound of a box opening, and then a scratching. The match flared, and a hand grew out of the dark. The hand lifted, and Silverman's face appeared, wavering, with wide, moist eyes. The elements of the carriage disappeared, and the face and the disembodied hand could have existed anywhere: in a cave, a cathedral, a hovel, a palace.

'Take us back, Simon,' she said.

Mason was standing now, looking down the carriage as that single small flame came towards him. Anita could not see him, but sensed that the man had awakened, and was watching.

'Will you come here, with us?' she called.

By the time he had joined them, the match was almost spent, the flame dwindling. He sat down opposite the boy as the dark returned. There was another scratching, and a new flame glowed strongly. The faces seemed to press around the light, as though it could feed them.

'I can't go on lighting one after the other,' said Silverman.

'You may have to,' said Mason.

Silverman lifted the match higher. The light gleamed on the sergeant's golden buttons.

'I'm glad to see we've got the cavalry,' he said. 'Oh, for a torch or a candle.'

'Just a minute,' said Calvin: 'I think I may be able to help you there.'

He stood up and felt his way to the rear of the carriage, and his seat.

'Now that the lights have gone, so will the heating,' said Mason.

'That's right,' said Silverman, watching the flame nearing his thumbnail: 'cheer us up.'

'It's best to know everything,' said Mason. He took out a cigarette and used the last of the flame. 'Then you're prepared.'

'I was never in the Scouts,' said Silverman, and struck another match.

Calvin returned, carrying a square parcel. Once again he sat beside Laura and began to tug at the wrapping-paper.

'Thought this might amuse my kids at Christmas,' he said.

He took out the box and lifted the lid. There was a smell of newness. The others leaned forward. Inside the box was a dismantled table-decoration, consisting of a circular base with holes for candles and spars, three golden metal angels and twelve small candles of differing colours, housed in plastic sleeves. He took out the base, put three of the candles in the holes, set up the thin golden spars, and hung the angels. Then the dark came again, and he waited for Silverman to light another match.

'Where shall we have it?' he said.

'Put it in the aisle,' said Silverman. 'On my suitcase.' Holding the match in his left hand, he lifted the case from the rack with his right, and gave it to the boy. 'Put it down there, Clive.'

The boy centered it in the aisle, and Calvin leaned forward and gently lowered the swinging angels.

'Matches?' he said.

Silverman fumbled for the box, but Mason was quicker.

'Here,' he said, snapped open a small silver lighter, and shifted forward.

'No,' said Calvin: 'I . . . I think I ought to light them.'

'Yes,' said Laura: 'it *is* his present.'

Mason grunted.

'No skin off my nose,' he said. 'Here.'

Calvin took the lighter, came off his seat, and knelt in the aisle. All except Mason crowded close to watch – the sergeant sitting back, like a father observing his children – five faces in almost near-darkness, faces that glowed warmer as each candle was lit, and the dark pushed back. The flames, caught by sudden small draughts, bent and then wavered upright, each with its thin, lengthening cap of smoke. Calvin closed the lighter, and sat back on his heels. The candles burned strongly now, their small fire heated the air – and the angels began to fly.

There was an almost audible sigh of pleasure from the half-open mouths. The light; the slowly flying golden angels; the bright stems of the candles: the watchers forgot where they were, and the magic worked again, and they were back in some half-remembered innocence, a childhood when everything was believed, and parents killed nightmares, and the days were as coloured as the candles, as warm as the flames, as golden as the angels.

Clive alone experienced another dimension: he looked at the candles, and saw another thousand ranged behind them, his hand with the long taper going from one to the other; cold stone under his black, highly-polished shoes; and then the faces of the priests, old and young; and the wafer and the wine, the flesh and blood he could no longer accept; and a picture of a small boy in a darkened pew, making a woman's shape out of a warm candle-end. The same smell of melting wax: the guttering battalions at the rear of the church, the holders caked with a hard whiteness like frozen snow. He looked from the flames to the slowly spinning angels, and thought of all the wasted time, all the smooth girls: heaven receding at the speed of light; but, likewise, hell . . .

'Cheap,' said Calvin, 'but effective.'

Anita, looking at the brightness and the movement, shook her head.

'Not cheap,' she said. 'Beautiful.' She lifted her head and smiled at him. 'Thank you.'

'Don't waste the candles,' said Mason. 'There's no telling how long we're going to be here.'

His words took away some of the glow. The unseen carriage reformed in their minds, and winter came back. Laura shivered again.

The boy looked at the sergeant. There was comfort in the uniform, the stripes, the light-reflecting buttons.

'Think we'll ever move again?' he said.

'The power's gone, son,' said Mason. 'The lines are down. We won't move again: not that way. He came forward from his seat. 'Better nip two of these out.'

'No, leave them!' said Silverman, more urgently than he knew. 'Let them burn.'

'We've got to plan,' said the sergeant, slowly and carefully, still leaning forward, hand outstretched. 'Got to imagine we're here for a long time. Space things out – just in case.'

'Leave them,' said Silverman: 'one's not enough.'

'It'll be better than nothing,' said Mason. He looked down at

54

Calvin, who was still kneeling in the aisle. 'They're your candles.'

Calvin looked at the wavering flames, the turning angels.

'We'll let these burn out,' he said. 'We've got nine left; your lighter; matches. Let's enjoy it.'

Mason withdrew his hand. It was always the same: there was no shape to anything. People were disorganised: they got what they deserved.

'Don't say I didn't warn you,' he said, sitting back. The angels were now a toy, too simple to contemplate.

The candles burned slowly, but too fast for the watchers. All eyes were on the thin, melting columns, as if hypnotised, entranced.

'We're wasting time,' said Mason.

Calvin lifted his head.

'Suggest something,' he said.

'We don't just sit around,' said the sergeant. 'We'll regret it, after. We ought to check what we've got between us. Get everything together, to hand. It's going to be a long, cold night.'

'Unless we're rescued,' said Laura.

'Unless we're rescued,' agreed Mason. 'Which we won't be yet, if this weather keeps up.'

One of the candles had melted faster than the others. It was sinking into a circle of watery wax, its ragged flame gasping for life. It went out; and a final wisp of smoke faded away to nothing.

'He's right,' said Silverman. 'My wife has finished the coffee. We've got one sandwich.'

'And the champagne,' said Anita. 'Don't forget that.'

'Yes, we have some champagne,' said Silverman. 'If the worst comes to the worst.'

'One sandwich, and some champagne,' said the sergeant. He looked at Laura. 'And you?'

'Are you taking command?' said Silverman.

There was a silence. And in that silence, the group acknowledged, for the first time, that there were individuals here, strangers, personalities; unknown pasts, rages, desires, all hidden – until now, or later; or never.

'I'm used to it,' said Mason.

'I'm an art teacher,' said Silverman, and even to his own ears it sounded pompous. 'I give orders, too.' And he smiled at the strangeness of his words. 'No, I don't mean that. I've never ordered anyone in my life. I . . .'

'Anyone mind if I *do* take command?' said Mason. He looked at the faces, one by one, in the growing dark as the candles faltered; and Calvin sensed a contempt behind the question, a dismissal.

'Yes, I do,' he said. 'We don't need leaders. We're all together, all in the same position. We'll just do what has to be done, by agreement: together.'

'Okay,' said Mason. 'What now?'

'We'll do what you suggested,' said Silverman: 'we'll gather together what we've got.' He looked at Laura. 'Anything for the pot?'

'I don't think so,' she said. She brought her two bags down from the rack. 'A few presents from people in the office. I expect it's the usual.' She pulled at the wrapping. 'Yes: bath oil, soap, perfume. Sorry.'

'Perfume burns,' said Mason. 'We may need it.'

'Thank you for that,' she said, resting her well-tended fingers on the now closed bags. 'They will be pleased.'

'You, Clive?' said Silverman.

The boy unzipped a pocket in his parka.

'Half a packet of gum,' he said, and held it out.

'One sandwich, champagne, and gum,' said Silverman. 'An assortment of riches. And what about you, sergeant?'

Mason thought of what his suitcase contained, and smiled in the near-dark.

'Nothing,' he said. 'A few cigarettes. Nothing.'

'And you . . .?' said Silverman.

'The name's Calvin. Ambrose Calvin.' He stood up. 'I'll go and see.'

As he returned to the rear of the carriage, the second candle died, and the second angel ceased flying. He came back in total darkness, until Mason's lighter flared.

'I was taking home some wine,' said Calvin. He put the tissue-clad bottles on the floor, near the dead candles and the unmoving angels. 'Two bottles of Beaune. And some chocolate for my kids.'

'What a provider you are!' said Anita.

'So,' said Silverman, looking at the light in the sergeant's hand: 'a sandwich, champagne, chewing-gum, chocolate, and two bottles of Beaune. We won't starve, and we certainly won't thirst.'

'We might get drunk,' said the boy.

'And what a way to go,' said Silverman. 'Right, we know who you are, Clive. And you, Mr Calvin. I'm Simon Silverman, and this is my wife, Anita.'

'Laura,' she said.

They all looked towards the sergeant.

'Mason,' he said. 'Gordon Mason.' He moulded some still-warm candle-grease in his fingers, pressed it on the base of the lighter, and fixed the lighter to the floor. He sat back. 'Now what?' he said.

They were silent, watching the single flame.

'It's burning very steadily,' said Anita. 'Perhaps the wind is dropping.'

'Or there are fewer draughts,' said Mason.

The inference made them avoid each other's eyes, and they looked into the dark that hid the ends of the carriage.

Laura leaned down and put a hand under her seat.

'The heating *has* gone,' she said. She straightened and pulled her fur collar about her throat. 'It's getting colder in here.'

And the others, hearing their own thoughts and fears given voice, looked at her as though they hated her.

2

The boy, alone in his seat across the aisle, held out the pack of gum.

'There are three left,' he said. 'Anyone want one?'

'I never did like the stuff,' said Anita. 'You see them on television: footballers, trainers, managers. Even when they're being interviewed – chewing away. Just like a lot of cattle. Terrible.'

'I'll join you, son,' said Mason. 'Thanks.'

'Anyone else?' said Clive.

Silverman rubbed his chest.

'Will it clear indigestion?' he said. 'I'll have one.'

'Anyone else?' said Clive. 'One left.'

There were no takers. The boy sat back, removed the foil, and folded the strip into his mouth. There was a strong smell of peppermint.

'If,' he said: 'I'm just saying – if . . .' He paused to fix the gum behind his teeth. '*If* it's that bad, and the snow goes on, and we're . . . covered – would we be *suffocated* – in the end?'

'There's a thought for a Friday night,' said Silverman.

'He's right to ask,' said Mason. Still chewing, he looked across at Clive. 'No.'

'That's a relief,' said Silverman. 'You're sure of that, are you?'

'I think we'd die of cold before the air gave out,' said Mason.

'There's no chance of that happening,' said Anita, briskly. 'They know we're here: there's probably a special kind of train coming along right now: a line-clearer, or something: a snow-plough.'

Mason chewed with his mouth open.

'You ever know weather like this?' he said. 'Supposing it's the start of a new ice-age? They say it's possible . . .'

'Are you always like this?' said Silverman: 'happy, constructive, a bearer of good tidings?'

'If you expect the worst, you're ready for it,' said Mason. 'It's something you have to learn.'

'On the battlefield, you mean?' said Silverman.

Mason looked at him.

'Not necessarily,' he said.

There was an uncomfortable silence.

'I'm sorry,' said Silverman.

'No offence,' said the sergeant.

Calvin leaned forward, his face taking shape in the small light.

'When my candles were burning and the angels were turning,' he said slowly, 'there was a kind of party atmosphere – didn't you feel?'

'I shouldn't waste any more,' said Mason. 'This'll burn for a while yet.'

'I wasn't thinking of that,' said Calvin. 'I was thinking: why not start on my wine? We could eat some of what we've got . . .'

'Sing carols . . .' said Laura.

'Spare us that,' said Silverman.

'I was only joking,' she said. 'Yes, why don't we have a party?'

'You got a corkscrew?' said Mason.

'Snag number one,' said Calvin.

'I've got a penknife,' said the boy.

'No, we'll leave the wine,' said Silverman. He took the gum from his mouth, rolled it into a ball, put it into the foil, and returned the foil to his pocket. 'I think I can manage without that, Clive – thanks all the same.' He stood up and reached for the rack. 'We'll have the champagne. No corkscrew needed for that. We'll toast my daughter's first-born. Why be downhearted?'

'Are you sure?' said Anita.

He looked down at his wife's shadowed face, and felt a surge of anger at the pettiness behind the question, the cramped life-

58

denying attitude he had borne all these long, uncreative years.

'You're not going on about the cost again, are you?' he said, the swift force of his words lifting other heads, other eyes searching for his in the dark.

Embarrassed at this public showing of a division, she said:

'No, of course not. I just thought . . . won't it be too cold? Aren't we trying to . . .'

'It won't be, once it's in us,' he said. He lifted the bottle and sat down again. 'Get the cup from the flask.' He unwrapped the tissue, took out the champagne, and began to twist the wire. 'We can always buy another, tomorrow.'

'Yes,' she said. She tried to brighten her voice, to share in the celebration. 'Now, what shall we have with it: the chocolate, the sandwich?'

'I don't want anything to eat,' said Silverman, still working at the wire. 'Just this will do me.'

'I *am* a little hungry,' said Laura. 'I'll have some of the sandwich, if I may.'

'Yes,' said Anita. She held out the open pack. Laura took one of the quarters. 'Anyone else?'

'Yes, please,' said Clive. He leaned across the aisle, took the second quarter, and removed the gum from his mouth.

'Nothing for me,' said Mason.

'I'll have some of my chocolate,' said Calvin.

'I'm not hungry,' said Anita. 'Could you eat two, Clive?'

'One's enough for him now,' said Mason. 'He'll have the other later . . . if he wants it.'

'Could you eat two, Clive?' she said again.

'I'll wait till later,' said the boy.

'All right,' she said, and closed the greaseproof over the remaining half.

There was a loud pop, and the cork struck the seat between Calvin and Laura, and dropped to the floor. She reached down and picked it up.

'Souvenir,' she said.

'Cup, Anita,' said Silverman. He held the foaming neck over the brim. 'Who's first?'

3

The carriage grew colder. The small flame of the lighter burned steadily, wavering gently at intervals. The snow seemed to have stopped: there was no longer that feathery rush and bluster at the windows. But the wind still soughed over the train, seeming now to come from the west. Each of the passengers had toasted Carol's health, and that of her child, and the bottle was now empty. The two quarters of the sandwich, and one chocolate bar, had been eaten; and the champagne was doing its work. They were not overly affected – individual amounts had been small – but their blood was fired; and, given the situation, they gladly succumbed to a welcome, liberating sense of lightheadedness. Bundled into their coats, their gloved hands deep in their pockets, they looked out at a world that still had its moments – and this was one of them. What a story they would tell – once it was all over. Champagne in a stalled train, in the middle of a blizzard! They knew a unity that a disaster, shared and borne, can bring; and they relaxed. One cold night in a lifetime: what was that?

And then the flame of the lighter struggled; and abruptly vanished.

Each pair of wide eyes stared into complete blackness, bounded by the whip-like crack and come-again of the wind.

A voice came out of that dark.

'Just sit still,' said Mason. 'We don't have to have a light. We can talk in the dark, for a time.'

'I'd like . . . some kind of light,' said Laura.

'We've got all night to get through,' said Mason. He lifted his watch close to his face, and read the luminous hands. 'It's only . . . twenty to eight.'

'Is that all?' said Anita. 'It seems ages.'

'All agreed?' said Mason, out of the dark. 'No lights until absolutely necessary?'

'As long as we go on talking,' said Laura.

'Oh, we can talk,' said Calvin. 'That chocolate's made me feel thirsty. I think I *will* start on my wine. I can feel my way . . .'

Laura felt him move away from her, and the sudden loss of that comforting human pressure brought a cry to her lips, but she smothered it. She heard the soft noise of the bottles, and then felt him brush by, on his way up the carriage. There was a sudden sound of smashing glass, almost visible on the air; and he came back.

'I broke the neck against a rack,' said Calvin. 'Penalty – twenty pounds. May I have the cup, Mrs Silverman?'

She felt around her feet for the flask, unscrewed the top, and held it out. His hand found it, and it was plucked away, into the blackness. There was a soft, liquid sound; and then they heard him drinking.

'Ah, that's better,' he said. 'Room temperature. Ha. Anyone want any?'

And so they all drank again, not out of thirst, but out of an almost desperate desire to weld the group closer together: the cup passing from unseen hand to unseen hand in the dark.

The wine seemed to dry Silverman's gums.

'Strong stuff,' he said.

'I've always liked Beaune,' said Calvin: 'when I could afford it.'

It seemed to work faster than the champagne. Calvin was back again, next to Laura, and she could feel the heat of his body, or the growing fire of her own. She thought how strange it was to be sitting in the dark, close to a stranger, slightly tipsy, with no promise of sex: simply a warm proximity, comradeship, brother and sister, father and daughter – but not the father she knew. She saw them waiting at home, perhaps watching a TV report: *Laura's out there somewhere.* The old, grey faces turning to each other. She shook her head, as though to dislodge a burr in the mind.

Calvin shifted, and she sensed he was looking at her.

'All right?' he said.

'Yes, thank you,' she said, and smiled at the thickness of her tongue. 'What shall we talk about?'

Silence. She tried to shape the faces, out there in the blackness, but found only the invisible, patrolling wind. She nudged Calvin.

'You start.'

He drank from the cup, the last of the wine.

'So you're an art teacher, Mr Silverman,' he said. 'What kind of art?'

'Fine,' said Silverman, and there was an unexpected pride there, surprising him. 'Fine art.'

'Painting, drawing . . .?' said Calvin.

'Both,' said Silverman. 'Life drawing, mostly.'

'And you enjoy it?' said Calvin, always interested in how people passed their days.

'Who wouldn't?' said Clive. 'Any more wine going?'

'We've finished the bottle,' said Calvin.

'You've got another,' said the boy.

'We may need it,' said Calvin. 'I was asking if you enjoyed it, Mr Silverman.'

'He wouldn't do it if he didn't like it,' said Mason.

And Silverman discovered a protection in the darkness, an armour in the champagne and the wine, and for the first time in many a long year found himself free to say what he truly felt.

'No,' he said. 'I don't enjoy it.'

4

He felt Anita stiffen beside him; but now he was past caring: this was the moment, *now*, in the darkness, to tell her what he had done, what he had decided. And, swiftly, out of this cold dilemma, out of blackness and blizzard and an apprehensive land, came winging a radiant bird whose name was joy. He had come to himself.

'Don't be silly,' said Anita. 'Of course you enjoy it.'

'No,' he said. 'I might have done, at first. But not any more.'

She gave an uncertain laugh.

'Don't listen to him,' she said to the unseen faces. 'He's one of the best art teachers around.'

'Again: not any more,' said Silverman.

He felt her turn towards him.

'What does that mean?' she said.

He rubbed his chest: there was a tightness there.

'I might as well tell you now, Anita: I gave in my notice today. I'm not going back after Christmas.'

In the silence the others waited for her response.

'You saw Derek today?' she said.

'Yes.'

'And you didn't ask him about the extra teaching?'

'I told you,' he said: 'I gave in my notice. I've finished.'

For a moment she forgot where she was. She moved away from his body and turned more fully to face another kind of darkness.

'You're mad, Simon. You didn't really . . .'

He sighed.

'I've wanted to do it for years, Anita: you know that. I don't want a long discussion about it. I've done it, thank God, and that's that. I'm going to paint.'

'And what are we going to live on?' she said. And then she felt those other faces about her. 'We . . . we'll talk about it later, once we're at Carol's . . .'

'We won't,' he said. 'She's got enough on her mind. And talking about what we're going to live on: what about you getting a job? You've sucked me dry for thirty years.'

'Sucked you dry?' she said. 'What have you ever given me?'

'Listen,' he said, patiently: 'I haven't got a lot of time left – I'll be sixty next year. My old man died at eighty-three, but you can't count on that. I've got, say, ten good years. Ten years to do what I want to do: paint full-time.'

'You can retire at sixty,' she said. 'Another year. Your pension . . .'

He threw up his hands in the dark.

'Oh, *fuck* the pension!' he shouted. Sweet anger was moving in, an anger that had been dammed for over a decade. 'We're talking about life. *Life* . . .!'

'Oh, don't be so juvenile, Simon,' she said wearily, the taste of the wine now stale in her mouth.

'Don't you see?' he said: 'it's not worth it any more. Watching others leave, and a new set of faces coming in. Year after year.'

'You're not good enough,' she said. 'You're starting too late.'

'Let's talk about something else,' said Laura. 'And could we have a light?'

'We won't talk about something else,' said Silverman. He put out his hand and found Anita's arm. She moved away; but he moved also and held her sleeve. 'Look, I've decided . . .'

'*You've* decided . . .'

'Yes, and I've done it. There'll be no going back, not this time. I'm telling you now, so you know. And I don't want this time with Carol spoiled. Accept it, and have done with it. Then we can move forward.'

She pulled her arm free in one swift gesture.

'You do what you like,' she said. 'But don't expect any support from me. All those promises . . .'

'Strangely enough,' he said: 'I don't care a damn whether you're with me or not. Carol's the only thing that's held us together this long, and you know it. I'm free at last, and that's all that matters.'

He was aware of a sudden tightness in his chest, but his

mounting exhilaration at the breaking of a cage, and an open, uncluttered landscape beckoning – this was the only reality, transcending all else. Until the tightness became a burning metal vice, and he gasped. He rubbed his chest fiercely, and gasped again.

'See?' she said, out of the dark: 'see what you've done to yourself? Made it worse, haven't you?'

The hot metal of the vice gripped even tighter, and he felt a strange sensation in his right arm: as if a shower of thin coins was falling from shoulder to wrist, growing heavier as they tumbled towards a hand that would not stop shaking. He gasped for the third time, seeming to bite at the air. In a brilliant second he knew what was happening to him. He struggled to his feet. And, as the vice crushed his ribs, he gave a high cry that was almost a scream, and fell forward across Laura's legs, and rolled to the floor.

____Part Four _____

Anita had felt him rear up and away from her, and when he cried out she found an echo of the same pain and terror rising in her own throat. She heard another cry, this time from the girl, and then Simon's body came down heavily on her shoes. Her hands went down into the darkness, and found his shoulder.

'Lights,' she said, and did not recognise her own voice. 'Let's have some lights!'

'He's got the matches,' said Mason. 'Where is he?' He came forward in the dark, almost tripped over Silverman, and fumbled about the coat until he found the matches. He struck one, and held it high. Faces came into view, so shadowed and shifting that a hundred others might have ranged behind them, eyes blinking, craning forward.

'Let me have the matches,' said Calvin. He took the box from Mason, pressed two candles into the holders, and lit them. As everyone looked at Silverman's head, the face slightly averted as though hiding or ashamed, two of the angels began turning. Mason dropped his match, trod on it, and moved back.

'Get him up here,' he said.

Calvin stepped over Silverman's body and grasped the heavy shoulders. Mason took the feet.

'Lift,' he said.

The boy moved aside as the two men shuffled the body around the flaring candles, and onto the seat. Anita pushed between them.

'Loosen his collar,' said Calvin.

But, kneeling now, looking at the closed face shaded from the light, she felt rooted to the floor, as though any further movement on her part would make things worse.

'Simon?' she said, and it could have been the voice of a child.

Calvin leaned over her. His fingers tugged at the knot of Silverman's thick, tweed tie; he pulled it free, and undid the button, feeling the warm flesh of the bared throat.

The boy, standing, said:

'Is he dead?'

'No,' said Mason.

Silverman was deeply unconscious. When he had cried out, it was anger that was given voice: a sudden rage at the prospect of an end, the almost certain coming of death; an anger that was more terrible than the pain. His fists had flailed the air before he fell, striking nothing as he dropped. Suspended now between two darknesses, he began to breathe heavily, a thin line of spittle marking his lower lip.

Anita lifted his right hand and placed it across his body. Then she lifted her own, equally shaded face, a face fighting for control.

'What are we going to do?' she said.

'Nothing,' said Mason.

The others, hearing that single, factual word, found not terror or despair, but, surprisingly, a sense of immediate relaxation, a lessening of responsibility. It was true: they could do nothing. Isolated here until the weather broke or rescue came, Silverman's collapse was simply another aspect of a continuing nightmare, which would end, sooner or later. Yet this relaxation brought its own guilt, and Laura crossed the aisle and put her hand on Anita's shoulder.

'Perhaps some of the wine . . .' she said. 'Instead of brandy.'

Anita shook her head, but not at what she had heard. Her fingers playing with Simon's fingers, she said:

'Never anything like this. Heart as strong as an ox: doctors have told him so.'

'Shall I try the wine?' said Calvin.

Useless to deny it, he felt a fierce animation. Out of the study now, and tested, his imagination saw not disaster, but conjured various ends: they floated before him, his to shape and make true.

'You can try,' said Anita. She took her fingers away, and shook her husband's shoulder. 'Simon?'

Calvin picked up the second bottle, went to the rear of the carriage, used the same rack, and came back with the wine staining his hand. He poured a little into the cup, and handed in to Anita.

'Can you . . . lift his head?' she said.

She let some of the wine trickle between his open teeth. Most of it ran out again from the side of his mouth. He coughed softly. She looked up at Calvin; and he let the head sink slowly back.

'Don't worry,' she said. 'I'm not the kind that breaks.'

It sounded so extraordinary, that they were all silent. And then Laura said:

'Or . . . or any of us, I hope.'

'At least he's alive,' said Anita. Again she laced her fingers with his. 'But what are we going to do?'

Only the wind answered.

They had doused one of the candles. The single angel glinted as it turned, but now was no longer childlike. Mason came back from relieving himself at the end of the carriage. On the way back he had tested the doors and the windows. They were held tight by the snow, or frozen fast. His fingers were beginning to feel numb. He put on his gloves again and banged his hands against his greatcoat as he sat down, opposite Silverman.

'Well?' said Calvin.

'They won't open.'

'None of them?' said Clive.

'You want to try?' said Mason. 'Go ahead.' His plan was being eaten away by time, and irritation was moving in. He brought out his cigarettes. Both Calvin and the boy took one. The smell was comforting.

'They know we're here,' said Laura.

The words faded like smoke.

Anita now had her head resting on Simon's hand. Her eyes were closed, but she did not sleep. She was listening to a pulse and, she told herself, a heart.

'There are people only a mile or so away,' said Anita, her eyes still closed. 'A town, streets, cafés. Amazing.'

'How long shall we give them?' said Calvin.

Mason's cigarette-end glowed in the dark.

'Before what?'

Calvin looked at Silverman.

'We'll have to try something.'

'What?' said Mason.

'Oh, I don't know. We . . .'

'The snow's stopped and the wind's shifted,' said Mason. 'But we're still half-covered. It's night. There are drifts out there that can drown a man. You going to try and reach someone? The doors won't open. Suggest something, go on.'

'Leave him alone,' said Anita. 'There's nothing we can do, not till morning. We all know that. We must keep as warm as we can, and wait. That's all we can do.' She patted Simon's hand, as though to reassure him. 'We'll be all right.'

'Should we try and get some sleep?' said Laura.

'You feel sleepy?' said Calvin.

'No. But if we could get off, time would pass more quickly.'

'It's too cold to sleep,' said Clive.

'It'll get colder,' said Mason.

'Let's try it, anyway,' said Calvin. 'Okay?'

Anita stayed where she was, her head resting on Simon's chest. Mason stretched himself out opposite, his head towards the window, his face burrowing into his upturned collar, cigarette in his mouth, arms folded. Clive moved over and took the seat vacated by the Silvermans, and curled himself tight.

'Shall we forget the proprieties, and share?' said Calvin to Laura.

She smiled in the dark.

'Why not?' she said.

'Why didn't I think of that?' said the boy.

Calvin and Laura lay down together, opposite Clive, and put their arms around each other, her head in the curve of his shoulder. He humped her closer, and her hair brushed his face. He lay back and looked up at the unseen carriage roof, which could have stretched away for miles. He felt the stirring of an erection, and smiled to himself.

'It has its compensations,' he said.

She made herself more comfortable.

'Yes,' she said, and closed her eyes.

'Goodnight, all,' said the boy.

Again only the wind answered.

They lay quietly, each in their own thoughts, and waited for sleep. Silverman, still unconscious, breathed loudly. The wind sang, the carriage creaked; and the single candle guttered, and died.

'Leave it,' said Mason, out of the dark. 'Save the rest.'

And now all eyes were closed.

But, half an hour later, sleep had not yet come; and, one by one, they opened their eyes and stared silently into the blackness, sharing their breathing wakefulness, if not their thoughts . . .

____ 2 _____

Don't die . . .

My hands are cold, but his are warm. How long? If, in the past, I had said yes to his dreams . . . But could I have gone against myself? I have a life, too. Denied myself, always. Yet he could die. And then what?

Don't die.

Things could be arranged, it isn't too late. There are always compromises. How many in a life? Somewhere people are laughing, in the warm. Sacrificed myself? Never. Denied each other, that's what we've done. Is it my coldness keeping him warm? He has never slept so deeply. I could put out a hand — he'd be awake in an instant. Such breathing . . .

The selfishness of the artist, I told my mother. She saw it as weakness. I was blind, then. Blind with love. He has been weak. He should have had the strength to trust. To push me aside. Would I have allowed that? Is that what I wanted? I'd have gone anywhere, if he had had the strength. Instead, I was the stronger.

Contempt, that was all I had. There is still time, Simon.

Surprisingly, I find I love. Need.

Don't die . . .

_____ 3 _____

In the name of the Father . . .

Listen how he breathes: you can hear it above the wind. If he should die on us. Never seen a dead person. A corpse growing colder in the dark. I don't believe any more, no. Not in hell or heaven or purgatory, thank God. Stories — like Andy said. Yet what happens, after? If I died here. If we all died. Unrescued. That film I saw about the Ship of Death: the travelling souls. Balls, all of it.

I threw the rosary in the canal. Thought it might float. It went down, into the greenness. Came away . . . liberated. Until later, and waking up in the night, the dark bedroom . . .

I could stretch out and touch her. She wouldn't let me lie with her. Would she? Slipped up there. Breasts under the coat . . .

What shall I say when I knock? She gave me the old come-on. No mistake. Had to get away. Never again. No going back.

Always uninvited. Never asked. I invite myself, then.

Pray? I won't pray.

Holy Mary, Mother of God . . .

No.

Her breasts under the coat . . .

Always an insult. Always used.

Even this: warming another person. Used.

To have been born a man. Yet the first time, the first touch: I was the leader. I unbuttoned my blouse and took his hand. He was trembling. How old? Seventeen. He didn't know what to do. Are there any left? No. They'd tear the blouse, scatter the buttons.

He had me once, like that: on the floor of the Boardroom. Late at night, everyone gone. Doors locked. And there was a smell of cigarette smoke in his hair, old cologne . . . Thrust and thrust. A hunger, a need, a surge. And, satisfied, the rolling away. He scorched his sleeve on the electric fire. I smelled it burning . . .

Seventeen . . . I saw him, years later, in the Strand, looking in the window of Gibbons' stamp shop, with a child. Thinning hair, worried-looking. And I thought of him trembling . . .

Thank you, Sheila − and good luck. It was as if I was looking at myself, down there on the floor: that fierce, possessive, triumphant look over his shoulder. He was faceless: they are all faceless. No one ever possessed me. Never will. After this is over, once I am home . . . No, not home. Once I have . . . visited − then I shall begin again. Yes.

I am getting cramp in my foot. Always, when I am cold . . .

'All right?' said Calvin.

'I'm getting cramp in my foot,' said Laura. She winced. 'I think I'll walk about for a moment. Excuse me.'

'Do you want a light?'

'No, I'll manage.'

She felt her way to the aisle, and was gone. When she came back, she said:

'Could I have a cigarette?'

'I was trying to give them up,' said Calvin.

Mason stirred in the dark.

'Here,' he said. The match was overbright in the darkness. They creased their eyes. She bent her head.

'Coming back?' said Calvin.

'No,' she said. 'I'll be all right, on my own. Thank you.'

The dark returned. There was a soft movement as they resettled. Then, once again, silence.

It was snowing then, too . . .

I never felt the cold, that day. The tropics in my blood. Summer in January. I had often passed their windows, stopping to look at the latest titles. Now it was my turn: up there with the Greats, one foot on Parnassus. It was a rabbit-warren of a place, like something out of Dickens. Yet other men had stood in the entrance-hall and travelled in the narrow, jerking lift: men I respected, envied, determined to join, and surpass . . .

It was strange seeing my typescript on his table: it looked dog-eared, battered.

It won't make any money, *he said.* First novels don't, normally. *He tapped the title page.* Novels like this: experimental.

It doesn't matter, *I said.*

He smiled wearily. God, how callow I was!

I was full of a sudden, overwhelming thankfulness.

There are thousands out there, *I said*: writing and hoping. I . . . I speak for them all.

He sighed.

I know, *he said.*

Je-sus!

Pigeons were flying over Trafalgar Square. I was a prince in my own land. Walking back to Waterloo the world was open and beckoning. The same old bearded bastard was playing his mouth-organ on the steps leading down to the Festival Hall. I gave him a pound. He didn't stop playing, but his eyes said it all. In Stockholm the Committee were sitting. The youngest recipient of the Nobel Prize. *My speech would praise the integrity of the individual. The King's hand, smooth with too much easy living. Not a hand blistered with devotion to a craft.*

Jesus Christ! And yet I believed it. Half-believed, hoped; aspired . . .

Out there, on the wide empty freeways, speeding towards and through a mythical America. . . . Diners and clapboard and the faces of sharecroppers' children. The black faces in downtown Atlanta . . . The girl hitch-hiking to Houston: sunlight on the blonde fuzz of her thighs.

And you? *she said.*

Paperback writer, *I said.*

Her eyes widened.

Should I know you? *she said.*
Of course, *I said.* Jake Barnes.
Gee! *she said, not knowing.*
Gee is a boy's word, *said Willie Loman.*
Jake Barnes is a boy's name . . .

____ 6 _____

I'm her brother, *I said.*

He nodded and led me down the corridor lit by one flickering tube. Everything was spotless, but the tube needed seeing to.

I must warn you, *he said, over his shoulder:* it's not pretty.

It never is, *I said.*

You'd be surprised, *he said.* Some look . . . beautiful, if I can say that.

But not this one. Not Barbara.

It was like the left-luggage at any station: rows of square doors with numbers. Clean surfaces everywhere. Smell of . . . disinfectant?

Ready? *he said.*

As I'll ever be, *I said.*

He took hold of the handle, and pulled. The long drawer seemed to go on for ever. She was wrapped in a white sheet. A label was tied to one of her toes. He looked up at me: a small bloke with a stained moustache – must smoke like a chimney in his job. And then he pulled the sheet down.

Her face was purple-green. There was a large bruise on her right cheekbone, and a clean wide cut near her mouth. Nothing could change the colour of her hair: deep red, like a flame. I had never seen her breasts: they looked . . . human, and sad.

Hit by barges or driftwood, *he said.* Been in about four days.

Yes, *I said.*

She *is* your sister?

Yes, *I said.* Barbara Mason.

Sorry, *he said, and began to pull the sheet back.*

Just a minute, *I said. And I leaned down and kissed her. For the first time. She was stone cold.* Okay.

The drawer went back too smoothly, as if it carried meat. The label caught, and he tucked it in with one finger.

You'll make all the arrangements? *he said.*

Yes.

You knew she was six months' pregnant? *he said.*

Like a blow in the gut.

No, *I said.* I didn't know that.

Sorry.

Has . . . has anyone else been here? *I said.*

No, *he said.* I'm sorry about . . .

Don't keep saying sorry, *I said.*

_____ 7 _____

Silverman had no thoughts. He existed in a dark limbo between life
and death, and knew nothing. But, slowly and painfully, he began
to move towards consciousness. Signals came and went and came
again from various parts of his body, like sparks in the brain,
stronger now, glowing and steady, until the mind lit; and he opened
his eyes. For a few terrified seconds he could not remember where
he was; and, staring up into blackness, he was convinced he had
died. There was a heavy weight across his legs, and this increased
his terror: something or someone had him trapped. He cried out, and
tried to rise.

His cry chilled their blood – it was so sharp and unexpected and
fearful. They were awake as never before, staring into the same
dark. Anita, jolted out of the first blessed stages of sleep, found
herself half-thrown by the twitching legs; and held fast to his
hands.

He cried out again, and she leaned over him.

'Hush, Simon,' she said. 'Hush, dear.'

It was a strange, motherly command, and it gave a strange
comfort to all. They moved through the dark to join her.

'Take it easy,' said Mason. He lit the remaining candle. The dark
stepped back, but only a fraction. For the first time they noticed the
vapour that came with their breathing.

And Silverman remembered. He looked down at Anita, the
weight gone from his legs, but centered like a bruise in his chest. He
coughed softly, winced, and ran a dry tongue over dry lips.

'Oh God . . .' he said.

'Give him some wine,' said Mason.

'Do you think that's wise?' said Laura.

74

'Give him some wine,' said Mason. He grunted in exasperation.
Silverman looked at his wife.

'Heart?' he said.

'It looks like it,' she said. 'Don't worry.'

'Don't worry, she says,' said Silverman, his voice a dry croak.
Calvin came with the wine.

'Can you sit up?' said Anita.

'Of course,' said Silverman. But other signals came now: ominous
pulses, laced with pain. 'I . . . I can't move this arm.'

'Could be a stroke,' said Mason.

Silverman tried to smile.

'Cheerful as always,' he said. 'I don't want you should feed me,
Anita.'

'Don't be silly,' she said, her arm around his shoulder. The
smooth, plastic rim of the cup touched his lip. 'Drink now.'

He drank, and there was something wrong. Something was
terribly wrong inside him. Something rebelled against the wine: it
was like drinking acid.

'No more,' he said. 'No. Let . . . let me lie back again. Thank
you.'

The cold formality of his words hurt them more than his cries.
They looked at the strong, pale face, the strong man cast down. And
Laura sighed. It was a loud sound in the silence.

'It's all the strain, Simon,' said Anita.

'You should know,' he said.

The condemnation was there, unhidden. They all heard it. She
pressed her face into his chest.

'Don't say that,' she said, and there were tears in her muffled
voice.

'I say it but don't mean it,' he said. His left hand came up and his
fingers touched her hair, pushed through it. He tried to laugh, but
all that came was a short, explosive grunt. 'I can see nothing down
here, gentlemen.'

Calvin put down the bottle and found the rest of the candles.
Soon three fresh ones burned in the holders. The light glared on
their faces, a feast.

'What are you doing?' said Mason.

'It's not a waste,' said Calvin. 'The man's . . . ill. There are three
left. Let him have his light.'

'Thank you,' said Silverman. 'Anita, you . . . you are making
me uncomfortable.'

She lifted her head from his chest. She sniffed, sat up, and blew her nose.

'Sorry,' she said. 'How are you feeling?'

The light hurt his eyes. It was suddenly too bright. He was no longer in command of his body. Only his mind seemed his own. He was fearful, but kept his voice steady.

'I'm cold, like everyone else,' he said. 'But not too bad. Alive, I think.'

'Of course you are,' she said. She patted his hand. 'What is the time?'

Mason looked at his watch.

'Ten to eleven,' he said.

'Still Friday,' said Silverman to himself.

'Still Friday,' said Mason.

Laura shivered and rubbed her arms.

'All night to get through,' she said.

'It'll pass,' said Calvin.

Anita stroked Simon's hand.

'Yes,' she said. 'What shall we do to pass the time?'

They were silent.

8

The boy's hand, resting on the rack, touched the paperback he had bought at the station. He picked it up.

'If you'd like to sit down,' he said: 'I could read you some of this. While the candles last. Or someone can.'

'What a good idea,' said Laura.

'That would take our minds off things,' said Anita. 'What do you think of that, Simon?'

Drowsy with shock and pain, he almost whispered:

'I don't mind.'

'What is it?' said Calvin.

Clive showed him the cover.

'*The Third Assassin* by Jake Barnes,' said the boy. 'It's not bad — as far as I've got. I can crouch down there, near the light.'

Calvin looked at something he had made, in the past, in the early, journeyman days, and was not proud of. He hated the whole glossy, bright, fluorescent production. He could not bear to hear it read: he did not wish to be reminded, especially today . . .

'I don't think so,' he said. He tipped the bottle and drank a little of the cold wine.

'It's about . . .' began Clive.

'I know what it's about,' said Calvin. 'It's not . . . that good.'

'Let him read it, please,' said Anita, still slowly stroking Simon's hand. 'We don't want to keep thinking . . .'

Laura sat down, across the aisle.

'Yes, go on, Clive,' she said.

Mason sat down opposite the long, stretched body of Silverman, and once again pushed his gloved hands into his armpits; the boy settled to the floor as though to a bedroom fire; only Calvin remained standing, holding the bottle to his chest with both chilled hands.

'No,' he said.

'What's the matter with you?' said Mason. 'Go on, son.'

Calvin lifted his head to the still-prowling wind.

'It's one of mine,' he said, almost reluctantly. 'I wrote it. And I'd rather not hear it.'

'Your name's not Jake Barnes,' said Clive.

'It's a name I use for some of my books. A pseudonym. I have proof in my suitcase, if you like.'

'You don't want to hear your own book being read?' said Anita.

Laura looked at the tall man with more than a casual interest.

'Perhaps he's being modest,' she said. 'Perhaps he'd like to read it to us himself.'

Clive held out the paperback.

'Yes, here . . .' he said.

'No, thanks,' said Calvin. He put the bottle to one side and sat opposite Laura. 'Leave it be, please.'

Silverman stirred under Anita's hand.

'Help me up,' he said.

'You're sure?' she said.

'Yes. I . . . I just want to turn . . . the other way,' he said. His breath whistled as he stood. 'Now, back . . . gently. Okay. Thank you.' He propped his head on the arm-rest near the window as Anita pulled his coat tighter around him. 'I . . . I can understand Mr Calvin's reluctance. I sold some of my paintings, once, way back. I wouldn't like to see them again. One moves away, right?'

'Right,' said Calvin.

'It got *me* interested,' said Clive. 'Made me want to see how it turned out.'

'I think it has the requisite number of hooks,' said Calvin. 'But, like Mr Silverman says: you grow away.'

'To what, in your case?' said Silverman.

Calvin saw Northumberland littered with Southern plantations, and shook his head.

'I'm . . . I'm working on something new at the moment,' he said.

'Under your own name?' said Silverman.

'Yes. For my sins.'

A pause.

'So you're a storyteller,' said Anita. 'Well, since you won't hear your own book read – tell us a story.'

'Yes, come on, do that,' said Laura. 'Go on – off the top of your head.'

'The kid couldn't have read for long anyway,' said Mason. 'Look at the candles.'

They seemed to be burning faster.

'Go on,' said Anita, wanting to be distracted from her husband's troubled breathing.

They waited.

Calvin settled himself against the window, and looked above the shifting glow that softened the faces of his listeners.

'Of course,' he said: 'this is what I might have tackled in the past.'

'What?' said Clive.

Calvin waved a cold hand.

'This,' he said: 'us. A version of the formula. Six assorted people, cut off from civilisation. Desert island, lifeboat, burning skyscraper; long-distance bus taken over by a madman. *Bridge of San Luis Rey* stuff.' He grinned in the near-dark. 'Of course, you'd have to be more than you are now. You're too ordinary.'

'Thank you,' said Laura.

'Oh, I count myself, too,' said Calvin. 'After today, believe me.'

'No one is ordinary,' said Silverman.

'I know a lot of ordinary people,' said Mason.

Clive leaned forward, his face brightening in the small flames.

'What would you make us?' he said. 'What would you make me?'

'You?' said Calvin, considering him. 'You'd . . . you'd be a normal-looking shipping-clerk. But this morning you went aboard one of the cargoboats in West India Dock, to collect a manifest. There was a strain of bubonic plague aboard. You're the next Black Death.'

'Hey, *great!*' said Clive.

Silverman gave a clotted laugh.

'And us?' he said. 'Anita and me?'

'You're real name isn't Silverman,' said Calvin. 'It's . . . Ivanov. Leon and Natasha Ivanov. You're a Russian national, a physicist working for the British government. The KGB are after you. You're going to a secret address in Portsmouth.'

'How right you are!' said Anita.

'My turn,' said Laura. 'Something romantic, please.'

Calvin looked at the shadowed face tucked into the fur collar, the glint of her eyes.

'You're obviously Sonia Radensky, a trusted member of the KGB, following the Ivanovs to Portsmouth.'

'True,' said Laura. 'How I miss my samovar.'

'And what would you make yourself?' said the boy.

'Me?' said Calvin. He laughed. 'Oh, I'm . . . I'm a transvestite who isn't ready to come out. I'm going to Geneva for the operation.'

'That wouldn't surprise me,' said Mason.

'Yes, and you, too, sergeant,' said Anita. 'What would you make the sergeant, Mr Calvin?'

Calvin looked at the dark shape huddled in the corner, the sudden glow of the cigarette, the subdued glimmer of the buttons.

'He'd have to be a killer,' he said. 'He shot his commanding-officer this morning, and now he's on the run.'

'Correct,' said Mason. 'I've got a machine-gun in my suitcase.' He half-stood. 'Want to see it?'

Calvin spread his hands.

'Well, that's as far as I can go,' he said.

'How would it end?' said the boy.

Calvin looked down at the uplifted face behind the dying candles.

'Buy the book,' he said.

*   *   *

One of the candles went out.

'Let *me* tell you something,' said Silverman. He tried to sit up, but slipped back again.

'It doesn't matter, Simon,' said Anita.

'But I want to tell you this: all of you. I'm . . . I'm stronger. Perhaps it's passed – whatever it was.' He propped himself upright, his elbows digging into the arm-rest, and settled. The second candle-flame began to waver. 'I want you to hear this. I want you to tell me what you think it means.'

'Don't tire yourself,' said Anita.

'Oh, leave me be, please,' he said.

The second candle went out, and the dark stepped closer, dousing Silverman's face. The voice spoke out of a dusky blackness.

'I had a dream . . .' he began.

'You and Martin Luther King,' said the boy.

'Quiet!' said Anita. 'Go on, dear.'

'I had a dream,' said Silverman. 'Not too long ago. The most vivid dream of my life. Listen to this. I dreamt I was in an Alpine village . . .'

'You'd gone for the same operation,' said Mason, and laughed.

'This is very important to me,' said Silverman. 'I'm not just passing the time.'

'Sorry,' said Mason. 'No more interruptions.'

'I've never forgotten it,' said Silverman: 'a highspot in my life, I tell you. Always some kind of talisman . . .'

'I don't remember you telling me,' said Anita. 'I'd have remembered.'

'I told no one,' he said. 'Until now.' The third candle went out suddenly, as if unseen fingers had pinched the flame. Silverman's voice now came from total darkness. 'I dreamt I was in an Alpine village. It was night. There was a cobbled street and lights from houses. I was standing to one side. A file of men went by, carrying climbing equipment: ropes and ice-picks, you know the kind of thing. I found myself bringing up the rear, and I had the same rope over my shoulder now, the same pack, the same ice-pick. We walked on through the village – no, *marched*, I would say: there was a kind of purpose, a directness . . .'

He paused, and the carriage shifted in the strengthening wind.

'. . . and then we came to the shell of a house. A tall, thin house, black against the night sky. And we went in. A complete shell: no floors, stairs – nothing. Like the interior of a . . . windmill, that kind of shape. And we took the ropes from our shoulders and linked ourselves together, and began to climb.'

'The *inside* of the house?' said the boy's voice, out of the same dark.

'Yes,' said Silverman. 'It didn't seem at all strange. We climbed up the walls, roped together, sheer. I enjoyed it: there was no danger of falling. And then, at the top of the house, there was a room. It just *came*, as it does in dreams. And we were all suddenly

80

very tired, dog-tired. I remember we untied ourselves and lay down on the wooden floor. And we slept. When I woke up, the others were still sleeping. I noticed there was a door to the left of the room, and under the door there was a line of yellow light. I got to my feet and opened the door . . .'

He paused, as if it cost him some emotion to continue.

'And . . .?' said the boy.

'Can you imagine?' said Silverman, and his voice had a kind of wonderment about it as he relived what he had dreamt. 'I was standing on a ledge, on the side of a mountain. In bright, clear, strong sunlight. It was a wide ledge. I went to the edge and looked down. All the people in the world were down there: tiny figures, crowds, looking up. Silently. Just the heat of the sun and the silence.'

He cleared his throat.

'And then I heard the most beautiful music. I can't tell you how beautiful it was – it's past description. It was a kind of chanting, backed by ancient instruments – dulcimers, that kind of thing. It was like . . . *drinking* beauty, you know what I mean? And around the curve of the ledge came a group of people, about twenty, twenty-five. They were as beautiful as the music: tall, bronzed, perfect; led by a man dressed in gold. Then the musicians appeared, and the music got louder. The man stepped forward and put his hands on my shoulders; and when I looked down at myself, I . . . I too was clothed in gold. And as he took his hands away, so a great cheer came up from the people of the world. And I felt a . . . sublime happiness. The cheering went on and on . . . When I woke up I remembered every detail; and I never felt happier in my life. That was the dream . . .'

Separate in their own darknesses, the others were silent. Until Clive said:

'And that's it, is it?'

'Isn't it enough?' said Silverman. He cleared his throat again. Coughed. 'Well, what do you think?'

'Just a dream,' said Mason. 'I've had better; worse. Crazy things happen in dreams: climbing up the insides of houses . . .'

'You see nothing else in it?' said Silverman. 'But, then, you're a military man, a military mind . . .'

'Doesn't mean you don't feel,' said Mason. 'I feel.'

'Too much cheese before you went to bed,' said Clive. 'Does it every time.'

'*Please*,' said Silverman, and there was pain in his voice, as if the boy tarnished the glory. 'Can't anyone be serious – just for a moment? It meant a lot to me . . . means a lot. What about you, Laura? You read anything into it?'

'Do you?' she said, feeling strange and alone: speaking into the dark.

'I have my ideas,' he said. 'Like to hear some more.'

'I never believed dreams meant anything in daylight,' she said. 'Astrology, all that stuff – it leaves me cold. Isn't climbing – ladders, and that sort of thing – isn't that supposed to mean something sexual?'

'Naturally,' said Silverman, in a dry whisper of a voice, almost lost in the sound of the wind: 'isn't everything? And you, Mr Calvin?'

'Again, I'm not one for symbols,' said Calvin. 'I don't like . . . interpretation. It could mean anything. Even too much cheese. It's very visual: something an artist would dream. Aside from that . . .'

'It's recognition, Simon,' said Anita, crouched by his side on the floor, chilled, holding his warm hand. 'If you had told me before . . . It's a desire for approval, Simon. A wish . . .'

He slowly took his hand away.

'No,' he said, in that same whispery breath of a voice. 'No, it's more than that. It's something . . . greater.'

She reached up to recapture his hand, but found only the angle of his arm. She pressed the thick cloth of his coat with cold fingers.

'Well, you tell me, dear,' she said. 'Tell us all what you think. What did it mean?'

They waited. The wind was strong, gathering to gale-force, lifting snow and sending it to hiss against the windows. The carriage groaned.

'Go on, dear,' she said.

Silence.

She pulled herself up by his arm.

'Simon?' she said. She rocked his body. 'Simon!'

And Mason was the first to move . . .

Part Five

1

The match flared over the closed face, and whitened the other, crowding faces. Anita rocked her husband once again.

'Simon, *please*!'

Mason passed the box of matches to Calvin.

'Light the rest of the candles.'

'There's only three left.'

'Whose fucking fault is that?' said the sergeant, his voice a mixture of desperation at ragged, undisciplined lives, and anger at this further complication of his plans. 'Get one lit, then. Get some light.' He pushed Anita. 'Out of my way, lady.'

She fell back, her spine hitting the edge of the seat behind her.

'I can help . . .' she began.

'You can do nothing,' he said. 'Keep out of the way.' He glanced at the dying match, now in Laura's fingers. 'Where's the light?'

'Coming, coming,' said Calvin. 'Getting mad solves nothing.'

'Oh?' said Mason, his fingers probing for a pulse in Silverman's neck. 'Where'd you hear that?' His chilled fingers began to tear at the buttons of Silverman's shirt.

Anita, slumped below him, began to push herself upright.

'What are you doing?' she said.

'Guess,' he said, shortly, and with a certain viciousness. 'He's gone, you know that?'

Two candles shone in the golden ring.

'Gone?' she said, and it was another whisper.

'Dead,' said the sergeant. 'Get them damned angels off and let's have some light here.'

Calvin removed the angels and lifted the bare circle high. Silverman's chest appeared, a fuzz of thick grey hair. Mason moved the body roughly to the right, straddled it, and began to press down with swift, urgent, jolting movements. Small gasps came from the dead man as the head swayed, and were signalled by small breaths which smoked. A blob of candle-grease hit Mason's right hand, but he did not pause. Calvin moved the circle an inch to the right. Now the blobs fell on Silverman's sleeve. The dead man breathed, but did not breathe. Anita took the limp left hand and cradled it to her cheek.

'Please,' she said softly, so softly that only she heard it.

Now Mason's own breath was hoarse with effort.

84

'Shall I take over?' said Calvin.

The sergeant did not reply, but worked on. Then he stopped. His left hand came up and wiped his mouth. He looked down at Anita, the hair that hid her face. Then he made his right hand into a fist, and brought it down hard on that grey chest. Everyone winced at the force of the blow, except the dead man.

'Oh God,' said Anita.

The fist came down again.

'Oh,' she said again. 'Don't.'

The fist came down with even greater force. The dead man seemed to surge up, then fall back. Mason rested his ear among the grey hairs, and listened. He lifted his head, and was silent.

'Mouth to mouth?' said Calvin.

The sergeant looked down with some distaste at the dark, beard-fringed lips. He heaved himself off the body, and stepped back into the aisle, treading on Laura's foot.

'Sorry,' he said.

'It's all right,' she said. The courtesies were almost laughable.

'You can try if you like,' said Mason to Calvin. He held out his hand for the ring of candles. Calvin gave it to him, and put his hand on Anita's shoulder.

'Excuse me,' he said: 'would you mind . . .?'

She did not release her husband's hand, but shifted back towards the door. Calvin knelt down, pinched Silverman's nose with two fingers of his right hand, and covered the dead man's lips with his own. He tasted wine and cigarette-smoke, and knew the cold smell of another human, joined in an intimacy only lovers knew. He gathered life-giving breath into his own lungs until they ached, then slowly but powerfully sent it jetting down into other lungs; and continued doing so, steadily, and with a certain pride and a touch of fantasy: the corpse reviving, the eyes opening, a man restored. He breathed on until his own lips were sore with the pressure, the hairs of the beard like blunt needles against his mouth. But nothing happened: the body did not twitch into life, there was no response, no answer. He took his stinging lips away, sat back, and, like Mason, could find nothing to say.

'You're giving up?' said Anita, sharply.

He looked at her. Her eyes were over-large, each holding a candle-shine.

'My . . . my lips are sore,' he said, and it sounded weak, a feeble excuse.

85

She came off the door, and got to her knees.

'Move, please,' she said.

'He's gone,' said Mason. 'I'm sorry, but . . .'

'Move!,' she said, and fastened her lips on her dead husband's.

The others watched and waited as the candles fluttered and grew shorter. To Calvin the urgent sound of her breathing was like that of a scared child's, working at an enormous balloon, closing its eyes for the bang. It was a comic image, not suited to the occasion, and he looked away, tucked his cold hands deep inside his jacket, felt the warmth of his body through his shirt, and moved his right hand down to his own heart: it beat strongly against his fingers, and he was comforted.

*　　　*　　　*

She had stopped now, but her lips still stayed on his. She said words against his mouth, but neither the dead nor the listening living could hear them.

Laura stepped across the aisle, and Calvin moved back to allow her to kneel and put her arms around that crouching, weeping body that seemed to be visibly shrinking. Mason took the candles away and rested the circle on the floor. The men looked at each other, read nothing there, and looked away. Once again the light began to go.

'Come on now,' said Laura, into Anita's hair: 'Come away now.'

'No,' said Anita.

'You can't stay there,' said Mason.

She lifted her head so swiftly that Laura was thrown back.

'I'll stay as long as I like,' she said. 'Will . . . will *you* stop me?'

'You can't hold a dead man,' said Mason.

'I can . . .' she said.

'There's nothing there any more,' said Mason. 'Nothing. You understand me?'

'Maybe he's gone to that . . . mountain,' said the boy.

The sentimentality sickened Mason. He knew men went nowhere but into the dark. Words came to his lips, but for the woman's sake he held them back. But to Anita the boy's compassion was another kind of light, and she reached out a hand. He leaned over and took it awkwardly, each feeling the other's coldness.

'Thank you,' she said. 'Thank you for saying that.'

He looked beyond her to Silverman's stillness. His first dead man.

'It's all right,' he said. 'Maybe he has.'

She released his hand.

'Candles are almost finished,' said Mason. 'Let's get him away from there.'

'Where?' said Anita.

Mason let out a breath.

'When these candles go,' he said, slowly, 'we've got one left, and your husband's matches. Right? We can't . . . plan with a dead man between us . . .'

'What have you got for a heart?' said Laura.

'I *could* tell you,' said Mason. He looked at her shadow-filled face. 'Look, it's not that I . . .' He started again. 'Look, we've got to be realistic. We can't help him now, and he can't help us.'

'I hope I'm somewhere near when *you* die,' she said.

'I won't care a damn, will I, one way or the other,' said Mason. 'Like him, there. You want to lie with a dead man all night?' he said to Anita.

One of the candles went out. She touched her husband's hand. It was losing some of its small warmth.

'It would be no hardship, believe me,' she said. 'But if he bothers you . . .'

'We won't move him far,' said Calvin. 'None of us are going anywhere.'

'All right,' she said. 'I suppose it's for the best.' She found her handkerchief and wiped her nose. 'Where . . . where will you put him?'

'Just forward a few seats,' said Mason.

She moved to join Laura as the two men stepped forward, their huge shadows curving on the roof. Calvin took Silverman's shoulders; Mason the feet. They lifted. The head lolled against Calvin's left arm. Anita's hands went to her mouth.

'Careful, please,' she said.

The boy moved the last guttering flame in its bed of grease, out of the aisle and out of the way. The men began to shuffle towards the front of the train, Mason going backwards. The flame, cowled by the jutting seats, went out. Once again there was complete blackness. Mason swore, the words lost in the cry of the wind, louder now in the dark.

'Can you feel your way?' said Calvin, the weight of the dead man pulling at his shoulders.

'Yes,' said Mason, and began to move again.

And then, without warning, blinding them all, every light in the carriage blazed.

*　　　　*　　　　*

The brightness, that covered them like deliverance, that caused sudden, sharp tears of thankfulness to prickle Laura's eyes, lasted only a matter of seconds; but in that short, seemingly arc-lit span, all were made motionless, as though a curtain had drawn back, to disclose a tableau: the interior of a night train; two men carrying a third; a boy crouched on hands and knees in a space between seats; two women, one old, one young, arms around each other, faces lifted. To Calvin, it was as if a flare had illuminated a battlefield, and caught in that falling, failing fire was the wide-eyed stare of his comrade, facing him across a dead man, perhaps the last enemy. And then it was darkness again, patterned by the fading echo of lights which had so briefly lived.

'Damn!' said Mason.

Calvin felt the body tugged away from him, and followed.

'At least we know they're trying,' said Laura. She squeezed Anita's shoulder. 'It could come on again any minute.' She herself was still shaken by what she had seen: the raw, cold, vulnerable faces of her fellow-passengers: did she look so defenceless, so *open*, too? 'Bear up,' she said, perhaps even to herself.

'For what?' said Anita. She moved out of the girl's grasp. 'Are you all right down there?' she called.

'Fine, fine,' came back Calvin's voice. 'Don't worry.'

'Don't worry, he says,' said Anita. 'What should we worry about?' She peered into the blackness, as if she might see the wind that tried the doors and the windows. 'Are *you* all right, Clive?'

'Yes,' he said. 'Sitting down. Okay.'

'Come nearer,' she said. 'Don't sit by yourself.' Her voice broke. 'Oh God, Simon,' she said. 'No, don't touch me, Laura.' The boy blundered against her, and she pushed him, more roughly than she intended, on to the opposite seat. 'There you are, Clive. Stay there, son.'

She bit her lip, and swallowed her tears.

'Do you want to see that he's okay?' called Calvin.

'See him?' said Anita. 'I can see nothing.'

'He's quite comfortable,' said Calvin, still feeling that heavy body in his tingling fingers. 'I mean . . .'

'I know what you mean,' she said. 'Later. Later I'll go and see him. Come back, now. Thank you. My God, what a night. Shall we have the last candle?'

'We'll keep it for emergencies,' said Mason.

Anita grunted.

'Emergencies,' she said. Her head turned restlessly. Her fingers plucked at her damp handkerchief. 'You said something about a plan . . .'

'There's nothing we can do till morning,' said Mason.

'We can talk about it now,' she said. 'Discuss.'

'I think we ought to sleep,' he said.

'I don't think I ever want to sleep again,' she said.

'I think we ought to try,' said Laura. 'It'll make the time go faster. And the lights *may* come on again. Who knows?'

'Who knows?' said Anita. There was a silence. And then she said: ''All right, we'll try.' She turned towards Laura. 'I'd . . . I'd rather be on my own. If you don't mind. Could you . . . move?'

'You're sure?'

'Certain,' said Anita. She felt the girl stand and move away. 'Thank you.' She stretched herself out and put her cold hands, childlike, under her right cheek. She closed her eyes. 'I won't say goodnight. I don't even know if I want the morning to come.'

_____ **2** _____

They lay separately, stretched out or curled against the ribbed padding of the seats, heads tucked into the collars of their coats, listening to the still urgent wind, the slither of blown snow, the complaint of the carriage. And, because of the cold and their own tireless thoughts, sleep was a long time coming.

Calvin could not feel his fingers or his toes. His ears ached, and there was a slight, bruising pain along his jawbone, joined at times by the jump of a nerve that seemed to fire every fibre in his face. Made alone by the dark, the breathing of others doused by the blizzard, he found himself thinking of Oates, that old schoolboy hero: companion of Scott on the last journey, lying awake in the shaking tent, crippled by frostbite; and then the decision: *Just stepping outside for a minute.* There was magnificence there: it still warmed his blood to think of it. And the equally magnificent silence of the others: that unspoken acknowledgement of another's free choice. The flap closing; the illustration in the history book: the bowed figure stumbling into the white eye of the storm, never to be seen again. The gesture, however futile the outcome.

The nerve woke again, and he shifted his head deeper into the join of the seat. Did they make men like that any more? Christ, no. It was a world empty of heroes. He thought of his own weakness at the hotel, and gritted his teeth. *You ask too much*, he said; but did not know to whom he spoke . . .

What if he were to die here, like Silverman? It was possible: rescuers coming too late, or never coming; a snowy mausoleum holding six stiff bodies: the Ice Age here without warning, moving towards a sub-zero Africa. What had he accomplished? Nothing he had done had ever truly satisfied him. What would he leave behind him? Two children: but even lunatics coupled. A few remaindered hardbacks; a few paperbacks yellowing in some back-street store. Nothing great. Just another journeyman.

Not any more, he told himself. No. Silverman had gone so unexpectedly, so *easily*. Just drifted away. The man who dreamed of mountains . . .

Sleep now, he said. But against his closed eyelids that bowed figure still stumbled on, a man who had given his life for his friends. Magnificent . . .

Across the aisle, Anita could not stop shivering. She thought the others must surely hear her fast, shuttling breaths, sense the small convulsions that shook her body. Her brain seemed numb, robbed of any emotion, save that, strangely, of indifference. Nothing mattered now. She was not concerned with rescue. She was not concerned with anything the world could offer. Still in a state of shock, even the imminent birth of her first grandchild meant nothing now. Whatever its sex, it was of another generation, another time. Already, in the womb, it was aeons forward, gone beyond a dead grandfather, an ancestor it would never know, gone into an ever-widening universe. What had held Anita's life lay a few feet away, in the dead shell of a man; and the past was as fixed and motionless as a fossil in rock; this cold, this shivering, merely a foretaste of the winter of the rest of her days . . .

It was then that she felt her stomach crawl with hunger. Still shivering, her hands pressed against her right cheek, she smiled. The needs of the body and the needs of the soul. The soul said *Enough*; but the body said *Live* . . .

But who needed her now?

She saw with a terrible clarity the never-to-come-again beauty of the world, and the preciousness of simply being alive. She had concerned herself with trivialities, and now, hard and painful as it was, she was learning the lesson.

But it was too late. Or so she told herself . . .

Curled into himself, his knees drawn up to his chest, the boy desperately needed to use the end of the carriage. But even the dark could not remove an old inhibition, and he curled himself tighter, and suffered.

It was the inhuman element he feared: the voice of the storm, a voice that cared nothing for steel and glass and the dead man, and the five remaining. Twice he had opened his mouth to call *Everyone okay?*: to hear their reassuring answers, to make contact, to know that they were there; but the words had died on his lips, as if killed by the cold, or by this evidence of his own frailty.

He opened his eyes. The blackness was so profound, it could be touched, felt, fingered. The borders of the train had disappeared. He lay on a ledge, travelling through space. Going where? Could it have been he that had died, and was speeding to judgement, an awesome light growing ahead, so strong now that he had to shield his eyes against it, and a powerful, commanding, questioning voice speaking out of the sun, through a flurry of angels . . .?

'Everyone okay?' he said.

The wind and the creaking carriage drowned the words.

'Everyone okay?' he said again, louder now, almost a cry, his head lifted into the Arctic air, fearful.

'Go to sleep, kid,' said Mason.

The voice could have been that of a god, so swiftly did it act like a benediction on the boy. He sank back with a sigh.

'Goodnight, Sarge,' he said.

There was no answer. But none was needed. A human voice had spoken, out of the dark. Someone was there. The boy closed his eyes. But another need asserted itself. He would have to make a move.

He swung himself off the seat, and stood up. Chilled to the bone, disorientated, he swayed forward, his hands grasped the rack in front of him, and the edge of his raincoat brushed Mason's face.

'What the hell now?' said the sergeant.

'Just going down the end,' said Clive.

Mason settled deeper.

'Have one for me,' he said.

*   *   *

A minute or so later – or it could have been hours, so timeless was the night – the boy came back. Mason, half-asleep now, caught the movement of clothes, a colder stirring of the air.

'All right, son?' he said, his voice muffled against his collar.

'Yes, thanks.'

'It won't be long until morning.'

'No. Goodnight.'

Mason shrugged deeper into his greatcoat, so deep that a button touched his cheek like the tip of an icy finger. He had been colder in his life: he thought of that exercise in Wales, two winters ago: hours wrapped in a groundsheet, waiting for an attack that never came; the sheet and the Bren gun ribbed with frost at first light. Everything had to be endured, fought. Animals laid down, gave up. He enjoyed being tested. He remembered Leicester-Brown, that tall, spindly, bespectacled National Serviceman, a graduate in Chinese Studies – *Jesus!* – falling on the assault-course, into a ditch full of barbed-wire, entangling himself further, blood spotting his denims as the strands tightened, the weak eyes filling with tears . . . The same on the firing-range, refusing to shoot at the target: *I am not prepared to shoot my fellowman, in any guise . . .* Mason grunted to himself, felt the warm breath fill what was now almost a cocoon . . .

Not prepared to shoot my fellowman . . . Falling asleep now, he saw the line of terraced houses (why did he see them as terraced?). He did not know the town, the avenue, the door bearing the number forty-two; he saw himself waiting for the door to be opened, but he could not visualise his victim. Somewhere now, in snow-covered Petersfield, a man was sleeping soundly who, tomorrow, would open the door to a stranger.

Mason smiled. Nothing would stop that confrontation. He looked forward to it. The night must end, the journey would resume . . .

He smiled himself into sleep.

Laura was at a party. There was light everywhere: streaming down from three great chandeliers. Talk, laughter; white-gloved waiters bringing champagne. Music was coming from another room. Lanterns lit a white balcony, ovals of shifting colours. He was there, dancing with Sheila, whose breasts rode above her red dress. Laura did not care: she looked up at her own escort. To her surprise it was Silverman, a younger Silverman, elegant, beard neatly trimmed. They danced out of the room, past the small orchestra; on into the garden . . .

But it was a winter garden. The trees were shafts of ice, with leaves that rang like glass. There was a moon, white-faced among the leaves, staring. The air was bitter, heart-stopping. She wanted to go back, and tugged at his sleeve. He did not move. Once again she looked up.

He had changed into a tall, rock-hard statue. Only his eyes moved, and they were red-rimmed and terrible – as if trapped inside that white, motionless head. And then, as she watched, the stone began to peel and slide away, and blood surged from within, ice-cold and staining her dress. She tried to pull away, but the hard fingers gripped. Her dress was soaking. And now she saw a thin film of stone sheathing her fingers, and moving on . . .

She screamed. And woke.

She stared into perfect blackness, her heart racing, the echo of the scream fading, lost in the wind. She sensed the others around her, and waited for their voices. None came. Like the boy, she wanted to speak, to call.

But she lay down again and pressed her face into the warm animal smell of her collar, and stayed awake for a long time, eyes wide open, thinking of a man slowly changing into stone.

Part Six

Mason woke. He had slept without dreaming, or did not remember the dream; and, waking, he lay still and silent inside his greatcoat, remembering where he was.

And then he became aware of light. It had been an ordinary circumstance in the past: the coming of day; but now there was something akin to a miracle pressing against the windows, marking the curve of the roof, acknowledging the thin haze of his own breath. He turned his face to the right, and heard the rasp of a day's beard against his collar. Calvin lay stretched on the opposite seat, closed face almost hidden. Mason quietly sat up. There was a faint blurring of frost on his coat, following the creases. He looked across the aisle. The girl was asleep, legs drawn up. There was no Mrs Silverman.

He swung his legs off the seat, and immediately seemed to break a fragile skin of warmth: cold pounced on his freed face and hands, set his ears burning. He rubbed his cheeks with his gloves, and stepped out into the aisle. The boy lay on a seat in the next row, only a spiky fringe of hair showing. Mason moved on, noiselessly.

Mrs Silverman was kneeling by the side of her dead husband, her head in the curve of his left shoulder. Unaware of Mason, she abruptly sat back on her heels, sighed, took a folded handkerchief from her bag, unfolded it and placed the white square over that unseeing head. She got to her feet, and turned.

Startled by Mason's closeness, her hand went to her mouth.

'Oh,' she said.

'You okay?'

'Yes, thank you.' Rubbing her arms now, her breath smoking, she looked down at the body. 'You were right, you know: there's nothing there. What made him what he was, has gone.' She lifted her head to Mason. 'It convinces me – the absence: that there's something after. Something has so obviously . . . *gone*. That's just the shell. I think we survive, somehow.'

'It's morning,' he said, turning away from her chilled face, the fiery eyes.

'Thank God,' she said.

Mason moved down the corridor to the others, and she followed.

'Let them sleep,' she whispered.

He nodded.

'Just checking,' he said.

They walked on to almost the end of the carriage, where the light was strongest. Here they stopped, and turned around.

*   *   *

Viewed from where they stood, the train seemed to have run into a gigantic snowdrift. There was a pearl-grey half-darkness at the furthest end, which the morning could not illumine. It extended to more than two-thirds of the carriage, then the snow-line began to dip, leaving the last three windows on the left side clear; those on the right still partially obscured. Yet nothing of the land could be seen: the snow-line might have dropped, but the frost was thick on the glass, and anything could have existed beyond those firmly-drawn elaborate fronds: a frozen sea, winter-locked earth, the strangest of planets.

Mason moved to the left, between the seats, and began to rub a gloved fist on the glass. It was like rubbing a slab of ice. Flakes of frost coated his glove, the fronds began to blur, and within seconds the cold burned through, numbing every bone in his hand, and moving down to his wrist. He worked on, cursing quietly. The frost seemed inches thick, layer on layer, and soon his fist assumed the heavy deadness of a tool, so alien did it seem to the growing warmth of the rest of his body. More flakes were moulded to the shape of his glove, or dropped to the floor, and still the window would not give up its secrets. Sweating now, a welcome, warming sweat, he crashed his fist hard against the glass.

'Come on, you bastard!' he said.

At last a small circle came, and widened. He peered through. But the blizzard had attacked the outer glass also, and all he could see was a division of whiteness, which might have been snow or the wall of an iceberg, or an unmoving river.

The sound of Mason's fist striking the window brought Calvin fully awake. He sat up swiftly, saw that the situation had not changed; discovered that he had one hell of a headache; and then was grateful for the light. He got off the seat and looked down the carriage. He saw Mason step away from the window.

'Anything?' he called.

'No,' said Mason.

'What's up?' said Clive, lifting his head an inch.

'Nothing,' said Calvin.

The boy came into the aisle, still half-asleep. He yawned.

'Good morning, all,' he said.

Calvin laughed, feeling the muscles of his face tighten.

'Good morning,' he said. He looked down at Laura. 'Shall I wake her?'

'No,' said Anita, coming towards him. 'Let her sleep.'

'I was hoping it might all go away,' said Laura, into her collar.

'It hasn't,' said Anita.

And Laura remembered the death. She pushed herself upright.

'How are you?' she said, and reached out a hand.

Anita took it, and sat down.

'Okay,' she said. 'I think.'

'At least it's morning,' said Laura.

'At least it's that,' said Anita.

Now everyone was sitting down, as if grouping together generated a kind of warmth. Laura patted Anita's hand.

'You're . . . you're taking it well,' she said.

'Not in the least,' said Anita. 'There's no point in breaking down. Not now. Come and see me next week: you'll see how well I'm taking it.'

'If there *is* a next week,' said the boy, and immediately regretted saying it. 'I mean . . .'

'We know what you mean,' said Mason.

Laura looked at him.

'I don't,' she said. 'Is he suggesting that we . . .' She left the question unfinished.

'Of course not,' said Calvin.

'Of course he is,' said Anita. 'I had a husband and a future when I started. Now . . .' She lifted her hands. 'Anything can happen.'

Laura gave a small, half-scared laugh.

'It's just a bad storm, that's all. There'll be snowploughs out, and . . . Now it's morning.'

'Let's hope so,' said Mason. 'But I've never seen snow like it.'

'At least it's stopped,' said Laura.

And they became aware, suddenly, of the silence that surrounded the train. The wind had gone, the carriage no longer creaked and groaned; there was no slither of snow against the windows. And to Calvin, straining his ears for the slightest sound, there was something more terrible, more to be feared, in such a silence. It was as if the train, and the listeners, were held in a fierce, unmoving grip, a fist of chilling iron that would never relent.

'Are we simply going to wait?' he said.

'No,' said Mason.

Anita took her hand from Laura's, and pushed it into the sleeve of her coat. She sat back.

'Oh?' she said. 'What are we going to do?'

'I'm not just sitting here,' said Mason. 'I'll have to do *something* . . .'

'We could play I-Spy,' said the boy. 'Hide and seek.' He snorted, embarrassed at his own childishness. 'Even pray.'

'Which wouldn't come amiss,' said Anita. 'What do *you* think, Mr Calvin?'

He looked at their faces. He saw weariness and the effects of cold and what Silverman's death had done to a group of strangers. The women's make-up had paled, and the true, vulnerable human self showed clear, sharpened by the chill air and by the fear of the unknown. His own imagination bred wolf-packs running through white suburban streets, and entire families frozen at breakfast-tables, undiscovered for centuries. He saw the stubble on the sergeant's face, marked the hollowed eyes of the boy, the restless fingers turning a raincoat button. He looked at his watch.

'It's five past seven,' he said. 'How long do we give them?'

'Who?' said Laura.

'What do you mean: *who?*' said Anita, too sharply.

The girl's question made Calvin shiver: as if black-winged angels of death, rather than rescuers, were speeding across country, to the train.

'The railway people,' he said. 'The line-clearers: anyone.'

Anita seemed to grow smaller as she bunched her body inside her coat.

'Suppose we give them an hour,' she said: 'what do we do then – if they're not here?'

'I'll go outside,' said Mason.

They looked at him.

'*Outside?*' said Anita. 'For what? What can you do? You can't get across those fields . . .'

'How do you know?' said Mason. 'We won't know what it's like out there until we open a door. Maybe the wind's cleared a section . . . Who knows?' He patted his pockets for his cigarettes, brought them out, and spoke as he opened the packet. 'I could maybe get down to the driver; or see if there's anyone in the other carriages.' He held out the open pack. Only the boy helped himself. Mason struck a match, lit his own and then lit Clive's. 'I could do that.'

'Of course there'll be people in the other carriages,' said Laura, the thought of a completely empty train too frightful to contemplate.

Mason looked at the thin smoke rising from the spent match.

'Not necessarily,' he said.

'Oh, come on,' said Calvin: 'there must be. I know few have got on, but . . .'

'I think the sergeant takes delight in picturing the worst,' said Anita. And then she remembered the worst had happened to her, and closed her eyes.

Mason turned the packet in his hands, looking down, creasing his eyes against the smoke from his cigarette.

'I'm trained to expect the worst, Mrs Silverman. Then things can only get better. That way I'm not disappointed.'

She nodded, her eyes still closed.

He looked up at Calvin.

'An hour, right? We give them an hour.'

'Agreed. If the others . . .'

Laura and the boy nodded.

'Now what?' said Anita.

'Breakfast,' said Calvin.

'Don't mention breakfast,' said Laura.

'There's still some wine left,' said Calvin. He dug his hand into his overcoat. 'And I've still got this.'

*   *   *

They looked at the chocolate in his open hand as if it had been newly created, as if they had never before seen such a marvel. Such blue paper, such golden words, such a shine of silver foil. Their mouths watered. They watched him unwrap the bar, and lifted their eyes to his face as if it housed the sun.

'All want some?' he said.

They nodded, each taking a piece. He stood up, found the bottle and the cup, and sat down again.

'I'll have the wrapper, Calvin,' said Mason. 'I'll save mine till later.'

The rest ate the hard, sweet chocolate, and washed it down with a mouthful of wine. They smiled at each, and, for a few moments, forgot the cold.

'Well, thank you for that, Mr Calvin,' said Anita.

'And for the last of the wine,' said Laura.

'Days of wine and roses,' he said.

'The roses will come later, will they?' she said.

'I'll get you a couple of dozen, if we get out of this,' he said. '*When* we get out of this . . .'

But the *if* echoed in their minds, and the cold came back.

Mason stubbed out his cigarette.

'All finished?' he said.

'Yes,' they said.

He rubbed his hands, and got to his feet.

'Right,' he said – 'exercises.'

'Exercises?' said Clive.

'Yes,' said Mason. 'Come on, find yourself some space. Move into the other seats, stand in the aisle.'

They looked up at him, their breaths smoking. There was something shrunken about them, some beaten quality that angered him.

'Well, come on!' he said. 'Liven yourselves up, for Christ's sake! Let's get your blood moving. Move!'

'Don't push it,' said Calvin, as they reluctantly got to their feet: 'there's still no leader here, remember that.'

'Okay, okay,' said Mason, dismissing it with a wave of a gloved hand. 'Right, sort yourselves out. You go over there, Calvin.'

'*Mr* Calvin, if you don't mind. And I'll go where I damn well please.'

'It's all for your own good,' said Mason.

'I've heard that, too – somewhere,' said Calvin.

Soon they stood, spaced about the carriage, facing the sergeant.

'Okay,' he said: 'fit?'

They did not answer him.

'Look,' he said: 'we've got to keep moving. What you people don't seem to realise is that people have died under these sort of conditions.' There was a silence. 'All right, I'm sorry, Mrs Silverman. I . . . I forgot.'

'I haven't,' she said, and her shoulders drooped. 'But I think you have our best interests at heart. Or your own. Carry on.'

He looked over at the boy: shaggy-haired and pale; at the tall girl, her head buried in the fur of her collar; at Calvin, his hands resting on the rack in front of him, waiting; and finally at Mrs Silverman, almost hidden by the high backs of the seats, eyes still bright against the white window behind her.

'Just a few simple exercises,' he said. 'Nothing you can't do. You'll be hampered by your coats, but don't worry about that. Just work up a head of steam.' He became brisk. 'Hands by your sides. Stand up, stand tall. When I say begin: raise your arms to shoulder height, and at the same time spread your legs; then together; and then repeat. Like this . . .' He demonstrated, slamming his hands against the sides of his greatcoat as his feet came together. 'Okay? Really bring those hands down. Work at it. Right. Begin! One-two, one-two, one-two, one-two . . . Good. Now, come on, put some beef into it. One-two, one . . .'

Fifteen minutes later they were exhausted. The carriage seemed to be full of the sound of their breathing. But Mason had been right: they sweated, were warmer, their hearts thudded, their bodies tingled, and the blood ached in their fingertips.

'Right,' said Mason, breathing hard himself: 'we'll try a variation . . .'

'We will not,' said Anita. 'We've . . . I've done enough, thank you.' She came back to the centre seats, dropped down into a corner, and opened the top of her coat.

'Out of condition: all of you,' said Mason. 'Want to carry on, Mr Calvin?'

'Make it Ambrose, will you?' said Calvin. 'I think we've known each other long enough: it seems like a lifetime. No, I think I've had it, too. For a while.'

'Make it Gordon, if you like,' said Mason. 'Okay, we'll call a halt. Maybe later.'

They grouped once again: Laura next to Anita; Calvin next to Mason; and the boy alone across the aisle.

Calvin was worried about Mrs Silverman. Still in a state of shock, she seemed to be over-controlled. She was picking at a thread in one of her gloves, and, sensing his gaze or his concern, looked up, her smile a hard pretence. He must divert her thoughts from what lay a few rows ahead. Then Mason spoke.

'Another half an hour.'

'What're we going to do?' said the boy, leaning forward.

'Wait till we get a door open,' said Mason. 'Then we'll see.'

Their breathing was more regular now. They faced each other; and were silent. The cold began to come back, strangely more chill on their sweating bodies. There was not the smallest sound from outside the carriage. Anita lowered her head and picked at the thread.

'Anyone experience anything like this before?' said Calvin. It was a clumsy attempt, and everyone knew it, including himself.

'I was stuck in a Tube for over half an hour, once,' said the boy. He sat up and thrust his hands inside his raincoat. 'Just outside Mansion House. Murder, it was. Just the sound of newspapers being turned.'

'What happened?' said Laura.

'Nothing,' said Clive. 'We started again, after half an hour.' He grinned. 'I go by bus, now.' Another silence. 'The next station's mine, you know that?' he continued. 'Another mile or so, and I'd have made it.' He shook his head. 'Amazing.'

'Are you spending Christmas at Witley?' said Laura.

'Yes,' said Clive. 'I'm . . . I'm staying with my girl-friend.' He bent forward again, looking at the floor, as if considering something; then he looked at Laura. 'No, that's not true, really.'

Anita stopped pulling at the thread.

'Oh?' she said. 'You've got some secrets, too, have you?'

'What does that mean?' said Clive.

'My husband giving in his notice like that,' she said. 'Never a word of what he was planning. What's your little secret?'

'Perhaps he doesn't want to tell us,' said Laura.

'Have you got some, too?' said Anita.

'We all have, haven't we?' said Calvin. 'That's what makes people interesting.'

'I haven't,' said Anita. 'I could never stand intrigue. I've always prided myself on being open and above board. It's safest.'

'You've never lied?' said the boy. 'Never?'

'Not that I'm aware of,' she said.

Clive looked beyond her to the frosted window that showed nothing.

'I'm a Catholic, see. *Was* a Catholic. My mother's very strong . . . I couldn't stand being at home this Christmas: Midnight Mass, and all that. There's a girl at the office: I pretended she'd invited me down for Christmas. She lives in Witley . . .' His voice tailed away.

'You mean you're just going to present yourself?' said Calvin.

'Yes. Well, I thought I might . . . But now . . .' He looked at Laura. 'What would you do if someone you only knew at the office turned up unexpectedly?'

'I don't know,' she said. 'It would depend, wouldn't it? Has she shown any interest?'

'No,' he said. 'Well . . .' He looked away from the window to her face. 'I'm not very good with . . . women. Girls. I was taught to close my eyes if I saw a girl coming towards me. And open them again after she'd gone by.'

'Why, for God's sake?' said Anita.

'In case I had . . . impure thoughts,' said Clive. And joined in that sudden burst of free, liberating laughter.

'Never,' said Anita. 'Not these days.'

'True,' said the boy. 'I was told by one of the Brothers that Christ's wounds opened again every time I had an impure thought; or when I lied.'

'Poor bastard,' said Mason: 'the Brother, I mean. Poor, twisted bastard.'

'I don't believe it any more,' said Clive.

'No sensible person would,' said Laura.

Encouraged by their sympathy, the boy said eagerly:

'Well, what do you think? When we get going again – you think I ought to take a chance? Just arrive there, on the doorstep?'

'Not a chance,' said Mason.

'Oh, I don't know,' said Laura. 'Perhaps she's secretly wishing something like that might happen. Perhaps she's been adoring him from afar, too. Yes, I should appear, Clive.'

'You see,' said the boy: 'I acted on impulse. My mother locked my bedroom door. I can't go back.'

'Well, I wish you all the luck,' said Mason. 'But I think we ought to start considering the here and now, rather than your love-life, son. That can come later.' He looked at his watch. 'We've got ten minutes left. Nothing's happened. Let's make a move.' He sat up straight and pulled the collar of his greatcoat tighter around his face.

'Let's look at the situation,' he said. 'There's not been a sight or a sound or any attempt at rescue, right? We've got no idea if there's anyone in the other carriages. For all we know we might be the only people on the train. Right again?'

'The driver and the guard,' said the boy.

'Okay,' said Mason: 'the driver and the guard.'

'Maybe we should pull the communication-cord,' said Clive.

'Grow up, son, will you?' said the sergeant. 'And how do we know that the driver and the guard are still around? Mightn't they have gone for help?'

The others considered this, only to feel further isolated. They rejected the idea.

104

'No, I don't think so,' said Calvin. 'They're as . . . confined as we are. Just waiting; as we are.'

'Why are you so intent in taking everyone away from us, Sergeant?' said Anita. 'You seem to want us to be more and more alone.'

'Of course not,' said Mason. 'The whole bloody train might be crammed tight. Champagne parties and discos in every carriage. I don't know. I just feel that we ought to face the fact that we *might* be alone. We can function better as a unit, without reference to anyone else.'

And in that instant, Calvin saw another aspect of the sergeant, perhaps the real man: a man to whom complexity was danger, subtlety a snare — action seen as perfection or an aspiration, shorn of all entanglements: beautiful in its simplicity.

'And so?' he said.

'So,' said Mason. 'We open a door and take a look at the land. Okay?'

'Okay,' said Calvin, and the others nodded.

'Another five minutes,' said the sergeant. He folded his arms. 'You make a lot of money from your books?' he said to Calvin.

'I've just sold one of them to a film company,' he said, and the words seemed empty.

'That'll bring you in a few bob,' said Mason.

'How much?' said Clive.

A small wind had come, and snow rustled against the east face of the carriage.

'Forty thousand,' said Calvin.

'You lucky man!' said Laura. 'What I couldn't do with forty thousand!'

Calvin looked at that cold-pinched face deep in its fur collar.

'What *would* you do?' he said.

'Oh, I'd take a cruise,' she said. 'A long, hot, sunlit cruise. White sands and green seas and, oh, everything that's the opposite of this. Expanding, for ever and ever.'

'And you, Clive?' said Calvin. 'What would you do?'

The boy's lips were dry, and beginning to crack. His tongue moved carefully over them as he thought.

'I think I'd spend two weeks in a brothel,' he said, and laughed at his own daring. 'One of the best. A two week course of instruction. Come out with some sort of diploma.' He laughed again.

'With that sort of money, you wouldn't need a brothel,' said Mason.

'It's chicken-feed, really,' Calvin found himself saying. 'What's forty thousand these days?'

'I wouldn't say no,' said the sergeant. 'What would *you* do, Mrs Silverman?'

She smiled thinly.

'It would come too late, wouldn't it?' she said.

Mason broke the quiet.

'Right,' he said: 'time's up. Let's go.'

They stood and looked up and down the carriage. Only two windows seemed relatively clear of snow. Mason led the way.

'We'll try this one first,' he said.

He stepped between the seats, and bent to the door-catch. He gripped the icy metal in gloved fingers, and pulled. It did not move. Using all his strength, he tugged again. It seemed welded by the cold, staying rock-hard and immovable.

'Want a hand?' said Clive.

'No, we'll try the other one first.'

But the second door was the same. Even with Calvin's help, the lock stayed frozen and firm.

The two men straightened, and stepped back.

'No luck?' said Anita.

'No,' said Mason. He kicked the door. 'It won't give.'

'You mean . . . we won't be able to get out?' said Laura.

'Not now,' said the sergeant. 'And these are the only two possible.'

Calvin felt a change in the atmosphere: a growing realisation that this journey could now, quite easily, be their last – as it had been for Silverman.

'We'll get out eventually,' he said. 'They'll get it open.'

'We can't wait for them – whoever *they* are,' said Mason. He bent down again and looked at the catch.

'Break a window?' said Clive.

'No, we can't do that,' said Mason. 'It's cold enough in here as it is. You can close a door . . .' He stood up. 'Hang on. I won't be a minute.'

He went back to his seat and looked down at the suitcase. He stood there thinking for a while, came to a decision, snapped the locks; and took out what was inside.

106

Part Seven

Calvin had once been asked to write a ghost story for an anthology. He did not believe in ghosts, but the money was good, and he had a professional's confidence that he could turn his hand to any literary exercise. So successful had been the story, so persuasive its atmosphere, that for two weeks following its completion he would wake abruptly in the night, woken by the slightest sound, staring into the dark, heart pounding, dry-mouthed, waiting for his own creation to materialise among suddenly unfamiliar furniture. Since that time, however diverse were the circumstances in which his characters found themselves, there was always that suspicion that, in the act of writing, he was making the future – and that, one day, he would literally find himself part of a situation he had brought into being: the outcome of which he knew only too well.

Thus, seeing Mason coming towards him down the snow-shadowed carriage, carrying a machine-gun, he recalled his half-joking declaration of the group's fictional roles – and found himself facing a potential killer.

The others, lacking his nervous imagination, saw only, in varying degrees of belief, a more normal sight: a soldier carrying a gun, a man with a trademark.

Clive was impressed. Echoes of the paperback returned, coupled with old movies: telescopic-sights, trigger-fingers, steely eyes looking down a barrel – plus a snow-held, stranded train.

'Hey!' he said in an awed voice: 'you really did shoot your commanding-officer!'

'That I did,' said Mason, smiling in that mask of cold. 'And you must be the next Black Death.'

'I suppose I must be,' said the boy. 'We're all doomed.'

Mason sensed Calvin's apprehension, saw a stirring of unease. He patted the cold metal of the gun.

'Don't worry,' he said: 'it's all above board.'

Calvin was not convinced.

'They allow that?' he said: 'taking a gun home – for Christmas?'

'Special duty,' said Mason. 'Nothing I can talk about. Let's just say I've got it, and I can use it.'

'Don't do anything stupid,' said Anita. She rubbed her hands and looked down the carriage to where Simon lay, hidden from view. 'You'd think they would do *something*: show that someone cared about us. How much longer?'

'That's what I asked myself in the Tube,' said Clive. 'It all worked out okay in the end. It just *seems* a long time, that's all.'

'It *is* a long time,' she said wearily. 'Longer than you know, son.'

'Right,' said Mason, looking at the door. 'It's a free country – I'll tell you what I have in mind: then you can say yes or no. Majority decision. I'm going to have a go at shooting the lock away. We may have to wedge the door afterwards. The only other alternative is just to sit tight, and wait. And, personally, I can't go on doing that. Any objections?'

They looked at each other. The wind was growing stronger, but not enough to rock the carriage. Blown snow sounded like gravel.

'Will it work?' said Laura.

'We can but try,' said Mason. 'All agreed?'

'I think I'd rather just wait,' said Anita. 'I'm very cold: I don't want it colder. And I know he's gone, but I don't want him . . . disturbed. I want him . . . taken care of.'

Laura put her arm around the shaking shoulders.

'Any other objections?' said Mason.

The others shook their heads.

'Right,' he said. 'Get well back. Go into another row. Get your heads down. There'll be a bit of noise.'

They separated, although Laura stayed with Mrs Silverman. They crouched down and cupped their hands over their ears. Calvin, far back, felt a sudden, unexpected claustrophobia – a confinement so intense, down there against the dusty seat, that he had to lift his head swiftly to gulp at the air.

'All ready?' said Mason.

'Yes,' they said, and braced themselves.

Mason stepped back into the aisle, aimed the Sterling at the lock, and fired. The sound, in that closed and silent place, was tremendous. It was at once shockingly metallic, breathless, and violent. Their ears rang, long after it had ended. Mason had used only five rounds, needing to conserve his ammunition.

They took their hands from their ears, and stood up. There was a strong, acrid smell, and a pale haze hung, not moving. They went to the sergeant and looked at what he had done. The lock was holed and buckled, fresh metal looking strangely vulnerable, as did the torn and splintered wood. Mason unclipped the magazine and handed both it and the gun to the boy.

'Here,' he said.

The gun was still warm. When Mason had held it, it seemed part of him. Now, in the boy's inexperienced hands, it looked incongruous.

Mason went to the door, lifted his foot, and kicked hard. It gave slightly, held by fragments of wood and the snow behind it.

'Together,' he said to Calvin.

And together they kicked it wider.

They were not prepared for the nature of the cold that entered. It was something so inhuman, that Anita cried out for the door to be closed again. But Mason would have none of it: shocked as he was by the cold's severity, there was no turning back now.

'Move away, if you like,' he said. 'Take her,' he said to Laura.

But Anita summoned some strength.

'I'm all right,' she said. 'Now what?'

Mason went to the gap, and looked out. An icy wind explored his face. He set his teeth, and then his lips, and looked up and down the track. What he saw, surprisingly, cheered him. Or at least left him less afraid.

What he had thought was a giant snowdrift − bringer of the shadow at the end of the carriage − was merely the thick covering of windblown snow over the engine and the first two carriages. The train itself was held by a succession of high, fixed, white curves, with above them a scattering of thinner snow like frozen surf; and yet it stood, apparently without wheels, on a hidden track, manmade and still impressive, surrounded by an unmoving whiteness that stretched to the horizon, where the sky was another expanse of white tinged with yellow, like old ivory.

And it was the land that scared him: a land that seemed to smoke in the wind. The snow had obliterated everything: hedges, fences, the divisions of fields, embankments, ditches. He had expected to see some trees standing out against the sky, the hint of a house: the angle of a roof. But there was nothing but this cold and neutral plain, going on and on, uninterrupted, to the edge of the world.

He pulled himself back into the carriage, brought back that frozen mask of a face, and tugged at the door until it stayed closed, held by ragged woodwork.

'Well?' said Laura.

He took the gun and the magazine from Clive, and told her what he had seen. And then they all moved back to another row, and sat down.

110

'Any further forward, are we?' said Anita.

'At least we know it's not a snowdrift,' said Mason.

'And how does that help us?' she said.

He felt the coming of anger, the hot words, but, remembering the death (how soon he had forgotten the dead man), he spoke quietly.

'It means they can get to us more easily,' he said. 'From either way. It means once the power returns, we can move.'

She looked down at her hands.

'But when?' she said.

'You'd have thought helicopters . . .' said the boy.

'Who knows the state of the airfields?' said Mason. 'Who knows what's happening out there?'

'I read a book once,' said Clive: 'about this group of people exploring an underground cave, and when they came out they were the only people left alive on the Earth. A disease from outer space had come and gone.'

'And what happened?' said Laura.

'They had to start all over again,' said the boy. 'They were the beginning of a new civilisation.'

'You see what a great responsibility we have,' said Calvin.

'How'd they make out?' said Mason.

'It didn't tell you in the book,' said the boy: 'it finished with them choosing mates, and moving off to populate the Earth again.'

Calvin laughed.

'You're going to be busy, Laura.'

She smiled.

'Of course, it had to be me,' she said. 'If only we knew we weren't alone.'

'We aren't, are we?' said Anita.

'But how do we *know*?' said Laura. 'It's the . . . being apart . . .' And was surprised at her own need: she who had convinced herself she needed no one.

Mason stood up and put the gun and the magazine in the rack to his left.

'There's only one way to find out,' he said.

'And what's that?' said Anita.

'Go and visit,' said the sergeant.

2

They looked up at him. At that dark, narrow, stubbled face, thinned even more by the cold, half-hidden in the greatcoat's upturned collar.

'Good idea?' he said. 'It'll pass the time.'

'How can we do that?' said the boy.

'I don't know yet,' said Mason. 'Let's go and see.'

Anita yawned.

'I'll stay here,' she said. 'I feel . . . very sleepy.'

Mason knelt in front of her and took her gloved hands in his.

'Don't go to sleep,' he said.

In the silence her eyes widened.

'It wouldn't come that quickly,' she almost whispered, her wide eyes on his face: 'would it?'

'Let's not take any chances,' he said. 'We don't want to lose the head woman of the tribe.' He patted her hands. 'Just keep awake. Try.'

'Yes,' she said.

'We've got to keep occupied,' he said. 'Got to keep active. We've all got things to do, outside.'

And to Calvin there came an image of a prison made of ice: of blue, glassy locks and keys and bars, and thin columns that rang if you touched them.

'What do you mean,' he said: 'visit?'

Mason led the way to the broken door.

'I thought I'd climb out and get to the next carriage.'

'For what?' said Anita.

'Just to have something to do,' said Mason. 'To check that we're not alone.'

'And what will you do if you get there?' said Anita. 'Just wave and say hello?'

'Why not?' he said. 'It would cheer them up. Break the monotony. Look, you don't understand. I can't be . . . passive.'

'We could go on talking,' said Calvin.

'I couldn't,' said the sergeant. 'No, let me try.' He searched in his pocket and brought out the small piece of foil-covered chocolate. 'In case I don't come back, share this between you.' He laughed, and handed it to Clive.

'Can I come with you?' said the boy.

'I'll try it on my own first,' said Mason.

'If you're going anywhere,' said Calvin: 'wouldn't getting to the engine be better than just checking on a carriage?'

'All right,' said Mason – 'I'll try the engine. I'd have to pass a carriage, anyway. Agreed, then? – I'll have a go?'

'You'll go along the track?' said Calvin.

'We'll see how deep the snow is,' said the sergeant. He turned to the door, and tugged it open.

They gathered in the gap, Mason in front and the others craning their necks. He looked down. The snow was over the rim of the carriage. He recalled occasions when he had seen men working at the side of the track, and closed his eyes, calculating relative sizes.

'I know this part of the line well,' said Calvin. 'The embankment slopes away here. It's deceptive. You could drown in that.'

'And what if you go?' said Anita, her voice trembling. 'You'll only get soaked, and it'll have to dry on you, getting colder all the time. You're stupid to even think of it.' And then, sharply, came the memory of how often she had said those last words to Simon. 'Oh, do what you like,' she said now, and turned away.

'Can I have your belt, Clive?' said Mason.

'My belt?'

'The belt of your raincoat.'

The boy passed it over. Mason draped the buckle-end over his right wrist, threaded the belt through, and tightened it. He gave the other end to Calvin.

'I'll just over the side and test it,' he said. 'If I can't feel the ground, I'll have you pull me up.'

'You're taking a chance on my belt, aren't you?' said Clive.

'We'll soon know, son,' said Mason. 'Let's go.'

He sat on the rim of the doorway, turned, and gently lowered himself down. He was not aware of the coldness at first: the crisp whiteness received him, allowed him to go deeper, Calvin holding the end of the taut belt; and then the snow began to work at his body, seeming to numb the ankles first, and then slowly to capture his legs, and move on . . . Soon he was shoulder-deep, and still his feet had found no firm ground.

'Okay,' he said, and was embarrassed at his own croaking, nervous voice: 'pull me up.'

Calvin tugged at the belt. It complained, and there was a faint tearing of fibres. Mason felt the hard buckle bite deep into his wrist,

113

and tried to force his body to follow his up-stretched arm. The snow let him go, inch by inch; and then he was being pulled over the rim, and on to the floor of the carriage.

He stood up immediately as if to show no harm had been done; and also to loosen the aching grip of the buckle. He stamped his feet and beat the snow from his coat. It fell in clean white slabs that broke on the floor, image of that tameness on store windows: but the reality was murderous.

'Satisfied?' said Anita, a shrunken figure over by the far window. 'Could we have the door closed now, please?'

'No, to both,' said Mason. 'If we can't go that way, we can try another.'

'How?' said Laura.

'Over the top,' said the sergeant.

'You've seen too many movies,' said Calvin.

'And you've seen too many hours at a desk,' said Mason. 'I'm on an assault-course twice a week . . .'

'Don't boast,' said Calvin.

'Not a question of boasting,' said Mason – 'a matter of fact. I'm the fittest person here. What's the point of life if you don't test yourself?'

'I don't want to be tested any more,' said Anita. 'I want that door closed.'

'You could kill yourself up there,' said Laura. 'You could slip, and . . .'

'You can kill yourself crossing the road,' said the sergeant. 'Don't worry: if it's too bad, I won't go on.'

He gave the belt back to Clive, and began to take off his greatcoat.

'What are you doing now?' said Anita.

'I'd be lumbered with a coat,' he said. 'It'll be drier for when I get back.'

'You're mad,' she said. 'All you men are mad. You'll freeze to death.'

'It'll take more than a winter to kill me,' he said. He looked at Calvin. 'You're in charge while I'm away.'

'Balls,' said Calvin.

Mason laughed.

'They'll probably be the first to go,' he said. He spread his greatcoat over a rack, smoothed his gloves towards his wrists, stepped to the doorway, and turned to face the interior of the

114

carriage. Without his coat he looked too thin, the smartness of his uniform with its silver buttons a sudden tinsel against the glaring whiteness behind him. 'I'll need a lift.'

Calvin took off his own gloves, and held them out.

'Here,' he said: 'put these over yours. You'll need them.'

'Aren't you going to stop him?' said Anita.

'People should be allowed their own follies,' said Calvin. 'I must have read that somewhere.'

Mason finished tugging on the gloves.

'Thanks,' he said. He put his hands above his head and looked up. 'Now, lift.'

Calvin and the boy bent down, grasped the blue trousers, and straightened.

'Take it easy!' cried Mason. 'Christ, you're not launching a rocket!'

He grasped the outer rim of the door and heaved himself out into the air. Even as he brushed the snow away from the roof with his right hand, he felt the brutal metal strike through the gloves on his left. He hesitated, but only for a second.

'And again!' he shouted.

Now Clive and Calvin were gripping his shoes, the melting snow. Grunting, they pushed him higher.

'Okay!' he called. 'Let go now!' They released him, and the shoes vanished. They heard a scrabbling and a scraping above their heads. 'I'm standing up!' he shouted. 'It's not too bad. Close the door now. I won't be long.'

Calvin slammed the door shut. There was a further scraping as the sergeant made his slow way along the roof. And then there was silence.

The others moved back a row, and sat down: Calvin next to Laura; the boy next to Anita. From where Calvin sat he could see the machine-gun and the magazine through the mesh of the rack. He shook his head.

'You shouldn't have let him go,' said Anita.

'I wasn't thinking of that,' said Calvin.

'What were you thinking of?' she said.

'It doesn't matter.'

'Thinking about the gun, weren't you?' said the boy. 'Funny you thought he was a killer.'

'He's on no special duty,' said Calvin. 'I'd bet on that.'

'Go on, frighten us some more,' said Anita. 'When I think of yesterday morning: how everything was . . .' Her voice tailed away. She put her arm around the boy's shoulder. 'Shift up, Clive,' she said: 'let's warm each other.'

'Shall we do the same?' said Calvin.

'Why not?' said Laura. 'I'm going to bear your children, so why stand on ceremony?'

'True,' he said, and settled her against him, first the fur of her collar, and then her hair, brushing his face.

They listened to the small wind finding the cracks.

'He's got some guts, anyway,' said the boy. 'It takes some – to try that.'

'He's a fool,' said Anita. 'All men are fools. Never content . . .'

Once again her voice tailed away, and she closed her eyes.

_____ 3 _____

Mason, balancing on the end of the roof, wrapped in a bone-bruising cold, debating whether to make the leap to the next carriage, or to turn back, accepted that Calvin was right: he *had* seen too many movies. It had been a heart-stopping, slipping, crouching progress – one could hardly call it a walk – and his legs ached with the strain. He looked at the unmarked snow on the next roof, and then down at the equally unmarked gap below him. And then, without further thought, he leapt.

It was in reality a simple leap: he cleared the gap easily. It was the hard reception on the other side that jolted his knees and then his hands. His whole body reacted to the hurt, as if punishing him: throwing him further forward, so that now he lay fully-stretched, his hands frantically searching for a hold. He felt himself sliding to the left, and forced himself down into the snow, his fingers finding a ribbed section of metal, and gripping, holding. He lay there for a few seconds, until the damp snow began to get at him, then he carefully got to his feet, going up in stages, until he was fully upright, yet still teetering, as though the leap and the hard landing had disturbed his sense of balance. He wavered there, arms wide, like a wire-walker, until his breathing became more normal; then he brought his hands gently to his sides, took another deep breath, and resumed that old crouching position; and moved forward.

He did not go far: about a third of the way. Then he came down as carefully again, dashed the snow away until the grey-blue roof appeared, then banged three times with his fist. Slabs of disturbed snow near the cleared patch broke away and began to drift to the sides, to slither and to fall.

'Anyone there?' he called, using the full force of a sergeant's voice.

Nothing. Not a sound. As if his voice was the only human cry in the universe. The wind took it away until it too was nothing: as if it had never been.

He banged again.

'Hello!' he shouted. He listened keenly, his head to one side. Only another small slither as more snow dropped from the curve of the roof.

Again there was no response. He stood up, and moved further along the carriage. Almost at the end, he stopped and repeated the same action: the banging and the shouts. The same silence.

He stood up. Ahead of him was the engine, a darker shape than the carriage, and more deeply covered in wind-blown snow. Beyond the engine stretched the same universal plain, to a lightening horizon. He shivered. His feet were icy, his hands and ears tingling; his face hardening, fixing a last expression. He inched towards the end of the roof, cupped his frozen, wooden hands around his mouth, and directed the shout at the distant cab.

'Hallo *there*!'

Nothing. He tried once more. And then slowly dropped his arms. He measured the gap between the carriage and the engine. It was the same: perhaps even narrower. But by this time he was more cautious: he could still feel the raw stinging of his knees. He shouted again, but it was a last formality. He would not go on to the engine. He had proved a point. Now was the time to return. He looked once more into the gap, then began to turn away.

It was then that, as his eyes moved over the snow beyond the engine, he saw something: a mark on that otherwise undisturbed white. Crouching down, his hands gripping the end of the roof, he pushed his head forward, to see more clearly. And it was what he thought it might be: his fears were justified.

It was an upraised human arm, thrusting out of the wind-banked snow, and a gloved hand with wide-spaced fingers sought for a hold in the swirling, indifferent air.

Crouching there, on the end of the carriage, unaware now of the cold metal striking through his gloves, he continued to look at the arm and the unmoving fingers. The sleeve was blue, with a thin red line circling the cloth above the wrist. There were no marks from the cab to the arm. Some time had elapsed. Whoever it was, was past helping. He began to stand upright, and it was like unlocking metal: as though he were encased in thin armour; or was now a robot, his blood gone to mercury. He turned to face the way he had come; and, even more carefully now, he started back.

The gap he had leapt before seemed to have widened. It was a chasm, and his mind, and then his body, rebelled. But he forced himself to the edge, gathered all his unwilling strength and flagging purpose – and threw himself over.

His right hand hit the roof first, slid, and something under the thin scrabbled snow ripped open his gloves. Then his other hand landed, and then his knees. He winced and cursed, stayed on all fours for a while, and then lifted his right glove. Both pairs were torn, but the skin was unmarked.

He got up, and it was as if he were now an old man. His whole body trembled, saliva dripped from his open mouth, and his breath roared.

'Get moving, you bastard!' he said, and even his voice sounded aged, forced through shaking teeth. He shuffled along the roof, dragging his feet into his own footprints, until two rough tracks led to, and reached, the more disturbed snow of his climb. Once there, he rested, crouching like an animal. He looked along the length of the train, listening to his own heart, the pulse in his ears.

It was then, looking to the west, that he saw a second mark on the land. But whereas the dead driver's hand – if it *was* the driver's – had sealed the inhumanity of the day, this new sight made him stand erect – and the house grew as he grew, more than a roof now: a hint of snow-framed windows and a laden tree. It stood on a rise about a mile away; and, beautiful sight, a wisp of smoke wavered from a chimney, drifting to a sky which seemed packed tight with cloud.

He looked down at his gleaming shoes, and from them to the roof of the carriage. He knelt and banged with his fist.

'I'm back!' he shouted.

It seemed a long time before they answered: so long that even he, the least imaginative of men, saw a carriage strewn with death. Then, muffled, came a cry, and he felt his shoulders drop. He heard the grating sound of the door opening, and then Calvin's voice.

118

'You okay?'

'Yes,' he said, and, froglike, turned his body about and slid slowly over the edge, his legs dangling until he could grip the rim of the roof, and feel other hands gripping his ankles.

'Easy now,' said Calvin. 'Take it easy.'

The hands moved up his body until they reached his waist. Now the edge of the doorway appeared, and he dropped his arms. Calvin and the boy swung him into the carriage. He stood, suddenly weak and shaking, as Calvin edged behind him and pulled the door shut. Mason dropped to the nearest seat and closed his eyes. Anita, his greatcoat ready in her hands, wrapped it around him, and stood back. He opened his eyes to a curve of faces; and their cold, pinched, fragile ordinariness warmed him, and he smiled.

4

To Calvin the man had changed. Beneath the smile there was a *beaten* quality: the face more drawn, although only perhaps with cold, the stubble more pronounced, like a shadow. Mason could not stop shaking. He pressed his elbows to his sides, but it was no use. The shaking became a shudder. He held his lips tight, and smiled with a closed mouth.

'You are a fool, you know,' said Anita, but there was a hint of respect in her voice.

'I know,' said Mason. 'Anyone got any brandy?'

'We're out of brandy,' said the boy. 'You were a long time.'

'I wasn't thinking of the time it took,' he said.

'And you're hurt,' said Laura.

Mason looked down at himself.

'Your hand,' she said.

He was about to say it was only the gloves that were torn, but what he had thought was unmarked skin was a long razor-thin cut across his palm which had opened; and now there were beads of blood on his greatcoat, and the torn flesh, now recognised, began to sting.

'It's nothing,' he said.

'Just a flesh wound,' said Calvin, echoing many a movie; and grinning.

'Right,' said the sergeant.

119

'Take the gloves off,' said Anita. She bound the cut with one of her handkerchiefs, noting the tallow-white of the fingers. Mason held up the ragged leather.

'Sorry,' he said.

'It's okay,' said Calvin, but his own hands were numb inside the pockets of his coat.

'Thanks,' said the sergeant to Anita. His lower lip had cracked, and his tongue probed the hard edges. He put his hands inside his coat, and sat back wearily.

'Well?' said the boy. 'What did you find out?'

The others, seated now, came forward, as though Mason brought news from a far battlefield; of the ending of a seige: bright banners appearing over the horizon's edge, food and wine promised, great fires roaring and cold banished for ever.

Mason, looking at their faces, saw the seeds of hope, and was silent. What should he tell them? The fact that he could lie: that he could say the train was full of optimistic, singing passengers; that the driver was confident the power would soon return – this never entered his head. It was a question of reality plus morale: yet wasn't the truth always the best? You could always build on the truth: it was like rock under your feet. Yet he was still undecided: acknowledging, perhaps for the first time, that others were not so strong as he.

'Well?' said Anita, and he thought of her husband back down the carriage: that silence always on the edge of things . . .

'I . . . I got to the next,' he said. 'I banged hard, and called . . .'

'We heard you,' said Clive.

'Did you? Well, they didn't. Or couldn't. Not a sound.'

'No one answered?' said Laura.

'No.'

They looked anywhere but in each other's faces.

'So there's no one in the next carriage?' said Anita.

'You heard me call – they didn't,' said Mason. 'Make your own picture.'

'It doesn't surprise me,' said Calvin. 'There must be others in the other carriages.'

'Must be,' said Clive, looking at him, and following the lead.

'Did you get to the engine?' said Anita.

The wind had dropped, and the silence ached in their ears.

'No,' said Mason. 'I was freezing up by then. I had to make the jump back. I didn't try it.'

120

'You call to the driver?' said Clive.

'Yes.'

They waited.

'And . . .?' said Laura.

'He might have heard me,' said Mason. And then he chose the truth. 'All right: the driver's dead. I think it was the driver.'

'What do you mean?' said Calvin.

Mason told them what he had seen. They never took their eyes off his face, as though his words were food. Anita was almost triumphant: there would be no rescue. Simon was the first to go, and the others would follow, eventually.

'What d'you think happened?' said Clive.

'Come to reassure us; to check the depth – anything,' said Calvin. 'You're sure he was dead?'

'I didn't go down and feel his pulse, if that's what you mean,' said Mason. He had thought that, inside the carriage, the chill might lessen on his bones, but he still felt encased in ice, the cut singing in his palm. 'Did you eat the chocolate?'

'No,' said Clive. 'You want it?'

'Yes.' He unwrapped the foil and looked at the last piece. 'Well, here goes nothing,' he said, and took a small bite. 'Pass it around, son. Finish it off.'

Calvin was left with almost a crumb, but the taste was beautiful: it lingered, and he treasured it.

'Shall we move away from the door?' said Laura.

Mason stood up, and Calvin helped him on with his greatcoat. They walked back two rows, and sat down. This time Clive sat with the women: the group was coming closer together.

'So,' said Calvin, 'let's see how we're placed.' He looked at his watch. 'It's five past ten. We've been here . . . what?'

'About fourteen hours,' said Mason, nursing his hand, sucking the last of the chocolate taste from his teeth.

'Fourteen hours,' said Calvin. 'The storm seems to have died down. Someone must be working, somewhere. It's bad about the driver: but I suppose he should have stayed put. We've no food and no drink. What have we got?'

'A box of matches,' said Mason.

'And ourselves,' said Laura.

'And the gun,' said Clive.

'Ah, yes,' said Anita: 'let's not forget the gun.' She looked at the sergeant. 'If the worst comes to the worst, we've got a way out.'

121

'I'd take the cold,' he said. 'It's slow, but it's . . . comfortable. A sleep, and then a longer sleep.'

'I don't think we ought to dwell on that sort of thing,' said Laura. 'Let's be . . . positive, for goodness sake. Fourteen hours is a long time, but, after all, this *is* a suburban line: we aren't out in the wilds.'

'It feels like we are,' said Clive.

Anita rested her head against the patterned seat.

'I think we ought to accept the possibility that we might not come out of this,' she said.

'Never!' said Laura, vehemently. 'You must be joking.'

Anita opened her eyes.

'Is my Simon joking?' she said.

'Well, that's different. I mean . . .'

'He was very much alive this morning,' said Anita. 'And so was the driver.'

'I'd try for the house before I got to that stage,' said Mason. 'I wouldn't just sit around here waiting for death.'

They looked at him: at a man who appeared infinitely weary, who cradled his hand inside his greatcoat, his uniform marked with dark patches, his shoes gleaming with wet snow.

'What house?' said Laura.

Mason glanced up at the roof.

'Coming back, I noticed one. Over to the left, on top of a rise. We wouldn't have noticed it from this side. The chimney was smoking.'

Laura smiled.

'There you are, you see?' she said. 'We're not completely alone. There are people out there. How far would you say?'

'I'd say about a mile.'

'Yes,' she said, 'I'd try for that, too: if things got really bad.'

Anita came forward and studied the sergeant's face.

'Could we see it from the other side?'

'We might,' said Mason. 'If we could open a window, a door.'

'We opened it before,' she said: 'the window.' She pushed herself off the seat. 'I'd like to see it.'

'Okay,' he said.

'I'll stay here,' said Laura: 'you can report back.'

The others went to the rear of the carriage. The snow-line had dropped a little from the frosted glass; and, as Calvin and the boy forced the window down, the rise appeared, white and unmarked and deep.

'Let me see,' said Anita. She rested her hands on the metal strip, and pressed her face into the bitter air. 'I can't see a house. Where?'

Mason joined her. He looked at the edge of the rise. There was no house.

'It must be back, over the edge,' he said.

'Remember, he was on the roof,' said Calvin. 'He'd see more. We're down in the dip here.'

She stared at the ridge, as if her hope might build walls.

'Wouldn't we see the smoke?' she said. 'You said there was smoke.'

Mason looked at the sky, and waited a few seconds.

'Drifting back, perhaps,' he said. Had the snow lied? Was the house a mirage? But no – he had seen it: seen the angle of the roof, the windows, the laden tree, the smoke. He spoke more positively. 'It's there. Just over the rise. I'd make for that.'

'Close the window,' she said, and turned away. She walked slowly back, down the carriage.

Calvin and the boy pushed at the strip until frost filled the space. He put his hand on Mason's shoulder, and whispered:

'You're sure?'

'Why would I lie?'

'Comfort?'

'I tell you I saw the bloody thing.'

'Okay. Fine. You'd have trouble getting up there.'

'I'd give it a go,' said Mason. 'I wouldn't rot here, pal.'

They went back to their seats. Anita had squeezed away from Laura, and was crouched in the corner, her mouth tight.

'We aren't children,' she said. You don't need to paint happy pictures of smoke coming out of chimneys.'

'It was there,' said Mason, calmly. 'It *is* there.'

'You were only trying to cheer us up,' she said. She was trying hard to control herself. She swallowed. 'Perhaps it's all planned.'

'What is?' said the boy.

'This,' she said, waving a gloved hand which returned to rest under the other. 'All of it: the storm, us being together; Simon. Perhaps God . . .'

'Don't make it worse than it is,' said Mason. 'We aren't children, remember?'

'Don't you believe in God?' she said.

'Two subjects I never discuss,' said Mason: 'sex and religion. Old army maxim.'

'Do you?' she said, turning to Laura: 'believe in God?'

'It . . . depends,' she said.

'Look,' said Mason: 'let's not get involved in that sort of thing, please.'

'All men turn to God at the last,' she said, and was faintly surprised at her piousness. 'You'd know something about that, Clive, wouldn't you?'

'Don't drag me into it,' he said: 'that's what I'm running away from.'

'What about you, Mr Calvin?' she said. 'Any higher thoughts?'

'Not about God,' he said. 'And certainly not at this moment.'

'It may be all the moment we have,' she said.

'No, I don't believe that,' he said. 'Like the sergeant here: I wouldn't sit and wait. I'd try for that house.'

'If it's there,' she said. She began pulling at the thread again. 'You see, I keep thinking: haven't we gone past being just . . . ourselves? Haven't we, situated as we are, gone past protecting ourselves? Haven't we – ought we not to be, *sharing* something?'

No one said anything.

'None of you feel it?' she said, looking up from her glove. 'Perhaps it takes a death to pull us up short.'

'Or to make us give in to superstition,' said Mason.

'Let's change the subject, then,' she said. 'We were talking about you while you were outside. Or Mr Calvin was. He doubted that you were on special duty.'

Stricken, Calvin moved back slightly, to face the sergeant.

'I'm sorry. It has nothing to do with us . . .'

Mason's hand was throbbing. He clenched his fist inside his greatcoat, and a fine, thin flame seemed to score his palm.

'You're right,' he said. 'It's none of your business.'

'But it *is*, don't you see that?' said Anita. '*Are* you on special duty?'

'Why the hell does it matter?'

'If you don't know that, then you needn't answer,' she said.

Baffled, he looked at her and shook his head.

'All right,' he said: 'have it your way. I have . . . I *had* a sister. We were very close. She got involved with a married man: an ignorant, unfeeling, sadistic bastard. She committed suicide two weeks ago. I'm going to Petersfield to see him. A kind of *special* duty. Are we any closer, Mrs Silverman?'

Her eyes were suddenly full of tears.

'If it's true, we are,' she said. 'Thank you.'

'It's as true as the house,' he said. 'Make your peace with that.'

An hour passed: an hour in which, perhaps unconsciously, they found themselves huddling even closer together – the boy between the two women and their arms around him; the men shoulder to shoulder, their faces almost hidden in the dark curve of their collars. Their breaths smoked; the only sound their shoes beating the floor at intervals, as they tried to force the numbness from their frozen feet. Mason was the only one whose eyes never closed. He watched the others, and if one began to breathe deeply or whose mouth stayed open, he would reach forward a shoe and tap their legs. They would wake with a start, then smile; but, even as he watched, their eyelids would begin to droop again – and finally he said:

'Right, let's be having you. A few more exercises.'

They reminded him of nothing so much as hibernating animals. They stirred in what warmth they had, and complained at the disturbance.

'No, thank you,' said Anita. 'I'm past exercising.'

'Later, perhaps,' said Laura.

'Not later,' said Mason. 'Now.'

Laura took her arm from behind the boy. It seemed detached from her body, until the blood started moving: then it began to ache, and her fingertips seemed full of tiny, needling sparks. She looked down at herself, and was horrified to see a thin coating of frost on her coat, as though she were slowly being consumed by something she did not wish to dwell upon. She beat at the cloth with her gloved hands until she was satisfied, then she sat up.

'May I have a cigarette?' she said. 'I feel like one.'

'Sorry,' said Mason.

'You have some left.'

'I know. But you're not a smoker.'

'I told you I feel like one.'

'I've felt like one for the past hour,' he said. 'I'll give you one after the exercise.'

Calvin pushed himself off the corner and took his hands from the pockets of his coat. The one without a glove was tinged with yellow, and the nails were blue. He sucked at it, but it stayed without feeling.

'Shall we try for the house?' he said.

'Who?' said Mason. 'You and me?'

'Well . . .'

'That's a last resort,' said the sergeant: 'when we know we're almost finished. Come on now, everybody – exercises.'

'*Please* . . .' said Anita.

'No excuses,' said Mason. He leaned over and grasped her hand. Standing now, he began to pull. 'Come on. You'll feel all the better.'

Reluctantly, they moved stiffly into the aisle.

'Spread yourselves out, like last time,' he said. 'Cigarettes for all, later.'

'I don't smoke,' said Anita.

'You'll do what you're told,' said Mason, grinning in that cold-narrowed face: 'or see the C.O. in the morning. Okay, ready? Same again . . . Ready, son?'

The boy had turned to face the back of the carriage. He waved his right hand, wildly.

'Listen,' he said.

'Don't matter about *listen* . . .' said the sergeant. 'Turn around.'

Clive waved his hand again.

'Just keep quiet a sec!' he said.

And the others turned their heads and listened . . .

Part Eight

1

At first they heard only the sound of their own breathing and that of their companions: a unified making of vapour. And then, above the human breathing, came a more urgent, whistling noise, instantly recognisable; and one that ended the vapour as mouths were closed and faces were turned to echo the same astonishment and hope as the noise grew louder.

'It's a helicopter!' said Clive.

Bodies were no longer stiff. Revitalised, they surged from the aisle to the broken door. Calvin was there first, and sent it crashing back with a shoulder-charge so powerful that the entire lock jumped from the splintered wood to drop to the snow.

He leaned out, feeling the hard press of their arms and hands behind him. His eyes searched the sky.

'Over to the left,' said Clive. 'See it?'

'No, not yet . . .' said Calvin. 'Yes! Yes, there it is!'

'Where?' said Laura.

He leaned away from the doorframe, and pointed.

'There!'

And now all their faces were free of the train, oblivious of the cold, lifted to packed, unmoving clouds.

Like a clumsy insect searching for some greenery in a never-ending white desert, the helicopter clattered on. It was flying parallel to the track, low, almost a mile away, and keeping a steady course. Their eyes followed it. Anita, the smallest of the group, stood on tiptoe.

'Is it coming this way?' she said.

'No,' said Clive.

'Well, do something!' she said. She began to shout. '*Help*! Oh, help us!'

'They won't hear *that*,' said Calvin. He pushed the boy back. 'You nearly had me out then.'

The helicopter was now immediately opposite them. But moving on.

'Oh, please do something!' said Laura.

Calvin twisted his head to look at Mason.

'What about the gun?'

'What about it?'

'Well, fire it, man! Quickly! Into the air!'

128

'They wouldn't hear it,' said the sergeant: 'the noise of their own engines . . .'

'Try it, please!' said Laura.

Anita had hurried to get the gun; and now pushed forward, holding it and the magazine.

'Here!' she said.

Mason swore and wrenched them from her.

'All right!' he said. 'Get back!'

They moved away. He clipped home the magazine, straddled the gap, leaned out as far as he could trust himself, put the gun to his shoulder, and pressed the trigger. The sound filled the day, obliterating the throaty song of the helicopter. His shoulder ringing from the shock, his eyes followed the insect body, the invisible props. Nothing seemed to disturb that steady progress, and he shook his head.

'No,' he said.

'And again!' said Anita. 'Go on!'

Lips pressed together so tightly that the flesh ached, Mason sent another burst into that birdless sky. And, even before the echoes clattered away, the helicopter tipped to its right and swung towards the train.

'Heard you the first time,' said the boy, now standing beside the sergeant.

'Is . . . is it coming?' said Laura.

'Yes,' said Mason: 'it's coming.'

And they crowded together and watched and waited.

It was a twin-prop military helicopter, seemingly fragile in the distance, but now, as it approached, seen to be heavy and ponderous: less a thing of nature than a construction of steel and glass and black oil, painted in the olive-green and ochre colours of camouflage, which against the whiteness suggested a hard, travelling jungle. As it came lower, so the snow beneath it seemed to be struck with terror: it writhed and shook and sought for escape, rising in spinning arcs, heaving itself off the earth, blinding the people in the open doorway of the carriage, coating their bodies with fine granules of ice that stung their eyelids and the insides of their open mouths. They stepped back; but only as a reflex. To surge forward again and peer through that shifting grey mist that held the paled image of the machine that spoke of liberation.

It came even lower now; and through the flying snow those who

129

were nearest – Mason and Calvin and the boy – saw a large open blackness in the body of the helicopter, and in that blackness stood a helmeted figure, looking down. Wisps of straw or hay were torn from the interior of the machine, to whirl and spin away.

'Cattle food!' shouted Mason, his words almost lost in the roar and the swirl. But Calvin heard, and nodded.

Now the helmeted man shouted, crouching down, one hand cupping his mouth.

'What did he say?' said Clive.

'Can't hear!' shouted Calvin.

'Make some sign,' said Laura.

'He can't get any lower,' said Mason. He leaned back against their bodies and cupped his own hands about his mouth.

'We can't hear you!'

But the helmeted man shook his head. Beyond him, in the front of the aircraft, behind windscreen-wipers clogged with snow, another helmeted face watched.

'Let me!' said Calvin.

He pushed forward, held on with one hand, and pointed to his mouth. And pointed again.

The figure in the gap turned and appeared to speak to someone inside the helicopter. Another figure appeared: a twin in helmet and army fatigues. They looked down, motionless. The disturbed snow was thickening on the side of the train, and on the bodies of the group in the doorway.

The men in the gap went away. The helicopter began to rise slowly, to drift to the right.

'What are they *doing*?' said Anita.

But no one answered, their hearts as chilled as their faces. Then the two men reappeared, carrying between them a long, black, tubular shape. To Calvin's heightened imagination the image came of a coffin for Silverman, or the trussed body of a dead airman to be dumped overboard into the snow. The men came to the edge of the gap, paused for two seconds as the helicopter continued to drift to the right; then tossed the shape into the air. It fell awkwardly, as though unwilling to go. To Calvin it even seemed to hang in the air a fraction. Then it fell faster, turning over twice before it hit the earth, almost opposite the door of the carriage, in the snow-whirled field. And the snow accepted it, until only one tilted edge showed, a black marker.

The men in the gap waved, and stood back. The pilot looked

through the half-cleared arc of his window and gave a thumbs-up. Then, whistling and scything to full power, the props spinning like water, the helicopter lifted itself higher, set course for those unknown farms where snow-caked cattle waited; and was soon miles away, a dot that eventually vanished: all that noise and white disturbance, that oily jungle-coloured metal and silent helmeted humanity, replaced once again by a silence so profound that it held the group in the doorway – five snow-dusted statues staring at folded, unmoving clouds.

2

But the statues came alive and moved, and the snow dropped from them or was dusted away, and they were human again and very cold; and they scraped the snowy floor clear, shut the door, and sat down. Anita felt the sharp air working its way through the hole the broken lock had made, and stood up.

'Excuse me,' she said, stepped over their feet, and crossed the aisle.

'Excuse me, she says,' said Mason. 'After all that, she says excuse me.'

Even she smiled as she sat down.

'Perhaps it's relief,' she said. 'There are other people in the world.' She tucked her gloves into her armpits. 'Well, how are we going to get it? You'd have thought they could have dropped it closer.'

'Or dropped it on a rope,' said Clive.

'They went out of their way to help,' said Mason: 'don't knock it. They did us a favour, and broken a few rules to do it, too, I bet.' He found he was still holding the gun, unconscious until this second that the metal had woken the pain in his hand. He unclipped the magazine, and glanced inside: two rounds remained.

'Still got enough?' said Calvin.

'For what?' said the sergeant.

'It doesn't matter.'

Mason stood up and put the gun and the magazine back in the rack. He peered through the window, but nothing could penetrate that frost.

'How far, do you think?' said Clive.

'Don't know,' said the sergeant. 'Couple of hundred yards, more or less.'

'What do you think it is?' said Laura.

'You sound like a child waiting for a present,' said Calvin.

'Well, it's the right season,' she said.

'It'll be some sort of survival kit,' said Mason.

'You ever done any of that sort of work, Sarge?' said the boy.

'No. I'm an infantryman.' He sat down again. 'Well, what do we do?'

And they all looked at Calvin.

He grew uncomfortable under their steady, unblinking gaze. He looked away from them. Cold as he was, he felt a trickle of sweat run down his left side. It was obvious, in some subtle, almost intuitive group-thought, that there had been a shift of responsibility, even perhaps of leadership, and he knew himself to be deficient in both, except in relation to his craft; and even that had taken a beating of late. He sat, looking away from the unmoving faces, and waited. But the silence continued, and he knew they would never speak, until he did.

'All right,' he said, finally: 'why me?'

'Well, it's certain the sergeant isn't going,' said Anita. 'He went up there, didn't he? It's he who's hurt. And the boy's not strong enough.'

'I don't know about that,' said Clive.

'Well, you're certainly smaller than Mr Calvin,' she said. And they waited.

'Mason?' said Calvin.

'I don't mind going,' said the sergeant. But even Calvin acknowledged the *drained* quality of the man. 'I don't mind giving it a go.'

'Of course you won't,' said Anita. 'Well, if a grown man won't . . .'

'I didn't say I won't,' said Calvin. 'Don't put words in my mouth.' He felt a sudden resentment, born of shame, at being pushed. 'What about you women?'

'*Us*?' said Anita, scathingly. 'You sit there, and . . .'

'It never ceases to amaze me,' said Calvin: 'the hypocrisy of women. They're forever standing on their rights, demanding equality in everything; but whenever it comes to the push it's *Yes, we like the old courtesies: the opening of doors, the chairs pulled away*

132

from the dinner-table, the single rose – we're frail creatures, really. Like now.'

'If that's a challenge, I'm happy to accept it,' said Laura. She got to her feet and tightened her coat around her. 'What do you want me to do?'

'Oh, don't be so bloody silly,' he said. He decided to be honest. 'Look,' he said: 'I'm scared. I admit it. If there's a helicopter around, other people could come at any time. I just don't fancy trekking over there in that depth of snow.'

'The helicopter's shifted some,' said the boy.

'You'd leave it out there?' said Mason to Calvin.

'For a while.'

'How long?'

'This afternoon, sometime . . .'

'We could be frozen to death by then,' said Anita.

Mason stood up now, and joined Laura.

'I'll go,' he said.

'Okay, okay,' said Calvin, wearily: 'I suppose I . . .' Then he changed his mind. 'No, why the hell should I? Why should I allow myself to be pushed by all of you? I'd rather sit it out for a time.'

'Suit yourself,' said Mason. 'Come on, Clive.'

Laura, the sergeant, and the boy moved to the door. Anita came from across the aisle to join them. She had to pass by Calvin, sitting alone at the end of the seat. She looked down at him.

'I won't say excuse me this time,' she said.

He looked up into that scornful face.

'You're excused, lady,' he said.

Mason opened the door. The cold, fastening on their damp clothes, chilled them to the bone. There was no wind. The land was as still and as silent as the day before creation. Everything seemed to be waiting for a sign, an action, a human voice. They stood in the gap and looked at the tilted black marker.

'It . . . it seems further away,' said Laura.

'No,' said Mason. 'It's where it was.' He looked at Clive. 'Well, it's belt-time again, son.'

'Let me go first,' said the boy. He pulled the belt free of his raincoat. 'If I can stand, then it'll be okay for you.' He handed the belt to Mason. 'Or I don't mind going the whole way.'

'No, I'll go down first,' said the sergeant.

'You can't go with that hand,' said Anita.

133

'Christ, it's only a scratch,' said Mason. He began to thread the belt over his wrist. Then a hand touched his arm.

'Okay,' said Calvin, behind him: 'you all know I couldn't live with myself. You're too bloody noble, all of you.'

'Nobility doesn't come into it,' said Anita. 'And I'd have been more impressed if you'd said yes straight away.'

He ignored her. He took the belt from Mason and placed it over his own wrist.

'I read in the *Reader's Digest* once about this guy who crawled through a mine-shaft with a smashed leg,' said Clive.

'Oh, yes?' said Calvin, tightening the strap.

'He said the greatest bravery was acting in spite of the greatest fear,' said the boy. 'Well, something like that.'

'If there weren't *ladies* around, I'd tell you what I think of that,' said Calvin. He moved to the rim of the door, turned to face the others, crouched down and began to lower himself over the side. 'All my money goes to the RSPCA – remember that.'

Mason took the other end of the belt, and knelt in the gap.

'I'll see the Queen is told, if you don't make it.'

Calvin's feet entered the snow. It seized upon his ankles, and he gasped.

'Are you okay?' said Laura.

He lifted a fearful, strained, and now half-smiling face.

'Oh, sure,' he said. 'Great.'

3

He went deeper. Small crusts like frozen foam broke around his arms, but close at hand not a crack showed. He felt he was descending into a frozen sea that had no bottom. In desperation he kicked out, and then the cracks appeared, but no firm ground. Deeper and deeper he went, to his armpits.

'Hold it!' he called.

He hung by the taut belt. He slowly lifted his head. The fringe of faces looked down. He swallowed, and the stone stayed in his throat. His breath made one continuous cloud. He coughed, and it racked his chest.

'Nothing,' he said.

'Try a little more,' said Anita.

'*You* try a little more!' he said. And then he realised he was sweating. Sweating with fear. Fear was making him a furnace. 'It's no use,' he called. The buckle was like a mailed hand around his wrist. 'Pull me up!'

Mason made a sound in this throat: of anger or derision.

'Another inch, man!' he said. 'It'll take another . . .'

And then the belt tore above the buckle, and Calvin dropped.

*   *   *

He cried out, once. And it was almost a child's cry: short and high-pitched. Mason was left holding the swaying remnant of the belt as Calvin's head began to disappear. Then that tousled hair, dusted with fine snow, moved no further: his feet had jarred on solid earth. Encased as he was, still shocked and apprehensive, the sense of safety was beautiful, and he almost cried out again – this time with thankfulness. He shook his head to clear the snow around it, and shifted his shoulders. Gradually he made an ever-widening space around himself, until he stood in a deep circular trench. Gasping, he looked up.

'You see?' said Anita: 'that wasn't too bad, was it?'

'It would have covered you,' he said. He looked back at the black marker, then up again at the train. 'Shall I go on?'

'What else?' said Mason. 'Try and make some sort of track that we can follow, if we have to.'

'It took two of them to throw it out,' said Calvin. 'I doubt that I can manage it on my own.'

'Try,' said Laura.

'It's getting to me,' he said: 'the cold.' He gave a sharp, involuntary shiver. 'I think I'll need some help.'

'We'll watch,' said Mason. 'If you look in difficulty, we'll do something.'

It was as if they were disowning him; or, even more alarming, were content to observe passively his floundering progress towards what . . .? Down below them, at a disadvantage, he felt like a creature contemplated by giants, or placed upon white filter-paper by uncaring scientists, his every movement logged and timed. He turned around in his circular trench, paused, and then struck out for the marker. Once again the image of the sea came back: he was literally swimming through motionless, frozen tides of snow, his feet lifted and then set down in slow motion, treading an unknown depth until the reassuring earth was found again. It was achingly

135

wearying: he alternated between heat and cold, sweat and a numbing chill. Then, a third of the way, the earth was no longer there – and he went into whiteness that was another kind of dark, down and down.

He lashed out like a drowning man, and was fiercely angry: an anger that drove out fear. He dared not mouth the obscenities his mind created: he was suddenly all vital, desperate movement – and his feet found something: not earth, but something hard and unyielding that at once was support and an opportunity to launch himself up, and out. He broke into the air and spluttered and, eyes closed now, fought his way out of the dip, until his feet found a slope and thinner snow cleared by the helicopter. He stood to full height and pulled the snow from his face. Below him were the ribs of a fence, like the uncovered brown bones of a dinosaur.

He swayed and gasped until his eyes cleared, and he saw that the others had not moved from the door of the carriage.

'*Bastards,*' he said to himself. '*You bastards.*'

Then he heard Mason call:

'Okay?'

He was too furious to answer. He spun around to face the marker, trembling with cold and the icy slide of melting snow at his collar and sleeves. He started out again, still shaken by those seconds of suffocation, the slope offering him a falling level of snow, until it was breaking around his knees. But it was still a slow and clumsy progress, and now his legs were empty of feeling: he lifted stiff, wooden limbs that grew heavier with each thrusting stride.

But with each of those strides came a determination that at first surprised, then cheered him. He spoke to the snow, and the day, and the silence, as if it could hear him.

'*Go on,*' he said, the words hardly audible, but forced out at the start of each breath: '*go on, try it. Try and stop me. Just try.*'

He ploughed his way to the marker, his arms swinging from side to side, the snow falling before him as though he were now in the shallows: ahead the sand, the shore, the island, and home.

And then he was there. He almost fell on the long curve of the container, and he pillowed his head on his arms, and closed his eyes, his lungs pumping like bellows and every sinew singing. Resting, he heard a sound on the air, like dragged-back shingle, and lifted his head, and turned. The others were cheering from the train, their arms waving. He did not acknowledge the salute, but stayed propped against the container, until his breath steadied. He pushed himself upright, banged his arms and his stinging hands across his chest and sides, looked away from the train, and considered what he had reached. It was about eight feet long and two feet wide, covered in dull, black, waterproof plastic, machine-stitched at each end. White military-style stencils said *S.K. MK.II 2433D* in two narrow bands. There were two zips running half its length, and at each end of the container was a thick loop of brown webbing.

He finished brushing away the rest of the snow; then looked back at the train. They were still grouped in the gap, watching. His eyes travelled along to the engine. He could see no upraised arm, no dead driver. He looked back along the train, across the gap, to the two remaining carriages. The white windows showed nothing. Standing as he was, slightly above the track, the train was almost a model: the land around and behind it, all powerful.

He bent down and slipped his right arm into the loop of webbing nearest the track. He took a deep breath, and tugged. He had expected a great weight, but the container moved comparatively easily, the snow acting as a runner. He was helped by the slope, and he blundered on, the container swaying from side to side behind him. And he was exultant: almost daring the cold to be more vicious, the weight increased a hundredfold.

When he got to the deeper snow and the bones of the fence, he stopped. He was soaked and he sweated and his breath roared, yet he had never felt more alive. It was going to be tricky here, but . . .

'Hang on!' shouted Clive. 'I'm coming to help!'

He heard his own voice whip across the last fifty or so yards.

'You'll do nothing! You'll stay there. Don't you move!'

The boy was halfway out of the gap, one leg trailing. Mason pulled him back.

Calvin flexed his right arm once again, and slipped it back inside the loop. He went forward and down again into the dip, and the container scraped behind him. It hit him in the back of the legs, and forced him against the fence. He clambered over and up, cowled in snow, edging towards the track.

He could not see the train, but he called:

'Don't anyone come, you hear?'

The loop at the far end of the container had caught on a fence-stub. He had to move along and release it. Then back to the front, and on . . .

Back came the unspoken obscenities that served as spurs. He was completely unaware of anything but the task. He battled on and up, out of the dip, pressing into the path he had made earlier. Then, as he felt gravel shifting under his feet, he heard, above the sound of his own progress, a faint, frenzied tapping.

It was only another whisper on the air, above the whisper of his body through the snow and the sliding of the container, but it was there; and, pausing, his shoulders sagging, he looked up from the start of the track.

Someone in the third carriage was trying to attract his attention. His eyes moved from window to window, until, behind the same grey-white frosted glass, he caught a darker movement, and what might have been a raised hand. There were no human features: just a blur on the glass, a shadow, and what might have been a hand. Then the tapping ceased, as if the unknown person knew Calvin was watching, and, behind the glass, waited for a response. But, deep in the snow beside the track, what could he do but painfully raise his left hand in greeting, then let it drop. As he dragged himself on, he heard the tapping begin again.

He reached the end of the gravel and the start of the buried sleepers, stubbing his right shoe on the wood. He looked up, his right arm still hooked to the webbing. Beyond the rim of the carriage-body the four faces looked down at him above snowlined, foreshortened bodies. Their faces reflected his own triumph. Mason and the boy were kneeling on the edge now, their hands outstretched.

'Great!' said Clive. 'Hey, great!'

Calvin suddenly felt his age. His throat was sore. The snow at his wrists and ankles burned like acid. Yet nothing would stop him completing what he had set out to do. He dropped the loop from the crook of his arm, the imprint aching in the flesh like cramp, took one step back, and wrapped himself around the end of the container.

'Want a hand?' said Clive.

'He's okay,' said Mason, seeing an echo of his own single-mindedness in Calvin's straining face. 'Let him be.'

The forward loop rose slowly to the gap, to be grasped instantly by the boy, and then by Laura. Calvin felt the weight leave his arms, and released them. The container rose swiftly, tipped, and was dragged into the carriage. Calvin heard it drop, and then all the faces returned, and the gap was full of hands. The boy was almost out of the carriage, smiling, hair all over the place, the white fingers straining.

'Jump up!' said Mason.

138

Calvin shivered. He seemed to be rooted to the snow. The boy was hanging down now as Mason held his ankles. Calvin made one upward lunge. His frozen hand missed the fingers, and he fell ignominiously back: the hero flat out in the snow, like an insect unable to rise. He summoned up the last of his strength and his purpose, clambered to his feet, went under the beckoning fingers again; and jumped, and held.

The boy felt his wrists would break: the cold seemed to have made them brittle. His teeth dug into his bottom lip as Mason pulled him back. Then Calvin felt other hands grasping his shoulders, and he followed Clive on to the floor, to lie there sprawling and gasping as someone moved his feet, and the door was slammed.

Hands lifted him bodily now and placed him upright on a seat. He sat back, and like Mason had done on *his* return, began to shake convulsively. The faces around him were immediately sympathetic, yet also fired with a kind of pride, as though he had brought honour to the whole group, and they shared the warmth.

'Congratulations,' said Anita. 'You never know until you try, right?'

He smiled in his shaking face.

'Right,' he said.

Laura touched his gleaming coat.

'You'll catch pneumonia if you keep this on,' she said, and began to pull at the buttons with stiff fingers.

'Shall we see what we've got first?' he said.

'What?' she said, still intent on the buttons.

'Let's see what I've brought home,' he said.

In the midst of that shared warmth, they remembered: as if what he had struggled for was secondary to his safe return. They looked at the container lying at an angle in the aisle, among shaken snow. Mason stepped over it and motioned to Clive to take the other end. Together they lifted it, and placed it lengthwise on the seat facing Calvin.

'Want to do the honours?' said Mason, lifting the tab of one of the zips.

Still unable to control his trembling, Calvin shook his head, feeling drops of melting snow sting his neck.

'You . . . you carry on,' he said.

The others left him as they turned to the container. Sitting behind them, he heard the swift, satisfying sound of the two zips opening; and then the equally swift intake of breaths from four astounded mouths.

Part Nine

Like a blind man calling into the dark, Calvin said:

'What is it?'

At first there was no answer, so intent were the others on what lay before them. Then the boy, still with his back to Calvin, said:

'Come and see.'

Standing now, and weaker than he had ever known, he pushed his shivering body forward, and the backs parted.

Mason continued to plunder the container. Like a magician, he brought out a bewildering flow of riches, an abundance so unexpected that once again there was silence, save for Calvin's shuddering breath.

Spread before their eyes was a growing man-made bounty of thick blankets, sweaters, scarves, gloves and socks. There was a diversity of food in airtight packs, a selection of fruit-juices and a three-gallon can of water. Mason lifted out a large flask, and spun the cap. He sniffed.

'Brandy,' he said. He turned and handed it to Calvin. 'Get some of that down you.'

Calvin could not hold the flask steady. The boy placed his own hands over the wet gloves, and lifted. Calvin swallowed more than he intended. He choked and sneezed, the brandy stinging his mouth and his throat. He sneezed again and turned his head away, leaving the flask with Clive, who, taking an equally strong pull, felt himself robbed of breath as fire began to track his blood.

Laura and Anita were taking what Mason passed to them, and arranging it on the seat across the aisle. There were matches and cigarettes in waterproof bags, cans of Coke and a box of mints. Mason grunted at what came next.

'So help me,' he said: 'a Bible.'

Calvin was feeling better: the brandy was doing its work, and by an effort of will he had controlled his trembling.

'An evangelical packer,' he said.

Laura put it to one side.

'This is more like it,' said Mason, and held up a small, folding Primus stove, elegant in white metal, and a can of paraffin. 'Trust the Army: they know what's wanted.' He pressed his hand deeper, down to the base of the container. 'And look at this!'

It was a small, black transistor radio, complete with two extra batteries.

142

'Try it!' said Clive.

Mason switched on, spun the dial, passed a swirl of music, and went back. The radio had a bright, tinny quality, but to Calvin the sound was such that he felt as though his spine was melting. He sat down quickly.

'Let's see if there's some news,' said Clive.

'*No!*' said Calvin, and was equally shocked at the abrupt loudness of his own voice. 'Leave it!'

'But we could hear what . . .' began the boy.

'I said *leave it*!' said Calvin. 'Christ, I brought the bloody . . .'

'To the victor the spoils,' said Mason, and handed the radio to Calvin. 'You ladies get the rest of the stuff. I'll get cracking on the stove. Come and help me, son.'

Calvin sat holding the radio, his eyes closed, listening to Schubert. The contrast between his own situation and the world the music promised – and had always promised – was too much. Sharp tears prickled his eyelids. Beyond this stranded train, beyond the snow-locked earth speckled with dead and dying birds, the fixed ice of ponds, the uncaring sky and this inhuman season, an unknown pianist was playing Schubert. A dead artist lay a yard away, yet art continued, would transcend everything that nature hurled at humankind. Schubert was a man no more, but what Calvin heard now was stronger than any storm, any winding-sheet: strong enough to conquer even death. He nodded to himself.

He felt a touch on his knee and opened his eyes. The boy's face, flushed with the effects of the brandy, came forward with an uncertain smile.

'Could we try for some news now?'

'The bastards,' said Calvin.

The boy, bending, saw the wet eyes, smelled the brandy-breath, and became embarrassed. He looked away for a second; then returned to consider a man whom privation seemed to have made mad.

'What?' he said.

'Changing the location to the States,' said Calvin. 'What the hell are they on about? They can take a running jump – nothing's been signed yet.' He appeared to be speaking to someone or something *beyond* the boy; and then his eyes focused, and he smiled. 'Sorry, kid,' he said: 'you wouldn't know what I'm talking about. Sorry. What did you say?'

'I said could we try for some news now?'

'You know what this is?' said Calvin.

'No,' said Clive.

'Schubert,' said Calvin. 'Let this piece finish – then we'll try, right?'

'Right,' said the boy: 'anything you say.'

He straightened as Calvin closed his eyes again, watched the fingers increase the volume; and turned away from the bright, scattering notes that to him was merely another kind of noise: something to be endured until the news, and an authoritative voice bringing news of how the real world fared.

*   *   *

Mason was kneeling in the aisle, pumping the jets of the Primus. There was a fierce, heartening roar from the blue-white flames, and a growing smell of hot, new metal. As Anita folded the empty container, Laura joined him and held out her hands to the heat.

He glanced sideways at her, grinned, and continued pumping.

'Do something to earn your pay,' he said. 'Put some water in those pans and tip in those instant soups.'

'Yes, sir,' she said, gave a mock salute, and stood up.

'Clive,' he said: 'see everyone gets a shot of that brandy.' He looked away from Anita's weary face. 'Start with Mrs Silverman.'

She stood there, the folded black square held against her body, and watched as the boy filled the plastic cup.

'Thank you, Clive,' she said. She drank some, and shuddered. 'That'll be enough.'

'Drink it all,' said Mason. 'Get it down you.' He rested, and looked at Calvin. 'Must we have that so loud?' he said. Everyone looked at the closed face. 'Calvin! *Must* we have that?'

Calvin opened his eyes.

'Philistine,' he said. He sat up and turned the dial. Voices came and went: foreign voices from far, perhaps sunlit, capitals; and someone talking about cancelled football matches; and then pop music and country and western, and back to Schubert – but, as yet, no news. 'There'll be something at one,' said Calvin. He shrugged his sleeve off his watch. 'God, it's a quarter to three!'

'There'll be a news on Radio 2 at three,' said Clive.

'Leave the music,' said Anita. She gave the empty cup back to the boy. 'But softer?'

Calvin turned down the volume, and put the radio on the seat beside him. He became aware of the cold, clinging discomfort of his clothes. He stood up and took off his coat, and then his jacket. Then

144

he stepped around the stove, which now held a can of water into which Laura was shaking flakes of dried tomato soup, and began to sort through the pile of woollens on the seat. Anita put the black square in the rack above him. She came close and said softly:

'I don't think we've thanked you enough, Mr Calvin. There were times when I thought we might lose you.'

He held up a sweater and placed it against himself.

'Me, too,' he said.

She put her hand on his arm.

'Well, then, thank you,' she said, 'and . . .' Her hand slipped from his arm, and she fell away from him. She began to slump to the floor, but he held her, the sweater bunched against her back. Her head swayed to one side.

'Oh, no!' said Laura.

Calvin opened his fingers and the sweater dropped. He lifted that surprisingly light body and laid it on the seat. The others had joined him now, and Mason leaned down and pressed back one of her eyelids.

'It's all right,' he said: 'she's only fainted.'

'Only?' said Laura.

'I'm surprised she hasn't gone down before,' he said. 'Brandy on an empty stomach didn't help either.' He picked up the sweater, bundled it into a ball, and put it under her head. 'Wrap a blanket around her – that one there.'

Anita's eyelids flickered, and opened. She gave a long, deep sigh.

'Take it easy, Mrs Silverman,' said Mason.

Her gaze cleared, and she remembered.

'No, lie back,' he said. 'Don't worry.'

'Silly of me,' she said. 'Sorry.' She closed her eyes. 'I'll be all right. This blanket's . . . lovely.'

Mason motioned the others away.

'I think she might sleep,' he said softly. 'The brandy'll keep her going for a while, and it's getting warmer in here. Let's all get some dry clothes. And then that soup . . .'

2

. . .a region extending south from Norwich to Bristol is now completely cut off from the rest of the country. It is estimated that over six

million householders are without electricity. Telephone lines are down throughout this area, and public transport is at a standstill . . .

'Surprise, surprise,' said Clive, lifting his head from his soup.

'. . . *a number of trains are snowbound. Efforts are being made to reach these, but snowploughs and other railway stock are being hampered by the exceptional drifts, particularly in the Home Counties. Many motorists, caught in yesterday's worsening weather, have been found dead in their cars. The weathermen say that present conditions will prevail for at least another thirty-six hours.*

In the rest of Europe, too, the . . .

'I think we've heard enough,' said Calvin, and found another station. He made the music softer, and shrugged back into his blanket.

'God,' said Laura, 'I hope we aren't here for another thirty-six hours.'

'We won't be,' said Mason. 'They'll be here before that.' He leaned halfway across the aisle. 'She still asleep?'

'Yes,' said Laura. 'This soup is marvellous. Shall I wake her and give her some?'

'No,' said Mason. 'She'll feel all the better for it. Leave her.'

There was a certain homeliness about the carriage now. The stove sang, sending waves of warmth to reach the windows, and here the frost began to relent, the feathered fronds destroyed and drifting down in irregular shapes like miniature icefloes; and in the clearing glass the land grew and came closer, yet was still nothing but a white mask pegged below the sky, indifferent, lacking even brutality.

While Anita slept, the others sat wrapped in blankets, like four Indians around a campfire, their feet and hands in dry socks and gloves, sipping the last of the soup.

'Anyone want another biscuit?' said Calvin.

'No, thank you,' said Laura. She put down the empty paper cup. She yawned and stretched, the cowl of the blanket slipping off her shoulders. 'I think Mrs Silverman has the right idea. Anyone mind if I try to sleep?'

'You carry on,' said Mason. 'We'll wake you if anything happens.'

'Ha,' she said. She lifted the blanket around her shoulders again, nestled her head into the folds, and lay curled in the aisle. She closed her eyes.

146

Clive yawned.

'It's catching,' he said. He dropped his cup into Laura's. 'I think I'll join you.'

'Do,' she said, without opening her eyes.

'Wait a minute,' said Mason. 'I'll move out of your way.' He picked up the radio and shifted back on to the seat.

'Thanks,' said the boy. He lay down, pulled his blanket around his head, straightened his legs – and his feet touched Calvin. 'Sorry.'

'Hang on,' said Calvin: 'I'll move, too.'

He got back on to the seat opposite Mason, and together the two men watched the sleepers, the gentle roar of the flames and the quiet music adding to the silence; until Mason recognised the deep, regular breathing (echo of many a midnight guard-duty) – and stood, reached for the flask, gathered up two clean paper cups, and looked enquiringly at Calvin.

Calvin nodded, and held out a clean, army-issue glove for the brandy.

The cup was almost empty now, and Calvin felt fine. He almost sagged against the seat, the blanket draped untidily across his lap. His thick tongue moved over his thick lips. He laughed softly, shook his head.

Mason, equally comfortable, the blanket thrown aside, the collar of his uniform open, his gloved hands around his second drink, his mouth slightly slack, his beard darker by the hour, considered his companion.

'Penny for them,' he said.

Calvin looked up. Flushed, he looked almost boyish.

'I did it. I bloody did it.'

'Did what?'

Calvin stared at him. How soon could valour fail?

'Went out there, and came back.'

'Proud of yourself, are you?' said the slow, perhaps even contemptuous voice.

'Wouldn't you be? I mean, I know you're in the Army and all that, but . . .'

'It had to be done. If you hadn't made it, I'd have had to go out there and bring you in. You *and* the stuff.'

'You're denying it took some . . . guts?'

Mason swallowed some of his brandy.

'No, I'm not saying that. Things are always smaller when they're over: the heat goes out of them.'

Calvin felt glory depart from him at the speed of light. He moistened his lips again.

'Would you give up forty thousand for the sake of a principle?'

'I've never had that choice,' said Mason.

'But if you had.'

'No principle's worth forty thousand,' said Mason. 'Money rules the world.'

'Would you take forty thousand not to kill this man?'

Mason drank the last of the brandy, and put the cup carefully between his feet. He wriggled his toes in the warmth from the stove. He looked up, and it was the steady stare of a predator, or so Calvin told himself.

'Who said anything about killing?' said the sergeant.

'Then why the gun? Why the worry about using more ammunition?'

'Who said anything about killing? You've written too many paperbacks.'

'All right, all right. Would you take forty thousand not to do this . . . special duty?'

'You offering?'

'Theoretically . . .'

'I was never one for theory,' said Mason. 'Hard cash – and I'll answer you.'

Calvin shrugged. Below the two men, in the silence, the boy twitched in his dreams. Mason wrapped his own blanket around himself, drew his feet up on to the seat, and pressed himself into the corner near the almost-clear window, the white field.

'Think I'll settle for half an hour's kip,' he said. 'You could do the same.'

'I don't fancy sitting up all night,' said Calvin. 'I'll wait till later.'

Mason wriggled deeper into the corner, folded his arms under his blanket, and closed his eyes.

'We won't be here another night,' he said.

'Is that a bet?' said Calvin.

Mason, already half-asleep, grinned.

'If you like.'

'Forty thousand?' said Calvin.

Mason nodded.

'You're . . . on,' he said. Within a minute his head had dropped to his shoulder, his mouth had fallen open, and his breath was as deep and as regular as the others.

Calvin watched him sleep, and waited another minute. Then he lifted his own blanket from his thighs, put it to one side, and stood up. The radio played quietly: a well-known tune from a recent hit show. He whistled softly in tune as he stepped around Clive's legs. Standing now behind the seat, he held on to the rack with one hand, and reached over the gun to the magazine with the other. He unclipped the last two rounds. A thread from his gloved thumb had caught on the magazine, and he tugged it free with his teeth. He replaced the magazine, went to where his coat was draped to dry, and pushed the rounds into one of the pockets.

Before he went back to his seat, he pumped the flames higher; then he took up his blanket and pushed himself into his own corner.

What had prompted him to empty the magazine? He shook his head. He had acted spontaneously, purely out of instinct: as if the man whose life was the creation of fictions had stepped from those hermit pages, to intervene in an all too dangerous reality. He was tempted to return the rounds: he went as far as to grasp the edge of the blanket; but sat back. It was done now, whatever the consequences.

He had told himself he would resist the coming of sleep: if rescue came within the hour, his would be the voice that cried *Saved!* But the two sounds – the stove and the radio – were another kind of silence; and he found himself unable to control his eyelids – they grew weightier with every breath. Finally, he was forced to let them rest – and was lost . . .

3

The boy was the first to wake.

He opened his eyes and saw first the silver base of the stove resting on Calvin's magazine, and then the struts which led up to the ring of blue fire. Drowsy, the brandy still firing his blood, he looked beyond the stove to Laura's face. He had never lain so close to a sleeping woman, and a stranger. He felt a sudden excitement, which was not entirely sexual: it was simply the repeated promise of liberation, horizons stretching as far as the universe. He had survived, and help was on its way: he was not dead like poor old Silverman; he was no longer caged by his mother and that holy room, and by that other Mother and her milk-white saintly Son: he was his own man, and he could almost feel the fabric of a new world under his fingertips.

He shifted nearer, until he was inches from her half-opened mouth. He could see the faint gleam of teeth, the shine of her tongue, smell the food and brandy on her breath. If he moved a fraction closer, he could kiss her – but he did not dare. Instead, he rested his head on the floor and was content to watch an unknown woman sleeping: promise of the future, the as-yet undiscovered cities where other women waited for him in other rooms, in the great hotels, by the warm borders of swimming-pools, across champagne-littered tables, in speeding powerboats heading for shadowed villas, the face in the pillows as dawn lit the walls . . .

Laura opened her eyes. She blinked twice, but the face was still there: resting on the floor, below the flames. She closed her mouth. The face was smiling. She blinked again, and was fully awake.

It was the boy: that sleep-hazed face never so near. There were biscuit-crumbs between his teeth. There were small acne-scars, and a scattering of pale freckles. His eyes were too bright, like other eyes she had known in the past, that close.

Her body became hard. She did not move. His smile was uncertain now, and she felt a perverse power and pleasure in what she intended to do next. He seemed about to speak. She spoke first.

'Go away,' she said, and it was almost a hiss.

He lifted his head.

'You hear me?' she said, still holding herself rigid. 'Get away from me, you creep.'

His eyes widened and his mouth opened. He sat up, the blanket falling behind him.

'I wasn't doing anything . . .' he said.

'But you'd like to, wouldn't you?' she said.

'If that's how you feel . . .' he said, and scrambled to his feet.

She looked up at him.

'That's how I feel,' she said. 'You can never leave it alone, can you?'

Her face had changed: it was fierce and animal-like, as if he had blundered over some territorial line, a land only she was allowed to inhabit.

'I'm sorry,' he said.

'You'll learn,' she said. She flung the blankets off her legs, stood up, and brushed the flecks from her sweater in sharp, swift movements of her gloves. 'You'll all learn, one day.'

Their voices had woken Anita. She caught the angry bitterness beneath the girl's last words, and became frightened. She pressed herself up on her elbows.

'What will we learn?' she said.

Laura turned to her, immediately dismissing the boy from her mind. She sat down on the edge of the seat and took Anita's hands in hers.

'Feel better?'

'Yes, thank you.' Anita studied the girl's face. 'What was all that about? What will we learn?'

'It was nothing,' said Laura. 'Would you like something to eat? There are biscuits and sandwiches. We've all had some soup. I could warm some for you.'

'I'd rather have something to drink.' Her eyes moved to the front of the carriage. 'How's my husband? I mean . . .'

'Everything's all right,' said Laura. 'We've heard the news — they're on their way.' She sat back. 'I think there's some coffee. Would you like some?'

'Yes, I would. Thank you, dear. And a sandwich. Doesn't that stove look fine?' Her eyes lifted. 'And how are *you*, Clive?'

The boy finished folding his blanket.

'Okay,' he said, still stung and disturbed by Laura's reaction. 'I'll get you the sandwich.'

Laura paused in her search for the coffee.

'You won't,' she said. 'I'll do it. Leave it to me. Please.'

Defeated, he sat down next to Calvin's feet, his hands hidden under his blanket. He looked across the aisle to the beaded window.

'You think it's getting darker already?' he said.

4

They sat, crouched at the ends of the seats, around the stove. Calvin blew on his hot black coffee.

'It looks as though we've had the afternoon,' he said.

'That's what I thought, just now,' said Clive. 'Christ, I hope they get here soon.'

151

'So does the sergeant,' said Calvin. 'Forty thousand, remember?'
Mason nodded.

'I haven't forgotten,' he said.

'Forty thousand *what*?' said Anita.

Calvin explained.

'Then we'd better all pray they get here, sergeant,' she said.

'Everything welcome,' he said. 'I might have to pass around the hat.'

Anita shuffled closer to the stove, the movement of a suddenly old woman. She looked down at the flames, the small roaring.

'I know you won't like me saying this,' she said: 'but what are we going to do about the others?'

There was a silence between them.

'Others?' said Laura.

'You heard the tapping,' said Anita. 'You must have done. You all heard it.'

Calvin sighed.

'You heard it, didn't you?' she said.

He did not look up from his coffee.

'Yes,' he said.

'What tapping?' said Mason.

'Tell him, Mr Calvin,' she said. 'You must have heard it, sergeant. Or are you . . . pretending?'

'Pretending about *what*?' he said, irritation sharpening his words.

'Do *you* know what we're talking about, Clive?' she said.

'No,' he said. He held up the flask of brandy. 'Anyone want some in their coffee?'

They shook their heads.

'I think you'd be better off without it, too,' said Mason.

'I might as well live a little,' said the boy, and poured some into his cup. 'Cheers.'

'Tell them, Mr Calvin,' said Anita.

Since he had heard the tapping and seen the shadow on the window, guilt had grown behind Calvin's every thought and action, every drink of brandy, every morsel of food. He put his coffee to one side.

'There's someone in the carriage behind us,' he said. 'He – or she – saw me coming back with the stuff. He started tapping on the window.'

There was another, longer silence. All except Mason grew

152

increasingly uncomfortable. For his part, life distributed its favours and its horrors impartially: men survived or did not survive. There was a simplicity there: as simple and as unconcerned as nature. Then he thought of his sister, and what he intended to do in Petersfield – and he floundered. But not for long. There were always exceptions.

'So?' he said.

'Answer that yourself,' said Anita, and her face and eyes were stony. 'Look around you. Clothes and food and heat . . .'

'I say again – so? What do you want to do? Or, more to the point: what do you want us to do?'

The implied acknowledgement of her uselessness, her frailty, angered her.

'I for one couldn't stay here another night, knowing they were there, cold and without food,' she said. 'Could you?'

'You'd have thought they'd've come to us,' said Clive.

She swung to him.

'How?' she said. 'What if their doors are frozen hard, too?'

'Then how are we going to get it to them?' said the boy.

'I don't know,' she said. 'But we must make the effort.'

'We could be rescued any minute . . .' he said.

'I know you've given up what Christianity you had,' she said. 'But I haven't.'

Mason nodded down the carriage to where Silverman lay.

'He'll go to Heaven without your help,' he said.

'I can't believe what I'm hearing,' she said. 'People are out there . . .'

She was so angry she could not go on. She stood up, a small, defiant woman with burning eyes. She reached up to the rack and brought down the container. She shook it to its full length, opened the top, and began to thrust home the remaining packs of sandwiches.

'Okay, okay,' said Mason, wearily: 'for Christ's sake don't be so dramatic. Just stop a minute.'

She paused, one hand inside the long black funnel.

'Yes?' she said.

'Sit down.'

'I don't wish to sit down. In another hour it'll be dark.'

'Let's get this straight,' he said: 'what are you suggesting?'

She continued packing the container.

'I'm not *suggesting* anything,' she said. 'I'm doing something.

We share what we have.'

'How do we get it to them?'

'I would have thought that was obvious, Sergeant,' she said. 'We go down on to the track, go to the carriage, and shout.'

'And if their doors won't open?'

'If they're hungry, they'll get them open,' she said.

'And are we to try the other carriage, *and* the guard's section?' She was fighting for control.

'Look, Sergeant,' she said, her voice as slow and as patient as she could make it. 'Don't ask so many questions, don't put up such a smoke-screen.' She looked at the other three faces. 'Are you with me?'

Each one waited for another to speak.

'You mean you have to *think*?' she said, her voice rising. 'Then I'll do it alone.'

'We might have something to say about that,' said Mason. 'You're one among five . . .'

'Oh, we wouldn't allow her to go, you know that!' said Laura. Mason smiled.

'That's precisely what she's counting on, isn't it?' he said. 'She knows one of the men would volunteer.'

'No,' said Laura: 'I'd go. If I had to.'

Mason looked at Anita.

'Satisfied?' he said.

She was near to tears. She took her hand from the container and sat down.

'So we leave them, do we?' she said. 'We stay here, warm and fed and clothed – and we leave them?'

They sat in their separate silences as the evening crossed the horizon and slowly headed for the train.

5

Laura took the pan off the stove, poured the steaming coffee into Anita's flask, put back the pan, and reached for the top which served as a cup. She tightened it, and handed the flask to Mason. He put it inside the container, and rested.

'That's it, is it?' he said.

'Just about,' said the boy.

Mason closed the mouth of the container, and folded the smooth plastic until it was firm. He lifted it on to his lap, rested his gloved hands on top, and said:

'Well, who's going?'

Laura stamped her snowboots, pulled her collar around her throat, and pushed down the fingers of her gloves.

'I'm ready,' she said.

'You've made your point,' said Mason. 'Sit down. Now, who's going?'

'*Me*,' she said.

'All right,' he said: 'go ahead.'

'You can't let her,' said Anita.

Mason lifted his shoulders.

'What did I tell you?' he said.

'I'll go with her,' said Clive.

'I can manage on my own,' she said. She lifted the black bundle from Calvin's lap, pushed it under her right arm, and stepped to the door. 'Open it, please.'

Mason sat where he was.

'Are we all agreed?' he said. 'She goes?'

'I don't,' said Anita.

'Or me,' said the boy.

'Calvin?' said Mason.

'People should be allowed the choice,' he said.

'Two for, two against,' said the sergeant. 'It's up to you, Saint Joan.'

'Open the door, please,' said Laura.

Mason stood up and kicked it open.

The darkening day coloured the snow a glaring blue-white, as if lit from below by neon. There was no wind, and now there were no clouds. Frost was tightening the land, and a first star winked, high and chill. In other circumstances the scene might have appeared beautiful, but now there was a cold ferocity in the air, a suggestion of forces biding their time, strong enough to wait, in no hurry.

'Don't go,' said Anita. 'Let one of the men . . .'

'Don't let me down, Mrs Silverman, please,' said Laura.

She moved to the gap and looked out, turning her head to the left. The snow-spattered train stretched back, silent and ominous.

'Okay,' said Mason. 'Off you go.' He put his hand on her shoulder. 'I'll come down if you get into trouble.'

'Thank you,' she said.

She put the bundle on the floor, and turned to lower herself over the edge.

It was then that all of them heard a violent, splintering sound that shattered the silence, and caused them to stare at each other with equally shaken faces . . .

Part Ten

1

It was the sound of breaking glass. And it seemed to go on and on, as if an unknown rage would not be spent until every single shard was destroyed.

They joined Laura in the gap, and looked with her down the track to the next carriage. Glass was still flying from a window, punched or kicked out, to fall without a sound to the banked snow. They watched and waited, the bundle pushed behind them, their bodies close, hands on each other's shoulders, and necks craning. The noise stopped, a single sliver dropping to the track. The breath of the watchers hung in the air, their bodies even closer now as they waited: a silent, attentive audience.

A voice sounded from the broken window, but the words were lost. Then an arm appeared, and fingers sought the handle of the door. There was a sudden, muffled thump, as if someone had charged forward – and the door flew open, the arm swiftly withdrawn.

Heads appeared and looked down the train.

'Hey!' one of the heads called: 'you got any food?'

'Yes!' Mason shouted.

A man dropped from the open door to the track. He landed in deep snow, and flailed around, getting his balance.

'You okay?' asked one of his companions.

The man below him, waist-deep, surged forward, keeping to the body of the train, gloved hands touching the metal, steadying himself, moving on.

'I'm okay.'

Step by floundering step he approached the others. They watched him come. Soon they could hear the roaring gasp of his breathing, see what kind of man he was: a heavy, bundled body, a chilled white face under a patterned woollen cap, crossing the gap now between the coaches, looking up at intervals, hands dragging trails through frozen waves of snow fixed to the metal, disclosing golden numbers.

And then he was there, below them, gasping, his breath about his face. They took an involuntary step back, almost as if they desired to escape contagion.

The man lifted his arms.

'Help me up,' he said.

Mason pushed forward, knelt down, and said:

'We can pass it to you.'

The man, his chest heaving, wiped his mouth with the back of his glove. And once again raised his arm.

'I said help me up.'

'Move back,' said Mason. 'Come here, Calvin.'

Together they crouched down; and the man gave a clumsy leap, hampered by the snow. They found his wrists – and pulled.

The women were now way back, close together; the boy a little to the left of the stove.

The man lay across the gap, his feet outside the carriage. But he soon scrambled up, shaking himself free of their hands. Mason went behind him, and closed the door, gently. Then he stepped around, and joined the others. They waited again, bunched together, listening to the choked breathing that was not yet under control.

Neither was the man's rage. He looked from the flames of the stove, to the clear windows, the signs of food. He could smell coffee in the warm air, and perhaps even . . . brandy? He shook his head. Snow slid from his trousers and his boots. He swallowed.

'Had yourselves a time, haven't you?' he said. He rubbed his ears with numb fingers. His small, pale-blue eyes moved over their faces, and the eyes were hard. 'Quite a time.'

'There's . . . there's some brandy here,' said the boy.

'I thought there might be,' said the man.

He took the flask and tipped it to his lips. When he had finished, he held out his left hand for the cap. He fixed it tight, and put the flask inside his coat.

'We heard the chopper,' he said. He coughed and banged his chest. 'Yes, we heard that . . .'

'We were just going to . . .' began Laura.

'What sort of people are you?' he said: 'that you could spend so much time getting yourselves . . . comfortable? Didn't you think of us? Were you all so nice and cosy, eh?'

'That's not fair,' said Laura. 'I was just going to bring you some food. And hot coffee.'

'*You* were?' he said. '*You*? And what were these big strong, well-fed chaps here going to do? – let you go? Don't make me laugh.' He pulled off his wet gloves and warmed his hands over the flames.

'She's right,' said Mason.

'You were letting her go out there?'

'It's too complicated to explain,' said Mason. He lifted the black

159

bundle from the floor and put it on the seat. 'This is it. All packed, ready to go.'

'I believe you – thousands wouldn't,' said the man. He rubbed his hands and flexed the fingers. 'You left it bloody late, that's all I'm saying.'

'You can take it now,' said Anita.

He took off his cap, rubbed his face with it, and ran a hand through a fuzz of fine ginger hair.

'Take it now?' he said. 'I'm taking nothing back, lady. We're all coming in here.'

It was as if he had revealed his true self: masquerading under a flag of truce he had breached the walls, the siege was over, the city in enemy hands.

'Coming in here?' said Anita. 'How . . . how many are you?'

'Two men and a woman,' he said. 'Three of us. Don't you want us?' His voice was contemptuous. 'Want it all for yourself?'

'No,' said Calvin, but he too felt that something was in the process of being broken: almost a way of life. He was amazed and somewhat appalled at his own insularity, but there was no denying the fear of intrusion. 'But why bring them out? You can take it back . . .'

'With a broken window all night?' said the man, incredulously. 'And you here with a stove . . .' He looked around. '. . . and blankets and . . .' He dropped his hands. 'Christ, I've heard of selfishness in my time, but . . .'

'The radio says help's on its way,' said Clive. 'We won't be here all night. You won't . . .' His voice tailed away.

The man acknowledged the radio for the first time. He bent his head to the soft music.

'All modern comforts, eh?' he said. He shook his head again. 'I don't know. I just don't know any more.' He pulled himself together. 'Well, I just can't stand here passing the time of day. Not like some, eh? There are people freezing back there . . .'

'You want any help?' said Clive. 'I . . .'

'I wouldn't disturb you, son,' said the man. He pulled on his gloves and stepped back to the door. The torn wood crackled. He looked at Mason 'Your gun, was it?'

'Yes.'

'Handy, wasn't it?' said the man. 'Someone up there must like you.' He turned himself around in the gap. 'I . . . *we* won't be long.'

He dropped to the snow.

2

They stood together and watched him go. And he appeared to have none of the group's apprehensions about the wildness of the weather, the fear of being engulfed – but fought his way with an almost uncaring determination through the crumbling sides of the track he had made – and was soon at the open door of his own carriage, and calling.

Mason felt a hand tighten on his arm. It was Anita. Her face had a strained, pleading look.

'I don't want them here, Gordon,' she said.

It was the first time she had used his Christian name: proof of the fusion of the group.

'I know,' he said. 'But what can we do about it?'

'I don't know why I don't want them,' she said. 'It's not like me. I think . . . it's Simon. We've – all of us, I mean – have . . . shared. I don't want them prying, asking questions. The fact that he's there . . .'

'I know.'

'If we gave them the blankets, they could pack them in the window,' said Laura.

They were all silent, astonished at the bond they had discovered, and what they were willing to do to maintain it.

'That's an idea,' said Anita. She brightened. 'I'll get them.' She moved back to the seat, picked up the first blanket and began to fold it.

'I don't know,' said Calvin.

'Stop a minute, Anita,' said Mason. 'Let's get it straight. We don't want them, right?'

They looked at each other, and it was as if they were a family.

'It's our carriage,' said Clive. 'I mean . . .'

'We know what you mean,' said Mason. 'We'll take a vote. Laura?'

'The blankets would serve better than glass,' she said, convincing herself. 'Warmer, yes?'

'You don't want them here?' he persisted.

'No.'

'Anita?'

'For the sake of my husband,' she said. 'I know it sounds strange . . . No.'

'Clive?'

'Like Laura says: the blankets. And they won't have to wait long.' He looked down the track. 'Make up your minds. They're helping the woman out.'

'Calvin?' said Mason.

'I don't know . . .'

'You're out-voted, anyway,' said Mason. 'Stand aside, Clive.' He leaned out. 'Stay there!' he shouted.

The woman was halfway out of the carriage.

'*What*?' shouted the man.

'Get her back!' shouted Mason.

'No!' He tugged at the woman's legs, and she dropped to his side. He held up his hands to help the other man.

Now the three of them were standing in the snow beside the train, preparing to move forward.

'Blast!' said Mason. He turned. 'Let's get these blankets folded . . .'

'You're not letting them in, then?' said Calvin.

'What do *you* think?' said Mason.

'But . . .'

'If you don't want to help, just don't get in the way, man.'

Calvin watched as the blankets, neatly folded, were placed beside the black bundle on the seat.

And then the group gathered in the gap, and waited.

The three strangers came nearer, the woman scared and unsure, often stumbling, and helped up by the man who followed her. The horizon had gone now, merged into the coming night. The land still glowed.

And then the woollen cap was below the door, and the face lifted, breath smoking.

'What . . . what was all that about?' he said.

He was met by silence. Now the woman stood beside him: a small, white-faced, wispy-haired creature in a fur coat. The other man was tall, grey-haired, wearing large glasses that seemed to hide his eyes; he was dressed in a snow-bordered black overcoat, and bright tan gloves.

'Come on, Margaret,' said the first man. 'Come along here. I'll help you up.'

She moved in front of him. Her tilted face was as white as the snow. She tried to smile at the group.

The first man put his hands under her armpits.

'Hold it!' said Mason.

The man, still holding her, looked up.

'What?'

'You're not coming in,' said Mason.

The man gripped the woman, and lifted.

'Give a hand here, Sam,' he said.

The other man joined him. The woman rose to the gap, her fingers stretching.

'Put her down,' said Mason, quietly.

Her fingers plucked at the doorframe.

'I said *put her down*!' said Mason.

The straining faces of the men below relaxed, and they gently brought her back to the snow.

'What the fucking hell are you playing at?' said the first man.

The other man was speechless, his face a picture of disbelief. The woman shivered, and rubbed her chin into her collar.

'Let them in,' said Calvin, softly.

'Get the blankets, Clive,' said Mason.

'Come on!' said the first man: 'what the hell are you doing?'

The blankets were passed over, one by one, until each of the group held one. Mason crouched down.

'We're giving you these,' he said. 'We want you to go back. You can pack them in the window. You've got our brandy. We've made you hot coffee, and there's plenty of food. I can't see this train being here another night. Hold out your hands.'

'Not a chance, friend,' said the first man.

'I've never heard anything like it,' said the second. 'We're coming in − like it or not.'

'We're going to drop these blankets now,' said Mason. 'If you don't catch them, they'll hit the snow. Ready?'

Without waiting for an answer he dropped his, and the second man was forced to receive it. The others followed. The woman held hers close to her body.

'We can't go back there,' she said. 'How are we going to climb up?'

'You'll manage,' said Mason.

'We won't be going back, Margaret − don't you worry,' said the first man. He looked up at Mason. 'We'll stay here until you let us in.'

'Get my gun, will you, Clive?' said Mason.

'Your gun?'

'You heard what I said.'

Calvin was tempted to speak, to object − then he remembered

the rounds were safe in his coat pocket: was he about to witness the result of his own intervention? He pressed himself against the doorframe, settling to watch the next few minutes as though he had created them.

The boy took the gun and the magazine from the rack, pushed between Laura and Anita, and gave them to Mason. Still looking at the first man, the sergeant clipped home the magazine, then crouched down on the rim of the gap.

'Get their food, son,' he said.

He took the bundle in his left hand, held it out over the snow, and let it drop. He pointed the gun at the woollen cap.

'Get going,' he said. 'The sooner you go, the warmer you'll be.'

The first man stared at the barrel.

'What do you think you're going to do with that?' he said.

'What does it look like?' said Mason.

The man turned to the faces of his companions. They reflected his own incomprehension. He opened his mouth to say something, but then the nature of the day and his own situation impressed themselves upon him with a sudden, brutal clarity. Everything was suddenly alien: the earth itself, its former comforting landmarks blotted out by this cold, clinging, inhuman whiteness; the cold itself, working at his feet, his hands, his face; the stranded, unmoving, silent train; the faces of strangers above him, the pointing gun – this was not his world, the one he had left behind in the city. Perhaps this was the beginning of an age he had always dreaded: all stability gone, anarchy, the coming of the barbarians. The past was a warm, receding paradise . . . He shook himself free of more than snow, and looked up again at the sergeant.

'Look,' he said, and there was a new fear in his voice. 'I . . . we . . .' He could not go on. He shook his head.

Anita came forward.

'He'd never use it,' she said. 'Don't worry. It's all pretence.' She paused. 'You see – we have a dead man here.'

Her words made the day a shade darker, made the cold a swordblade on the faces that looked up at her. It was the seal of a new, nightmarish reality.

'A dead man?' said the woman.

'Yes,' said Anita. 'My husband.'

'He's in there?' said the woman.

'Where else?' said Mason.

The three, standing in the snow, blankets to their chests, looked

164

at each other. It was they who now felt the risk of an unnamed contagion: the watchers above them the guardians of a pest-house, a purpose behind their seeming lack of compassion, an excuse – the three even breathed easier.

'We didn't know,' said the first man. 'You should've said in the beginning . . . Still, I can't see it makes that much of a difference.'

'I'd rather go back,' said the woman.

'Yes,' said the second man. 'We'll . . . we'll take our chances. Come on.'

All the first man's anger had departed.

'Thanks for the blankets,' he said. 'And the food.' He handed his own blanket to the other man, and picked up the bundled container. 'Sorry to hear about . . .'

'That's all right,' said Anita: 'you weren't to know.'

Mason, still crouching on the rim, swung on his heels. He passed the gun to the boy.

'Put this away for me,' he said. Then he dropped down to the track. 'I'll see you get back all right.'

'You needn't do that,' said the first man.

But Mason had already taken the blanket from the woman, and was beginning to guide her through the divided snow.

And then it sounded behind them, far away but still clear: the high, double-call of a klaxon.

_____ 3 _____

They all turned their heads, as if pulled by a single wire. Eight pairs of eyes looked down the track, past the next carriage and the part-obliterated engine, past the hidden lines, and on to the misty ending of the day, this horizon not completely merged: an horizon that held the sound – and also, out of the mist, like the coming of morning, a growing point of light, like the birth of a sun.

The klaxon sounded again, and it served for all their unspoken words, their heart-lurching gratitude. Gathered together in two groups, they touched hands and shoulders, and smiled without looking at each other.

The light grew bigger, the sun enlarged, changing from a pale yellow to white, seeming to burn its way towards them, parting the snow that reared and fell in giant waves to either side. The klaxon called at regular intervals, and between the calls they heard the sound of the train itself: a hissing, drumming, thrusting strength that sang in every fibre of their shivering bodies.

Mason still had his hand on the woman's shoulder. Now he turned her completely around.

'You can't go anywhere now,' he said. 'They'll be here soon. Come in with us.'

'Thank you,' she said.

He turned to the two men. Their faces had a strangely blurred quality, as if the fine grains thrown up by the plough had drifted this far: they looked posed, like frost-bitten explorers, held until the shutter clicked – and then moving.

'Okay with you?' he said.

'Yes,' they said, like twins.

They took another look at the snowplough as it pressed towards them, then stood below the gap. Clive put the gun on a seat, and knelt down to help. The woman felt herself lifted, and then other hands grasped. She stood in the carriage now, saw the bright flames of the stove, and moved towards them.

Blankets were thrown up, and then the container. One by one the men were hauled in. Mason stood in the doorway and looked out, down the track. The plough was yards away now, and slowing – the waves small, smaller. And then it had reached the engine. The klaxon called – or rather, erupted: braying and violent, like a double shout of triumph ringing in their ears, echoing across the carriage and across the land. As he watched, he saw a group of men jump from the plough's engine and make their way towards the train. The boy joined him.

'What's happening?'

'They'll find the driver in a minute,' said Mason quietly. He reached out and, with one swift movement, slammed the door shut. 'We'll let them get on with it.'

The three strangers were like uninvited, uncomfortable guests. They grouped themselves around the stove, hands over the flames, and smiled uncertainly, their faces lit from below, behind them the growing dark of the carriage and the day.

'What about the brandy?' said Mason.

'None left,' said the first man. 'We all had a drink before we started out.'

Anita finished folding the blankets. Now that one part of the ordeal was over, another took precedence – and was perhaps more terrible and longer-lasting. She had to be busy, had to force this tremble from her bones before it overwhelmed her.

'Sit down, sit down,' she said, like an anxious hostess. 'Gordon, move that gun, will you?'

He picked it up.

'You had me worried out there,' said the first man.

Mason unclipped the magazine. He smiled.

'I'd've only gone for your ears,' he said. 'Nothing serious. I'll put it away.'

He moved down the aisle to where he had left his suitcase. On the way, he noticed that the magazine was lighter: lacking a weighted end. He tipped it towards himself, and discovered the rounds were missing. He stopped short, turned, and looked back at Clive. The boy was handing a sandwich to the woman. Mason decided to speak to him later, turned back, opened the suitcase and put the gun and the empty magazine inside. He closed the lid, snapped the locks, and put the case at the end of the seat. From where he stood he could see through the beaded window – now there was no division between the sky and the land: only the snow lining the edge of the windowframe glowed before the dying of the evening and the coming of night. Returning, he had to pass by the still silence of Silverman. The dead man's shoes looked incongruous, even comic, splayed and pointing to the ceiling. He touched the thin ankles: the socks covered stone. Beyond that window a beam of white light flashed, and he heard the voices of living men.

He went back to the others, circled the stove, and kicked open the door.

'Oh, *please*!' said the woman, her hands cupped around her steaming coffee.

'They're out there,' he said, and turned his face to the right.

Two men were making their way alongside the train, the leader carrying a large torch. They had paused at the crashing-back of the door, but now came on, pressing through waist-high snow. They broke through below the gap, and Mason closed his eyes as the light hit his face.

'You okay up there?' said one of the men.

Mason felt the others pressing around him. He opened his eyes and the men were encircled by the imprint of the light.

'We have one dead man,' said Mason.

167

The unadorned fact seemed to stun the men. They stood motionless behind the beam, their mouths open.

'You have?' said one, finally.

'That's what I said. You find the driver?'

'You . . . you know about him?'

'I'll tell you about it later,' said Mason. 'We're all okay, otherwise.'

'We're from the next carriage,' said the woman, behind him, leaning forward. 'There's no one else in there.'

'Right,' said the man with the light. It dropped from their faces. 'We'll just check with the guard — and then we'll take you into Witley. Ten minutes.'

'Thank you,' said the woman.

The men moved on, the snow dazzling in the beam.

Mason pressed himself back until he could close the door. The others were sitting again, blankets wrapped around their legs. The ends of the carriage were now completely dark, the only light the small, hissing flames of the stove.

The woman in the fur coat was slowly coming alive. Holding her coffee in her right hand, she loosened her collar with her left, the small fingers bright with rings.

'He's down there,' said Anita, from across the aisle, her joined hands tight between her knees, under her blanket.

'What?' said the woman.

'My husband. I thought you were . . . looking, wondering. He's down there. There's nothing to be afraid of.'

'I didn't think there was,' said the woman. 'How did he . . .?'

'Heart attack,' said Anita.

'Tsk, tsk,' said the woman. 'What we have to go through. Still, it won't be long now. I mean . . .'

'Yes,' said Anita. She parted her hands, pushed aside the blanket, and got to her feet. 'Excuse me.' She looked down the carriage. 'I think I . . .'

'Do you think you ought to?' said Laura.

'I won't have him much longer, will I?' said Anita.

'Do you want me to come with you?'

Anita put out her hand.

'No, thank you, dear. Good of you to offer. I'll be all right.'

She made her way past the stove, out of the circle of warmth, and down to Simon. Their voices began again behind her, suitably hushed. Bending into a dark made darker by the high seat-back, she caught the odd word or two: *tragedy* and *no* – or perhaps it was *know*. She rested her knees on the cold floor, and removed the handkerchief. His profile glowed faintly, as if she had turned towards him in bed. She did not touch him.

Once again, and for the last time, she admitted that she did not *have* him at all. There was nothing to have. All those Victorian heroines casting themselves on the hard chests of their dead lovers, fathers, brothers, sons. An indulgence in an ordered world. Nothing survived. Nothing heard or forgave . . . But still she spoke, whispering, her face no closer.

'I'm sorry, Simon,' she said. 'I'm very sorry.'

As if in answer, or retribution, the floor began to tremble, and then to shudder. She hung on to the side of the seat, her eyes on a head that was swaying from side to side. She could not bear it if it finally turned and . . .

The power throbbing through the carriage died; and the head was still.

Then it surged again, stronger now – and the lights came on.

She closed her eyes immediately, hearing the spontaneous cheer from those around the stove. Then she opened them, and looking above his head, dropped the handkerchief over his face. She pushed herself upright, and went back.

____ **4** _____

The light had brought more than cheers. It had also brought an eye-wincing glare, a white clarity which they at first welcomed, but now were forced to endure. For whilst the dark had served to reduce their separateness, to soften the effects of what they had experienced – this light showed everything.

It showed unshaven faces and weary, red-rimmed eyes; it showed slurred makeup and uncombed hair; it showed damp, dishevelled clothing and roughened flesh – above all, it parted them from one another, showed them once again as individuals, self-conscious entities that searched for combs or compacts or mirrors, hands that sought to fasten buttons, to tug at sweaters; and to blink like disturbed animals.

The light also revealed a general untidiness – empty plastic bags, used paper cups, crumpled newspapers, a litter of burned matches and hard blobs of candlegrease. The two older women, without reference to one another, began to gather and fold and straighten.

Anita brushed crumbs from her seat into her palm.

'We'll put everything into the container,' she said. 'Lift your feet, Clive.'

It was an echo of his mother's command – and the broken room came back, and a sudden, unexpected guilt that made his stomach lurch.

'Leave the Bible,' he said. 'I'll have it here.'

She leaned behind her, picked it up and gave it to him without comment, but her eyes were warm and she nodded, as if acknowledging a fact – one that he silently and furiously denied. The touch of the cold limp leather brought back everything he was desperately trying to forget and ignore – every nuance of the faith, every odour of sanctity, every cribbed and cabined life – and he was tempted to return it to her, to say on second thoughts . . . But instead he thanked her and walked down the bright carriage to his suitcase, and opened it, and thrust the book into the swirl of clothing – and slammed the lid. To find that Mason had followed him, and was holding out a hand.

The boy looked at him: at the creased dress uniform beneath the unbuttoned greatcoat, the general air of unmilitary disarray.

'Not you, too?' he said.

'What d'you mean?' said the sergeant.

'You want the Bible, too?'

'Don't make me laugh,' said Mason. 'No – I want the rounds.'

'The rounds?'

'From the gun. Two are missing from the magazine.'

'I haven't got them.'

'You didn't take them?'

'No. Why should I?'

'A souvenir . . .?'

'No.'

Mason looked down the carriage at Calvin.

'Okay, son,' he said. 'Don't worry.'

They moved back again, this time carrying their suitcases. Outside, unseen by all, the torchlight paling below the yellow windows, the two men were returning from the rear of the train, the guard still beleaguered behind his frozen door, moving on to the engine where another driver sat waiting at the controls.

170

There was a faint smell of perfume. Hair had been combed, and the women wore new faces. The floor was tidy, the flames of the stove were out. Already, from beneath the seats, warm air was breathing against their legs. The aisle divided the two groups, and in that growing warmth sleep weighted their eyes, and there was silence. Weary eyes closed against the white bulbs blazing in the white, curved ceiling. The carriage still trembled with power, and each in their separate ways they longed for the train to resume the journey, for the day to end, to be home. Or what passed as home.

Anita opened her eyes to find Laura looking at her. The girl half-smiled.

'What will you do?' she said.

'Do?'

'Your daughter. If you'd rather not talk about . . .'

'No, I don't mind. I don't consider myself . . . here. Most of me seems somewhere else. Do? What does one do? She needs me more, now . . . We go on, don't we?'

The train gave a sudden jerk forward. Fizzing bursts of light illuminated for an instant the white land. And again. The wheels slipped, spun, and gripped. A full-throated cry of triumph came from the klaxon. The train rolled towards Witley, picking up speed until the track sang.

Anita smiled.

'How's that for confirmation?' she said.

'I never thought I'd get out of it,' said the woman across the aisle. 'Never. You hear such stories. They all come back, don't they? You remember. Heaven knows what my husband's been doing all this time. Do you think they'll let us go on – past Witley?'

No one said anything.

'It depends,' said Mason. 'I hope they do.'

Calvin looked at the sergeant. Now that the group were to be parted, he ached to know the outcome. He could invent any last chapter – but he would like to know. He thought of the rounds in his coat. His fingers found them, and he smiled to himself.

Mason leaned across and tapped him on the knee.

'Thanks for the precaution,' he said. 'I'll have them now.'

'You will?' said Calvin. The bullets were warm and hard. '*What will you have, my friend?*'

'You emptied the magazine while we slept,' said Mason. He held out his hand.

Calvin brought out the rounds, and gave them to him. Mason

leaned down, brought up his suitcase, opened it and put them inside. They clattered to the end as he closed the lid.

'How clever of you, Mr Calvin,' said Anita. 'Do you normally think that far ahead?'

'He's a writer,' said Mason. 'He never stops thinking, do you, pal?'

'To no avail this time, it seems,' said Calvin. He felt cheated: back to being an understudy, no longer in the play. 'Will I read about it in the papers?'

'Read about what?' said the sergeant.

'And by the way,' said Calvin: 'you owe me forty thousand.'

'In the post Monday,' said Mason. 'Spend it in good health.'

'The Jews always had the best words,' said Anita. She looked down the carriage, and sighed. 'But how shall I tell her . . .?'

After ten minutes the train began to slow. The boy gripped the handle of his suitcase – somewhere out there an unsuspecting girl watched TV or read. He saw her face: shock turning to pleasure – the smile. Christmas in the country. Mathis on the hi-fi. Christmas morning and scattered wrapping-paper. Snowball-fights on the front lawn. Cold lips warming to fire . . . The handle was burning his fingers. He relaxed.

There was an incline now. All felt it, and the regulars recognised the run into Witley Station. Lights began to slide past the beaded windows. A patch of yellow came and went. The train stopped.

And hands began to pull at the doors.

5

The hands belonged to railwaymen and people from nearby houses who had gathered at the station to help. When they found that most of the doors were frozen fast, blowlamps were brought from the storeroom, and their bright blue tongues licked at the locks. The first carriage was empty; and by the time the fourth was breached, allowing five stiff, slow-moving, shivering travellers to be led away, two men had swiftly and silently clothed Silverman in a red blanket, lifted him free of the train, and lain him down on a table in a small room beyond the ticket-office.

Anita sat on a hard-backed chair before a fire of coal and logs in the waiting-room. The others stood around and drank more hot coffee spliced with brandy. Clive held up his cup.

'I could get used to this,' he said.

Anita leaned forward, above her a poster fluorescent with beach-umbrellas and a tropic sea, and spoke to the porter.

'Is it possible for me to use the phone?' she said.

'Sorry, lady,' he said: 'the lines are still down. Shouldn't think it'd be much longer though.'

'But we'll be able to carry on?' said Laura. 'I have to get to Liphook.'

He shook his head.

'I doubt it,' he said. 'Can't see anything more moving tonight. It's a case of just bringing them in, off the track.'

'What's going to happen, then?' said Mason, the confrontation forever postponed, sweet revenge needing constant refuelling.

'We're fixing you up at the village hall tonight,' said the porter. 'Bedding you down there. You'll be all right. Camp-beds, but there's heating and food. I think there's even a TV.'

'Who could ask for more?' said Calvin.

'Is Palmer's Lane, Chiddingfold, far?' said Clive.

'You won't be able to get even there,' said the porter, shaking his head again. 'Them side lanes – murder. I'm a Chid man myself: I'm stuck here, too. Have been, for two days.'

The door opened and a figure appeared in the doorway: a tall man in black; white clerical collar startling below a heavy, ageing face that came forward.

'Is the wife here?' he said, softly. 'The wife of the deceased?'

'Yes,' said Anita. 'What do you want?'

'Could I just see you for a moment, please?' he said. 'Alone?'

'Yes,' she said. She followed him out of the room. The door closed.

'I'll just go and check that phone again,' said the porter. 'I'll come back and tell you, if it's working.'

Calvin picked up the poker and stirred the fire. A log shifted, fell lower, and a burst of sparks rose to cling to the soot of the chimney, glowing. It was a homely sight, and it cheered him. He crouched down, the poker loose in his hands, basking in the heat.

'Looks like my great romance will have to wait another day,' said Clive, the brandy getting to him.

'Love laughs at snowdrifts,' said Calvin, still staring into the

173

flames. 'Battle through – I would.'

'Oh, sure,' said the boy. 'I'd like . . .'

The door opened and Anita returned. They looked at her. There was no change in that calm, controlled face.

'They're ready to take us to the hall,' she said. 'If you are.'

They gathered up their luggage. As they moved to the door, Laura put her arm around Anita's shoulders.

'Anything I . . .?' she said.

'It was just the arrangements,' said Anita. 'Just the disposing. Getting him home.'

They walked out of the booking-hall and into the forecourt.

Away from the warmth of the waiting-room, the night was black and bitter, and the wind had come again, whipping around the small, low building and numbing their legs and faces. A blue minibus waited, engine idling, headlights pointing at banks of snow. Beyond it another landscape was tinted grey, like a negative: the pressure of other, unlit snows on tree and wall and roof and carpark and obliterated squares of garden.

The priest was waiting at the open door of the bus. The group from the fourth carriage was already seated, still resentful at not sharing in the helicopter's bounty, but silenced by the fact of death and their own survival. The others ducked in and sat on the long seats, their wet shoes resting on and marking slatted wood. To Mason it spoke of many a military journey: boots on the ribbed floors of Army trucks, gloved hands resting on rifles, the baby-faces of new recruits, round and trusting. A man's life. A dead-end. He grew angry at the new, unexpected thought: *a dead-end?* Yet he knew it was true. It was a boy's world. The play-pens of barrack-squares. Ranks of toy soldiers marching and counter-marching while the real world burned, or drowned in winter. It was over, finished – time to move on. To what? A professional soldier, a professional baby-minder. He thought of Silverman . . . It was always too late, and yet it was never too late. While death had not come, everything was possible. The unknown man in Petersfield – that had to be settled first. And then . . .?

'All aboard?' said the priest. 'Right – take it away, Ian.'

The engine woke, and a smell of warm oil drifted back, over their faces. The chains on the wheels made for a bumpy ride. The headlights lit the wall of a garage, and then swung past laden hedges.

174

'Quite an experience for you people,' said the priest, the red light to the left of his head giving one side of his face a curiously Satanic glow.

No one answered him. Humped together like refugees, the returning cold had made them dumb.

'Any Catholics among you?' he said. He laughed, without humour. 'Come on now – own up.'

Another silence. The engine of the bus seemed to worry at the night: a high, fluctuating whine that never steadied.

'Yes, come on, Clive,' said Mason: 'own up.'

The brandy had not dulled all the boy's perceptions. He had seen the trap, but now it had swung open.

'I'm not a Catholic,' he said.

'He was, once,' said Mason, his mouth dry with too much brandy.

'Ah, a renegade,' said the priest. His large head with its black hat came forward, and the shadowed eyes sought the boy's face. 'I left the Faith for a time, too – when I was younger. Young as you. There's nothing dishonourable in doubt, you know.'

'Unless it lasts, eh, Father?' said Calvin.

'It *never* lasts,' said the priest. 'It comes and goes. But it never lasts.' He turned his head again to Clive. 'I can promise you that.'

It was like a sentence delivered by a sympathetic judge. All the boy's sense of liberation evaporated. He stared at the priest with a growing hatred. Words came, hot with denial, but he could not utter them. He swung his head sharply and looked out of the window, but the glass was steamy with warmth, and he could see nothing.

'I've never once blamed God,' said the woman in the fur coat. 'I think we're all being tested. All the time.'

'That's one way of looking at it,' said Mason. 'What do you think of that, Mrs Silverman?'

But she would not be drawn. The night would end, and all would be normal again. Nearly normal . . . She would fall from this suspended state, regain her humanity. Soon.

'Don't mock what you don't understand, Gordon,' she said.

'Amen to that,' said the priest.

6

Calvin had expected a draughty shack, the boards still redolent with the sweat of discos and the training of Scouts, but the hall was large, high, and well-made; warm and bright, and full of the talk of stranded travellers. There were lines of green camp-beds with folded blankets and pillows, a side table with a giant silver urn of tea, and plates of sandwiches, and in the far right corner a colour TV showed a Western that no one watched.

'Make yourselves at home,' said the priest. 'If you want to freshen up, there are facilities behind the stage. Just go around the steps to the left. If you'll excuse me one moment . . .'

He crossed the hall to speak to a woman who was making more sandwiches.

Seen from a distance the group appeared lost, and yet sufficient unto itself: unwilling to break and scatter. As if to emphasise this unwillingness, Anita put her suitcase on the wooden floor and began to drag one of the camp-beds over to the wall.

'Get four more,' she said. 'Come on. Bring them over here.'

Laura looked at Mason, and raised one eyebrow.

'Let's humour her,' he said, softly.

They each selected a bed, and began to push or drag it to the wall. The woman who had paused in the making of the sandwiches, now put down her knife and hurried over, leaving the priest in mid-sentence.

'Whatever are you doing?' she said.

'I can't stand regimentation,' said Anita. 'It's like a boarding-school I was at, once. Lines of tidy beds. We've separated ourselves, that's all.'

'Any objections?' said Calvin.

'Well . . .' said the woman, who loved an ordered world, one she could handle, and who herself had supervised the setting-out of the hall: 'well . . . I don't know. I . . . suppose it's all right.'

'Of course it is,' said Anita. 'It also makes for a little more room.' She felt a sudden ache for Simon's easy-going nature, his contempt for trivialities. 'Let's all be a little untidy, yes?'

'If you wish to be, don't let me stop you,' said the woman, thinking of her own uncluttered house, the dust-free surfaces. 'After all, you'll be gone tomorrow, won't you?'

And with that she marched away, to meet the priest in the centre of the hall, and to say something that made him lower his head in answer. The woman looked back at Anita, and then returned to her sandwiches.

'Well, I'm going to have a shave,' said Clive. He put his suitcase on his bed. 'Or shall I grow a beard?'

'I wouldn't advise it,' said Calvin. 'You'd look like something out of *The Red Badge of Courage*.'

'*The Red Badge of* what?' said the boy.

'It doesn't matter,' said Calvin.

The boy moved the Bible and took out his shaving gear.

'I'd like to borrow that after you,' said Mason.

'Didn't you bring anything?' said Clive.

'Left in a hurry,' said the sergeant. 'What have you got?'

'Electric,' said the boy.

'Pity,' said the sergeant. 'Never use 'em. Still, it'll do in a pinch. Hope you can find some points.'

'Me, too,' said Clive. He closed the lid. 'Won't be long.'

He walked towards the stage.

'Shall we?' said Laura to Anita.

'I suppose so,' she said. 'Yes, I'd like to feel a little cleaner. I'll get my things.'

Calvin lay on his bed, his hands behind his head, looking up into the dark of the rafters.

'You only had one thing in mind, then?' he said.

'What?' said Mason.

'Leaving in a hurry.' He turned his face to the long body in the next bed, the stained uniform. 'I'd like to know what happens. For my own peace of mind.'

Mason gave a short laugh.

'*Your* peace of mind.'

'Before the others come back,' said Calvin. He raised himself on one elbow. 'Will you let me know?'

'How?'

'I could give you my address.'

It was Mason's turn now to look up at the roof.

'You'd let me go ahead and do it – whatever it is?'

'Freedom of action.'

Mason looked at him.

'Even if it ended in the killing of a man?'

'I don't know the man,' said Calvin. 'You have your reasons.'

177

'I don't know him either,' said the sergeant. 'Why *did* you take the shells?'

'I thought I might . . . intervene.'

'I don't like writing letters,' said Mason.

Clive came back, bringing a fresh face and a smell of after-shave. He held out the razor.

'They have towels in there,' he said.

Mason swung himself off his bed, took off his tunic, folded it on the pillow, and took the razor.

'Cheers, son,' he said, and left.

As the boy lifted the lid of his suitcase, the priest came over.

'Everything fine?' he said.

'It will be, when we get out of here,' said Clive.

The priest dropped a thin, long-fingered hand to the open suitcase and lifted out the Bible.

'For a renegade, you still read the enemy's literature,' he said.

'It's not for me,' said Clive, defensively. 'It's for my . . . mother.'

The priest put the Bible back.

'I don't think you're lost to us, young man,' he said. 'No one ever is. See you later.'

Clive slammed down the lid and sat on the edge of his bed.

'Bloody, interfering bastards!' he said.

Calvin turned his face into the cool pillow.

'What are you going to do if she doesn't want you? he said: 'this dream child.'

'She can't turn me away,' said Clive. 'Not in this weather.'

'You sound like something out of *Peg's Paper*,' said Calvin. 'I can see her now: standing in the doorway, her finger pointing down the drive. You departing in tears and a flurry of flakes.'

'She wouldn't do that,' said the boy. 'Not to someone who works in the same office.'

'You're still going through with it, then?'

'I can't do anything else.'

'What will you do if she *does* say *Get thee gone*?'

'I don't know. I can't go back.'

'Haven't you any friends in London?'

Clive grinned.

'Only other altar-boys.'

'Well, I wish you luck.' Calvin straightened as he saw the women approaching. 'I'd like to use that razor after Gordon – if you don't mind.'

'No, you carry on,' said the boy. He looked up at Laura and Anita. 'Anyone want a sandwich?'

The back room, obviously used by a local drama group, held two giant mirrors surrounded by a blaze of white bulbs; two basins with smaller mirrors; and, beyond, two doors marked *His* and *Hers*. An elderly man was washing at one of the basins, his collar tucked away and his shirt open, showing a speckled chest. He rested his red hands in hot water as Calvin put the razor's leather case on the shelf.

'Take a look around you,' he said, his face a stubble of white hairs like frost.

Calvin looked around. He saw a confusion of wet, crumpled towels, tissues; and a floor awash and marked with footprints.

'So?' he said. He let the hot tap run, tested the water, and pressed home the plug.

'You'd think people'd be more tidy, more considerate,' said the old man. 'Take more care.' He rubbed soap on his hands. 'They wouldn't allow it in their own homes – why let it happen outside?'

'Exceptional circumstances,' said Calvin. 'Time of emergency – all that.' He hung his jacket on a peg, and took off his tie. He bared his throat and reached for the soap. It was green, and hard, and institutional. It took some time to raise a lather.

The old man dried his face. He took out his false teeth and let cold water run over them. The room still troubled him: he made wet, protesting noises which clarified once his teeth were back in place.

'Never understand it, never,' he said: 'people's untidiness. You off the train?'

Calvin rinsed the soap from his face and took a clean, dry towel from the pile: it smelled like the soap.

'Yes,' he said. 'And you?'

'Bus,' said the old man. 'On my way to Grayshott. Been here over ten hours. You like them electric razors?'

'It's not mine,' said Calvin, plugging in.

'I like my old cut-throat,' said the man. He rasped a hand over his chin. 'Could do with it now.' He pulled his collar free and fastened the top button. He put on his tie and reached for his jacket. 'Work in London, do you?'

'No,' said Calvin, the razor tugging at his beard. 'At home.'

'Know London, do you?' said the man. Dressed, he looked less ancient, but still, with that white stubble, like a tramp who had been given a good suit as a handout.

'Pretty well,' said Calvin.

'Know Carlisle Street, off the Strand? Near the Law Courts?'

'Can't say I do,' said Calvin.

'There's a gents' toilet in the middle of the street,' said the old man. He leaned against a table and folded his hands in front of him. 'In charge of that, I was, for fifteen years. Before that, in the one in Bothwell Place, near Oxford Circus. Know it?'

'Sorry, no . . .' said Calvin. The mirror was misting up, and he rubbed it with his fist.

'Been quite a day for me,' said the man. 'I finished – this morning. After thirty years . . .'

'In gents' toilets,' said Calvin.

'Yes. Not much of a job, some might say. But I enjoyed it. Every minute. Had my regulars: wash and brush up. Kept it like a palace. Spotless.'

Calvin rinsed his face again. Took up the towel.

'Like to see something?' said the old man.

Calvin peered between the folds of the towel. The man reached inside his jacket and brought out a long, blue presentation-case. He opened it. Inside was a gold wristwatch. It gleamed on blue silk, catching the light from the massed white bulbs. The old man took it out, reverently.

'Take a look at that,' he said.

It was heavy in Calvin's fingers. The second-hand danced along. He turned the watch over. An engraving on the back declared: *Presented to Peter Southern in recognition of thirty years of devoted service.* He handed it back.

'Congratulations.'

'Not many people have that given to them,' said the man. 'Given to me at County Hall that was, yesterday.'

Calvin folded the towel and put it neatly on the table. He pulled his collar free and fastened the top button.

'What will you do now?' he said.

The man sighed. He took one last look at the watch, and put it into the case.

'God knows,' he said. 'I'm not married. Got no family. Toilets was my life – all my regulars. Got a few quid from them, too. Had to teach a young chap the ropes.'

'The chains,' said Calvin.

'He won't stay. Who does – these days? A question of pride, right?'

'Right,' said Calvin.

180

The old man looked around the room and shook his head.

'Well, cheers,' he said. 'And a merry Christmas.'

'All the best,' said Calvin. 'You've made the world a cleaner place.'

'And that's the truth,' said the old man. 'I can say that – more'n some.'

Calvin followed him out. Behind them the massed white lights blazed on the same confusion.

It was late now, past midnight. The last TV news had spoken of more disasters, but a lessening of the severe weather. The last cup of tea had been poured and drunk; the last sandwich cut and eaten.

Laura put a finger to her lips as he approached. Anita was already asleep, bundled under her blanket, her head near a radiator. Calvin gave the razor to Clive.

'Thanks,' he said, softly.

One by one the lights began to darken in the hall, until only a central tube glowed, and the suddenly bright red of the Exit sign. Around the walls the hot radiators clicked and sang as other men and women settled on the creaking camp-beds. The priest moved silently by like a black ghost.

'Goodnight, everyone,' he said. 'God bless.'

Soon the whole group was bedded down. The boy, Laura, and Mason were asleep within fifteen minutes; but Calvin was still awake as a distant church-bell marked one o'clock: restlessly turning back and forth, thinking of thirty years' devoted service underground, below the grimy streets of London, keeping a fallen world clean.

_____ 7 _____

Mason opened his eyes. It was a reflex action to lift his watch to his face. Five to seven, as always. So spartan were the conditions, he thought for a second he was on an exercise, and a word of command, of arousal, almost escaped his lips. He sat up. Three women were quietly working at the table, and there was a beautiful smell of coffee and toast. Other men were awake and folding their blankets. He threw off his own and padded over in stockinged feet to the table. On the way he met the priest: freshly-shaven, a clean white collar, bright-eyed under those thick, shaggy eyebrows.

'Don't you ever sleep?' said Mason, his tongue like old cotton-wool in his mouth.

'I don't need much,' said the priest. 'If I get four uninterrupted hours, I'm fine.'

'Good for you,' said Mason.

'The train will leave at eight-thirty,' said the priest. 'The lines are relatively clear to Portsmouth. You may continue your journey.'

It was as if the words contained adrenalin. Power flowed through Mason: so urgent that he shivered.

'That's good to hear,' he said. 'I'm just going to get some coffee.'

'I've had mine,' said the priest. 'I'm just off to check the telephone.'

Mason joined the queue at the table, picked up a tray, and took five coffees back to the beds. The others were still deeply asleep. He woke them one by one, and put the cups into their hands. They sipped at the coffee, and thanked him, put the cups to the floor, and sank back into the pillows.

'Don't go to sleep again,' he said: 'the train's leaving at eight-thirty.'

Calvin looked at his watch.

'Bags of time,' he said. 'Leave us alone.'

The others grunted agreement.

'Have it your way,' said Mason. 'They'll be queueing for everything soon.'

He finished his own coffee and went to wash. The priest was coming from the right of the stage.

'Any luck?' said Mason.

'Dead as a doornail,' said the priest. 'I'll try again later.'

As Mason had suspected, there was a queue in the dressing-room. Once again, as he rested against the table, the military images returned: the ablution-tents, the tin-shacks, the light of early morning over Salisbury Plain; the maleness, the hard bodies under the showers. But here the bodies were flabby and white: the civilian indifference to the body's potential. He found himself, strangely, tired of men and their preoccupations. He thought of women: that legendary tenderness. He thought of Barbara – and winced again at the nature of her death . . .

When he returned, the others were out of their blankets and drinking more coffee, and eating slices of thick toast. Outside, in a morning that was still dark, the engines of cars were being tested.

He went over to the table and got his own breakfast. He sat on his bed and bit into the first slice. The taste was another assurance that he was back to normal: the track uncluttered, straight as an arrow – to Petersfield.

'So, we are moving on,' said Anita. She had slept too heavily, as though drugged. Her eyes were sore: the hall, and their faces, blurred often. She blinked again. 'We are splitting up.'

Like all survivors, they felt as if they had shared a lifetime. They experienced a sense of regret, however temporary. Calvin felt it most: the hunger to *know*, the need to halt and examine, before all drifted to oblivion – which was the basis of his craft. He opened his mouth to suggest that they exchanged addresses – but knew it was a juvenile exercise, nothing would come of it.

'We could write to each other,' said Clive.

'I don't think so,' said Calvin. 'Let us depart upon this hour, hostages to fortune.'

'Who said that?' said Laura.

'Some genius,' said Calvin. 'Me, probably.'

An hour later, they were ready to leave. Some of the motorists had already gone, trusting to gritted roads. Others had decided to take the train. They sat on their tidied beds and waited to be called.

And then the priest spoke from the stage.

'Ladies and gentlemen: the phone is working. Don't all rush . . .'

But they did rush, and a queue lengthened.

'Don't take too long,' said the priest, and came down off the stage.

No one in the group had moved: bound by some unspoken resolve, or need. The priest came across the wide, cleared space of the hall. He sat next to Clive.

'I understand you want to get to Chiddingfold,' he said.

The name seemed weighted with doubt, and the boy hesitated.

'Yes, I do,' he said.

'There are no buses,' said the priest. 'But I have to go there in half an hour. I can take you.'

Clive looked at that white, heavy face.

'Palmer's Lane,' he said.

'Yes, I know it,' said the priest. 'You may have to walk from the centre of the village, but . . .'

'Yes, thank you,' said Clive. 'I'll go with you.'

'Fine,' said the priest. He put his hands on his knees and grunted himself upright. 'Do you mind if we leave the hall now? There are a few things I have to find at the house . . .'

'Now?' said Clive. 'Yes . . . all right.' He picked up his suitcase, and held out his hand to Anita. 'Goodbye.'

She stood up, took his hand, and kissed him.

'Goodbye, Clive,' she said. 'Take care.'

'You, too,' he said. 'I'm sorry about . . . what happened.'

'I know,' she said.

He took the other, proffered hands; and yet stayed.

'Isn't it funny?' he said: 'the way we . . .' He shook his head.

'Goodbye, Clive,' said Calvin, almost brutally. 'Live it up, son.'

The boy grinned, and was suddenly much younger.

'I'll try,' he said.

'Ready, then?' said the priest.

'Yes,' said Clive.

'And I think you people ought to start making your way to the bus,' said the priest. 'God bless you all.'

'I'd like to use the phone first,' said Anita.

'Me, too,' said Laura.

'Do what you must,' he said. 'I'll tell Ian you'll be about ten minutes. Come along, then, Clive.'

The boy gave one final wave, and then walked away with the priest. They watched until the door closed.

'I think he's in for a shock,' said Laura.

Calvin laughed.

'Someone is,' he said.

A quarter of an hour later they were riding in the bus, through a morning whose sky was streaked with the coming of a pale, white sun. All except Mason had used the telephone, but none had spoken of what had been said. Already they were drawing apart from each other, as those other lives made their demands, evoked responsibilities. They looked out through clear windows at a world made sharper and clearer by the cold, and they were silent.

At the station the train had a battered look: the broken window of the third carriage, the splintered and smoky locks, the coating of unmelted snow. But the engine sounded powerful enough, and the track ahead gleamed silver.

'Think we'll make it this time?' said Mason.

'No more snow forecast,' said the porter. 'I'm seeing you off –

then it's me home to Chid. You'll be okay now.' He turned to Anita. 'They'll be coming for your . . . husband later this morning. Do you want a last . . .?'

'No,' she said. 'Just get me on the train.'

'Right you are, mam,' said the porter, briskly. 'You'd better all go up front. Nice and warm in there.' He opened the door. 'Good luck,' he said, as they filed past him. 'Are you the lot?'

'All that was in the bus,' said another man, not part of the group.

'Right,' said the porter. 'British Rail apologises . . .'

'Spare us the commercials,' said Calvin. 'And, by the way: thanks . . .'

The porter nodded, stepped back, and closed the door. He looked to the rear of the train, and then forward to the engine. He lifted his hand.

'Take it away, Jim!' he called.

The power increased, the klaxon gave a short, throaty shout, and the train lurched forward.

Soon they were making good speed through a silent, white, and, as the sun climbed higher, an increasingly beautiful land. But none of the group acknowledged the beauty: their thoughts racing ahead of the train to their differing destinations, and what awaited them there.

Part Eleven

Clive Parsons

___1___

As the dutiful page had followed King Wenceslas, treading in his master's snowy steps, so Clive followed the priest as that dark shape with its wide-brimmed hat led the way to the Presbytery. Not that the boy felt dutiful: he had gone from one fake Father to another, he still carried the Bible in his suitcase, and he would have to endure pious talk all the way to Chiddingfold. And, with a quick sense of unease, he realised that today was Sunday.

'Are you not taking Mass this morning?' he said to the black back: said it with a kind of eager hopefulness – that the Church itself might be capable of change, given the circumstances.

'Yes,' said the priest, without turning his head. 'Oh, yes. A little later today, because of the weather. At ten o'clock. I shall be back well in time. Oh, yes, there's always Mass.' He stopped and looked back. He smiled in that cold face. 'You're welcome to stay. I'll run you there, later: to Chiddingfold.'

'No, thanks,' said Clive.

'I forgot: I'm dealing with a renegade,' said the priest, and turned his head to the front again. Clive, who had also stopped, followed on.

They had to climb a small slope. The snow was deep here, and the priest used the thin wooden fence to pull himself forward and up. Soon Clive's shoes were soaked, and his jeans were fastened wet and cold to his legs.

'How much further?' he said.

The fence creaked.

'Just a walking distance,' said the priest.

'I know,' said Clive: 'but how far?'

'You can see it now.'

The boy looked beyond the black shoulder, and there, at the top of the slope and to the right, was a plain red house with no holiness about it. At the top of the slope the snow had been partly cleared, and there was room now for Clive to come alongside. But he preferred to hang back until the short, cleared drive was reached, and they walked on red, gleaming ashphalt to the door. The priest kicked the snow from his shoes, and, puffing slightly, brought out a key on a long silver chain. He fitted the key into the lock and turned it.

But someone was already opening the door, and the priest was drawn into the house by the silver chain. The woman was short and country-looking, and dressed for outdoors. She looked beyond the priest to the boy, and back again.

'All gone, Father?' she said. She nodded at Clive as she closed the door. The priest shook the snow from the ends of his coat.

'Yes, Mrs Prentice,' he said. 'All gone.' He looked at the boy. 'I don't know your full name, young man.'

'Clive Parsons.'

'Clive Parsons – Mrs Prentice, my housekeeper,' said the priest. 'Mrs Prentice – Clive Parsons, one of the stranded. He's coming with us to Chiddingfold.' He took off his hat and smoothed his hair. 'I think I'll get changed now, Mrs Prentice – it'll save time.'

'Do you really think we ought to go?' she said. 'It's not all that important. If he were only on the phone . . .'

'Of course it's important,' he said. He shook his coat again. 'Mrs Prentice's aged father lives in Chiddingfold, Clive. Alone. He's been a bit under the weather. Haven't we all? Ha. I'm just running her there, before Mass.' He waved to a closed door. 'You can wait in there for a moment or two. Have you managed to contact your friends in Chiddingfold?'

'No, not yet.'

'You'll find a telephone in there. Give them a ring, tell them you're on the way. Put their minds at rest.' He took off his coat and handed it to Mrs Prentice. 'I'll go upstairs.'

'Is there a local directory . . .?' said Clive. 'I've . . . forgotten their number.'

'On the window-ledge behind the telephone,' said the priest.

'I'll get your other coat, Father,' she said.

'Thank you,' he said.

*   *   *

The room was cold. The whole house was cold. Clive nodded: it was typical – bear with it down here, there would be roaring log-fires in Heaven. And the other place. There was a bachelor mustiness: a combination of polish and pipesmoke and leather bindings; perhaps even a whiff, an aftermath, of incense. Dark wooden panelling, a gleam of silver, a scattering of crucifixes, a small-paned window showing a winter garden, a snow-covered bird-table from which hung the empty shell of a coconut, motionless on frost-furred string.

He took up the directory, put it on the table, and turned the pages. He found the number, and, repeating it to himself, returned the directory to the ledge. As he dialled he heard the priest moving about in the room above his head.

It was a long time before someone answered. A breathless woman's voice.

'Three three six.'

Clive turned and faced the garden. Nothing moved out there.

'Could I speak to Dorothy, please?'

'I'm afraid she's still in bed. Who is that, please?'

'Clive. Clive Parsons.'

The line hummed for three seconds.

'Who?'

'Clive Parsons. I work with Dorothy . . . in the office.'

'Oh.'

'Hasn't she . . . ever mentioned me?'

The woman gave a soft, embarrassed laugh.

'She may well have done. This is her mother. I'm afraid we're all sleeping rather late today, Mr Parsons. I've only just got up, myself. We had rather a late night: Dorothy's engagement party. We're all feeling the effects.'

Clive turned to face the room. He leaned against the ledge, the cold air from the glass of the window chilling his neck.

'Engagement?'

'Yes. To Harold Rimmer. You're surprised?'

'I . . . I wouldn't know him. Yes, I'm surprised.'

'We all were. Completely out of the blue. Is it important? I *could* wake her, but . . .'

'No. It's not important.'

'Where are you phoning from?'

'London.'

'Awful weather.'

'Yes.'

The line hummed.

'Well, give her my congratulations.'

'I will. Shall I get her to ring you back?'

'No. It doesn't matter. I'll be in touch.'

'Yes, very well. Have a happy Christmas.'

'And you,' said Clive. 'Goodbye.'

He reached to his right and put down the phone. Still leaning against the ledge, he folded his arms. He was still standing there when the priest opened the door, dressed for Mass, the white vestments startling against the gloom of the hall.

'I'm just going to get the car out,' said the priest. 'All well?'

'No,' said Clive.

The priest came further into the room and peered at the black shape of the boy against the window.

'Why not?'

'They can't put me up. Not this weekend.'

'Why ever not?'

'Personal reasons.'

'After you've come all this way? After what you . . .'

'They . . . they tried to contact me. It doesn't matter.'

'Well, that is unfortunate. What will you do now?'

Clive rubbed his arms.

'Go back to London, I suppose.'

'That'll be difficult. Trains are few and far between. And today *is* Sunday. Look, you stay here until I get back from Chiddingfold. After Mass, we can have a spot of lunch together. And then decide. How does that strike you?'

'All right,' said the boy.

'Good. Yes, I'm coming, Mrs Prentice. I don't think I'll be more than half an hour, Clive. I *can't* be more than half an hour. Make yourself at home. The kitchen's at the end of the hall: make yourself· a cup of tea, if you like. There are books around, magazines . . . All yours.'

'Thanks.'

'See you later, then.'

'Yes.'

The priest smiled and went back into the hall. The front door closed, and Clive saw two figures move past the window which faced the road. There was the sound of a garage door sliding back; and then the choked whirring of a cold engine. Then the roaring. The car, a black Mini, came into view and rolled slowly forward. It paused; then turned to the left. And was gone.

2

As if released, Clive pushed himself off the ledge and once again rubbed his arms. He moved to the large electric-fire housed in the chimney-breast, and snapped down the two switches. The bars crackled, as though the dust of years ignited; then began to glow. He warmed his hands, and walked into the hall. He soon found what he was looking for: a small white disc set into the wall, which controlled the central-heating. He turned it to *High*, and moved on to the kitchen. It was a long white room, shadowed by a tall black, leafless tree whose trunk was streaked with runnels of snow. The two fluorescent tubes flickered and steadied, and the morning stepped back. Clive filled the kettle and plugged it in. He found a tray, and set it with teapot, milk-jug, sugar and a cup and saucer. The kettle began to sing. There was a heater above the window. He switched it on.

Waiting for the kettle to boil, he went into the high, cold pantry. There was the usual collection of tinned food, ranked like an army on the shelves. Turning, he discovered another shining army: the silver throats of a score of bottles of Communion wine. He smiled, and lifted one from the rack. He went back into the kitchen and switched off the kettle. He pushed a knifeblade under the thin foil, and peeled it away. There was a corkscrew hanging among other implements. He put the bottle between his knees, thrust home the screw; and tugged. He put the cork in the red plastic bin, and tipped the bottle to his lips. He drank steadily, until he choked. Still carrying the bottle, he went on a tour of the house.

The Mother of God greeted him at the head of the stairs, watching him, unsmiling, from her blue alcove. He lifted the bottle in acknowledgement, and drank some more. The house was warming-up: waves of hot air came from the thin, cream-painted radiators. He went into the first room. It was the housekeeper's bedroom: scent of woman, a display of dried flowers, a black crucifix above the plump white pillows. Christ lifted a warning finger from above the mantelpiece.

'And you, J.C.,' said the boy.

The priest's room was at the end of the landing. The same orderliness of a lonely man in a sinful world. There was a brown wardrobe with a half-open door. The suits smelled of incense: an air more real to the boy than the breath in his lungs. He fingered the black cloth. There was a drawer of black vests; another of white, clerical collars.

He smiled again, put the bottle on a small, round table, took off his raincoat; and then his parka. There were patches of sweat at his armpits. He fitted the vest to the front of his shirt, took a stud from the box, and carried it, and a collar, to the mirror next to the window. He fastened the collar, and looked at himself. His face burned, yet he appeared starved: the collar a loose white yoke over the smooth silk. He made the sign of the cross.

'Go and sin no more, my son,' he said.

He bowed at his reflection, and turned away. His fingers had almost grasped the bottle – when his heart leapt at the sound of the telephone. He swung around, and looked at the extension beside the bed. He lifted the bottle, drank some of the wine, and, holding the bottle against his chest, he leaned against the pale flowers of the wall; and waited.

But the ringing would never end. He washed more of the wine around his teeth, pushed himself off the wall, and lifted the receiver.

'Yes?' he said.

'Father Chambers?' said a woman's voice.

'No,' said the boy, looking at clean, white bed-linen where a holy man slept.

'Could I speak to Father Chambers, please?'

'No,' said Clive.

'Who is that speaking?' said the woman.

'Father Parsons,' said the boy. And smiled a wide, satisfied smile.

There was a silence, full of doubt.

'Father *Parsons*?'

'Yes.'

'Where is Father Chambers?'

The boy finished the bottle, and threw it on the bed.

'Are you there?' said the woman.

'Yes,' said Clive. 'Why . . .' He burped. 'Pardon. Why do you ask?'

'This is Mrs Wade. Where is Father Chambers?'

'Father Chambers is dead,' said the boy, and closed his hand over a sudden, wine-tasting laugh.

'Dead?' The woman was horrified. 'My God . . .'

'That's the name,' said Clive.

'But . . . *How* . . .?'

'Killed in a car accident, going to Chiddingfold. Mrs Prentice, too.'

'I . . . I can't believe it.'

'True,' said the boy. 'Pray for him. For them both.'

193

'What . . . what about Mass?'

'I'm taking it,' said Clive. 'That's why I'm here. Now, if you don't mind, Mrs Wade. There are things I must do.'

'You sound very young,' she said.

'I'm not long out of the seminary,' he said. 'But I know what to do.'

'Yes, of course,' she said. 'I didn't mean to infer . . .'

'Ten o'clock, Mrs Wade,' he said. 'I'll see you there.'

'Yes, of course,' she said. 'Poor Father Chambers. What a loss. Is there anything I can do?'

'Pray for his black soul in purgatory, Mrs Wade,' said Clive, and put down the telephone. He laughed aloud, swayed, and almost fell on the bed. He picked up the bottle and peered at it. 'Another dead man.'

He made his way down the stairs. The house was like an inferno. He stumbled through the kitchen, and into the pantry. He pulled another bottle from the rack, ripped off the foil, and was about to return for the corkscrew – when he saw the candles.

They, like the Communion wine, were racked against the wall. There were altar-candles of varying sizes and thicknesses; votive candles in bundles of twelve; and packets of round night-lights. Above them, on the top shelf, were large boxes of matches. He swung towards the kitchen.

'Back in a minute!' he said.

The corkscrew seemed reluctant to enter the cork. It swayed about, its sharp point hitting the neck of the bottle. He threw it across the kitchen, and then tapped the bottle against the sink. The neck broke, and the wine gushed out. He found a glass and filled it. Carrying the glass, he went back into the pantry. He drank a mouthful of wine, put the glass on a shelf, and began to fill his arms with candles. He went back into the kitchen, and arranged them on every flat surface he could find.

Then he lit them, one by one.

He stood back. It was beautiful. The flames wavered, caught by some small, invisible draught. They shone and they glittered and they danced, reflecting each other in the white gloss paint of walls and cupboards. The kitchen was an altar.

It was not enough. Why not the whole house?

He had found his purpose. Everything was suddenly clear and positive: a revelation. He filled another glass from the broken bottle,

194

took one swallow, and dashed the rest into the sink.

He went back for more candles.

He started upstairs, with the priest's bedroom, and soon it was an echo of the kitchen: bright flames everywhere, adding to the jungle heat. Sweat poured off his face. He stripped off, until he was naked but for the black vest and the collar. He stepped over his ripped shirt and went to the housekeeper's room.

He had to make several journeys to the pantry, but at last every room on the first floor had its share of burning candles. The heat was intense, but he gloried in it, unhampered by his clothes – that white body leaping about the landing, leaving a line of flames behind him.

The telephone rang again, but he did not pause to answer it. It rang for a long time; and then it stopped. By that time he had finished the landing, and, singing loudly, was returning with more candles, to light the study . . .

3

Mrs Prentice finished wiping the inside of the windscreen, and put the rag back in the glove-compartment. Ahead, the broken snow of the road was brown with slush from thrown salt and speckled with grit.

'You could have stayed,' said Father Chambers. 'I'd have called for you later.' He started the engine. 'Is your door closed?'

She tried it. It was not. She slammed it, made a circle in the glass to her left and waved to a face in a window of the cottage.

'Now I know he's all right, I don't have to bother,' she said. 'It was nice of the Reynolds to pop in. He's stronger than you think.'

The priest released the brake.

'Indestructible – country folk,' he said. 'All well, then?'

'Yes,' she said. 'You'll have to hurry.'

'Plenty of time,' he said.

He followed the tracks of other vehicles and soon reached the frozen village pond, the snow-covered seats. He settled back. It was a straight road home, now . . .

She watched the black trees tick by, the huddled farms. She shivered.

'You'll be able to feed three, won't you?' said the priest. 'I know it's unexpected, but . . .'

'We'll manage, Father,' she said. 'I've got a nice piece of lamb.' She looked from the brutal, empty land to his white hands, rock-like on the steering-wheel: the strength there, the certainty: a certainty she found so difficult to share, faced with this botched and violent world. 'You're too trusting, you know: leaving him there, alone.'

He felt the car drifting to the right as the wheels found another stretch of ice. He waited, and then there was firm ground, and the hill leading to Witley. In the bay window of a large snow-hooded house a lighted Christmas tree cheered him. The old festival, the old story, the old love . . .

'He's a Catholic, Mrs Prentice,' he said. 'Was a Catholic, *is* a Catholic. Perhaps he's been . . . roughly treated. You never know. They come back – in the end. Perhaps today is the start: we never know the result of our actions. We have to act . . . *as if*. You understand?'

She did not answer. Then she said:

'*As if* He's there, you mean?'

'No, of course not,' he said. 'I didn't mean that. I meant as if glory was possible, in the next minute. I find that . . . exhilarating. That's why I let him stay.'

'Yes, Father,' she said.

It was difficult negotiating the hill. Frightened, she clung to her seat as the wheels spun and the engine roared and laboured. They passed one car that had dropped back into a drift, three people standing beside it in the road, hands in armpits, grave-faced, as if they contemplated the death of a favoured hireling.

But at last they were there, cresting the brow, the house sturdy and uncowed by the season, standing there before the black tangle of the trees, home and safe: and even the winter would relent, one day . . .

The priest drove straight into the garage, and cut the engine.

'I don't think he'll want to come to Mass,' he said. 'But he might. If he doesn't, you'll keep him happy, won't you?' He turned that craggy face to her, and smiled. 'He might even give you a hand with the lunch.'

'Will he?' she said. 'You don't know your teenagers, Father.'

'There are always exceptions,' he said.

They got out, feeling the chill off the whitewashed walls, and slammed their doors the harder. The garage door swung silently behind them, and they trod the path to the door.

He put his key in the lock, Mrs Prentice a little to his left, and still on the path. The door swung open.

A giant breath struck his face. A breath so hot that he staggered back, cannoning into the housekeeper. Recovering, shaken, and full of a growing astonishment, he stepped into the furnace of the hall. And there, before his widening eyes, dozens of candles shone and glittered and beamed: on the floor, on tables, on ledges, and on every stair – mounting up to a flame-bordered, naked man, who, with black vest and white collar askew, came flying laughing shouting leaping down towards him, a torn Bible in one hand and a broken crucifix in the other . . .

And Father Chambers knew, beyond all doubt, that Hell had finally broken through, and it was Lucifer Himself that now fell, clawing, upon him . . .

Laura Stone

1

Once outside the station, she hardly recognised the place. There was a new supermarket, all glass and bright metal, and open this early on a Sunday morning, the snow cleared from the entrance, and piled. It was empty of customers: two check-out girls in crisp blue uniforms were leaning across from their machines, talking to each other. Beyond them the gathered bounty of the world waited to be carried away. Then there was a new car-showroom: fluorescent figures startling on the windscreens of expensive foreign models.

It was only when she reached the end of the street, and turned right to discover the same flat fields and the white war-memorial, now grey against the snow, that she acknowledged that she was home. She did not regard it as *home*: it was merely the place in which she had spent her childhood and her youth. In London (how many days, years, ago?) she had grasped at the memory of this narrow road, as a token of stability: but the hard brashness of the supermarket and the sleek, exotic lines of alien cars now unnerved her: nothing was the same for ever, nothing lasted – adapt, or perish.

Yet once she entered her parents' street, not a half mile from the station, she saw ahead of her the child she had been – dragging a sled on which a miniature snowman shook, swayed, and crumbled.

The house was the only one whose doors, window-frames, gutters and drainpipes were painted green. Where the snow had not been, or had fallen, the colour showed – as if spring or even summer pushed forward. The gate had been repaired: the centre strut was less weathered, and the green was brighter and fresher. She might have taken it as an omen, but life had taught her differently. It still squeaked as she pushed it open.

The smell of the privet hedge brought everything back. It was suddenly overpowering. She gasped, and almost ran to the door with its semi-circle of stained-glass. As a child she had thought it beautiful: the sun lived there, divided, like the facets of a jewel. Now it was merely suburban.

Without further thought, without preparation, she rang the bell.

It was like a cave. And at the start of the cave stood a woman, disguised as Laura's mother. Age had disguised her, and the years had weighted her shoulders, bending her forward; and the hand that came out was carved from mottled wood.

'Laura,' said this woman, the voice was a whisper among grasses. 'Laura, my dear.'

She took the mottled hand. It was warm and dry. It drew her into the hall, and left her for an instant to close the door, and returned. Laura kissed her mother, and it was like pressing her lips to warm paper.

'Such a time,' said her mother, moving back, always too abruptly from any show of affection. 'We were so worried.'

'I'm here, now.'

'So you are. At last. What an experience.'

Laura followed her mother deeper into the cave. Had it always been so dark? Plants were everywhere: fronds reached out and brushed her arms. Then light came fitfully from the living-room, and grew within the two, tall, glass-panelled doors leading to the conservatory: more stained-glass and more plants.

'Are you hungry?' said her mother, the fingertips of her left hand resting on the closed lid of the piano.

Laura could not answer for a moment. The room seemed to have a physical presence. Once again she felt she could not breathe. She put a hand to her throat, and gave a choked cough. The sound was loud.

'Are you all right?'

'Yes. I'm not hungry. I'd like a bath.'

'You coughed. Are you still smoking?'

'No. I gave that up. A long time ago. Where's Dad?'

'Gone to get the Sunday papers. I'm surprised you didn't see him. He's been longer than usual.'

'How is he?'

'Are you interested?'

'Of course.'

Her mother took her hand from the piano.

'He's . . . difficult.'

'In what way?'

'I'll take you to your room. How long are you staying?'

'Is there a time-limit?'

Her mother went slowly before her up the stairs. Her legs were very white and laced with thin blue veins. Her red slippers were too large.

'Of course not. Stay as long as you like.'

'How is he difficult?'

'Who? Oh . . . Was he ever easy, Laura? It's been harder, since he retired.'

'No hobbies?'

'He listens to music. Stays in his room for hours. He has *his* room now, did you know that? Likes to be . . . *apart*, as he says.'

'You have lots of plants.'

Her mother paused on the landing. Her fingers smoothed a healthy leaf.

'All my children,' she said. She opened the door and stood aside. 'All ready for you.'

It was like stepping into the past, or a dream of the past. It was the bedroom of a dead girl. There were dolls on the pillows; and the front of a doll's-house gaped, showing tidy, never-lived-in rooms. There were woollen bears and monkeys and rabbits, staring speechlessly from the window-ledge. Her mother, smiling, stepped around her, went to a table, and lifted a mother-of-pearl box. She turned a key, and lifted the lid. The harlequin spun before his mirrors, and the tune sealed the past, and the nightmare.

'Remember?' said her mother.

'Why?' said Laura.

'Why what, my dear?'

Laura waved a hand.

'All this . . .' she said.

'Isn't it nice?' said her mother, looking around as the harlequin still spun in her hand, and the tune played on. 'I thought of it as a kind of homecoming. It's been so long. As a welcome. I brought them all down from the loft, yesterday – while you were in that awful train. Not knowing if you were coming . . . if something had happened. They were so dusty. But they're clean now – and happy to see you.' The harlequin clicked to a stop. 'Like it?'

'I can't sleep here,' said Laura.

Her mother's face was destroyed. The light draining from it. 'Why not?'

'I mean . . . the dolls. On the pillows.'

'Oh,' said her mother, her voice swift with relief. 'Oh, they'll have to come off, dear. Of course.' She put down the music-box, and went to the bed. She lifted the dolls, and held one forward. 'Remember Nancy?'

Laura looked into the bland, forever-unchanging face. The tiny

200

white teeth. The eyelashes. The hard, blue, unmoving eyes.

'Yes,' she said.

'Take her,' said her mother. The face came nearer.

'Not now,' said Laura. She put down her bag. 'I'd like that bath now, if you don't mind. With no rubber duck.'

'No rubber duck?' said her mother. 'I don't think we even have . . .' Her face cleared. 'Oh, you are funny, Laura. No rubber duck. That *is* funny, dear.'

2

She had intended taking her time over the bath: to laze and loll in hot, perfumed water, letting the grime and the tension of the journey slide from her body, to drift away. But there was no bath-oil, and consequently no perfume. There was only a bar of pink soap that finally released a thin lather, and she had to make do with that. Rubbing it over her shoulders and upper arms, she looked about her. The bathroom was more spartan than she remembered: two well-worn toothbrushes stood upright alongside a mangled tube of paste. There was a razor and a can of foam. A bottle of mouthwash. Nothing else. The square mirror reflected blue tiles, on which transfers of smiling fish had almost faded. She had memories of laughter here: part of the dream?

There was a knock at the door, soft and tentative.

'Nearly finished, Laura?' said her mother.

'Yes. Fine.'

'Your father's back.'

Laura rinsed her shoulders.

'Would you like dinner early, dear? We usually have it early. Around twelve. Shall I put it on now?'

'Anything you like.'

'We haven't got a great deal. We . . .'

'I'll have what you've got. Don't worry.'

'We can go shopping tomorrow.'

Laura looked at the door, at the towelled house-coat and the tartan dressing-gown hanging from separate hooks.

'We don't have to talk through the door, mother. I'm getting out now.'

'Yes, all right. I'll go and start dinner, then.'

Laura was thankful that the mirror showed only her head and shoulders. It seemed . . . appropriate. Why? But she knew why, and as she dressed, she found herself trembling. She took great care with her makeup: as if it constituted some protection. Or war-paint? She smiled, picked up her comb; and in another minute she was ready.

She opened the door. Already there was a faint smell of cooking.

'Pull yourself together, girl,' she said softly.

Straightening her shoulders, she walked slowly along the landing and down the stairs. Reaching the living-room, she strode in, and opened her mouth.

'Hallo, Dad,' she said.

But he was not there. Folded on the table were the *Sunday Times* and the *Observer*. A closed spectacle-case waited nearby. Turning, she found him behind her.

'Hallo, Laura,' he said.

Time had been kinder to him. He was still tall and thin. The moustache was greyer, but still immaculately trimmed. The eyes, still pale as milk, tried to stay as unblinking as hers, but shifted away. Then were forced back. He rested his hands on her shoulders. She fought to stay on the same spot.

'Why are you trembling?' he said.

'Cold.'

'It's a hot-house,' he said. 'The damned plants.'

She closed her eyes as his face came forward. He kissed her cheek.

'You've put on weight,' he said, his hands still lightly on her shoulders.

'All that good living,' she said. 'Only around the hips.'

He took his hands away and nodded.

'You survived, then?' he said, moving past her into the room. He picked up the papers and the spectacle-case and carried them to an armchair.

'Survived?'

'The dreaded winter,' he said, sitting down. 'The train . . .'

'Oh, yes – I survived.'

He stood up again.

'Forgetting my manners,' he said. 'Like a drink? Bit early for me, but . . .'

'What have you got?'

'Only Martini,' he said. 'As always.'

'I'll have a Martini.'

'Right,' he said. He moved to the cabinet and opened the doors. There was a clink of glass.

Her mother came back, peering in.

'Everything all right?' she said. 'She looks tired, doesn't she, Nigel?'

'She's bound to look tired, isn't she?' he said, his back to her. He turned and held out the drink. Laura took it. 'I'll join you,' he said.

'Do you think I could have one?' said her mother.

'You don't like Martini,' he said.

'I . . . don't mind it. It's a celebration, isn't it? It's been ten years, Laura. Ten years.'

'I know,' she said. She lifted her glass. 'Merry Christmas.'

'Don't tell your father anything about what it was like,' said her mother: 'in the train. Save it till dinner.' She took her own glass. 'Thank you, dear. Merry Christmas, everyone.' She took one sip, and carried the glass to the kitchen.

Her father moved the papers from the chair, and sat down.

'Thank you for the long letters,' he said. He drank a little of the Martini, and pressed his moustache with his thumbnail.

'Glad you enjoyed them,' she said.

'Do sit down,' he said. 'Why did you never write?'

'I phoned. There were Christmas cards, birthdays . . .'

'Your mother would have liked more than that.'

Laura's chair creaked, and she could feel the springs.

'Not you?' she said.

He considered her, holding the glass in both hands.

'Do I look sixty-one?' he said.

'No.'

'Good. *What*, do you think?'

'Early fifties.'

'As much as that?' he said. 'God.' He drank the rest of his Martini and put the empty glass on the floor. 'I'd like you to see something,' he said. 'Come along.'

Carrying her own drink, she followed him out into the hall, and up the stairs. He turned to the left, and, at the end of the landing, took out a key. He unlocked the door, and pushed it open.

'Go in,' he said.

The room did not belong to the house. It was painted in white and yellow, and, with the light from the snowy fields outside, had a kind of luminosity. There was a divan bed with a plain yellow cover; two pale blue, comfortable-looking chairs; an expensive hi-fi system with two large speakers set in opposite alcoves; a range of LPs and cassettes in three white-painted units; elegant lights and curtains, and a bookcase full of bright paperbacks; a bowl of fruit that glowed.

The door closed behind her.

'You keep it locked?' she said.

'Always,' he said. He went and sat on the windowledge. 'What do you think?'

'It's . . . elegant,' she said.

'That's the word,' he said. 'Thank you.'

'How long?' she said.

'How long have I had it, you mean?' He spun the key in his fingers. 'I started it not long after you left.'

'You and mother don't sleep together?'

'Not for years.'

She sat in a chair: it *was* comfortable.

'It must have cost you something.'

'I was given a small golden handshake when I retired.' He stood up. 'Like to hear something?'

'Yes.'

He walked his fingers through the LPs.

'How about some Debussy?' he said. 'String Quartet?'

'Fine.'

The music *was* the room, or the room the music. He sat in the other chair. The light from the window lit one side of his face. Once he had been handsome. The music relaxed him, and his face grew older. She saw his lonely life, but felt no pity.

He allowed it to play for a few minutes, then reached over and turned down the volume.

'Shall we talk about it?' he said.

'If you like. We can't go anywhere until we do.'

'True,' he said. 'Do you understand, now? You obviously didn't at the time.'

'I . . . I understand the need,' she said. 'The . . . needs of men.'

'Not of women?' He shook his head. 'Not you?'

'Perhaps you froze that,' she said.

He was torn with conscience.

'Oh God, I hope not. Shall I tell you . . .?'

204

'No. I can imagine.'

'I only kissed your breasts,' he said. 'But you know that.'

She smiled, but it did not warm her face.

'If mother could hear us . . .' she said.

'You've seen her,' he said. 'The damned plants. The dolls. I'm a sensual man, Laura. I'm . . . starved. I need . . .'

'The drug wasn't strong enough, was it?' she said. 'Or you couldn't wait . . .'

'I couldn't wait,' he said. 'Are your breasts still as beautiful?'

She half-rose from her chair, but settled back. Ten years ago she had been a profoundly shocked virgin. Now . . .? For months she had felt his lips on her nipples. Not any more. Other lips had found them, and moved on . . .

'You poor bastard,' she said. She drank the last of her cold Martini. 'Can't you find *anything*? You could buy it in Portsmouth. The barren landscape he inhabited made her bones ache. 'Buy it,' she said. 'For Christ's sake, go out and buy it. Or leave her, and find someone else.' She made a sound of contempt. 'You had to use your own daughter?'

'I wouldn't do it to my own daughter,' he said.

3

The music was the only sound in the world, the slowly-turning record the only movement. The white garden listened.

'What does that mean?' she said.

'It means I am not such a bastard, Laura,' he said. 'It means, in one way, that we *are* . . . separate. You see, you were adopted at six months.'

Immediately, he was a stranger. He was a strange, lustful man in a strange house. His words had cut a thousand ropes. He smiled, came off his chair, and put his hands on her knees.

'You see, *now*?'

'Take your hands off me,' she said, so quietly she hardly heard them herself. 'Get back there.'

He took away his hands and sat on the carpet.

'I'm not yours?' she said, wonderingly. 'Or hers?'

'Not by blood,' he said. 'By love, perhaps . . .'

She laughed.

'By custom,' she said. 'Why did you never tell me?'

'I wanted to,' he said: 'often. But your mother thought it would . . . change you. Distance yourself from us.'

'*Distance* me?' she said. 'What about drugging a daughter, and . . .'

'Not a daughter,' he said.

The full realisation was getting to her at last. She found she was trembling again, but not with dread.

'It's true?' she said. 'I *was* adopted?'

'Yes,' he said. 'Your mother couldn't have any children.'

'All that talk about one day a brother,' she said. She looked down at him, her eyes wide. 'So I'm . . . *free*?'

'There's no such thing,' he said. 'Ask the expert.'

'I'm free,' she said. She got out of her chair, and moved to the door. 'Listen to your music.'

'What are you going to do?' he said.

'Going down to see mother.'

'Laura . . .!' he called.

But she was running along the landing.

In the kitchen her mother was sitting at the table, peeling potatoes. She looked up.

'You've been very honoured, Laura,' she said: 'seeing his room. He won't . . .' She looked over her shoulder. 'What *are* you doing?' She looked at her husband as he entered the kitchen. 'She's turned off the cooker.'

He leaned against the doorframe.

'Yes,' he said, and there was a finality about the word.

Laura sat next to the woman who was not her mother. She took the knife away and held the cold hands.

'We're not having dinner here,' she said. 'We're going out.'

'Out?' said this strange woman. 'How can we go out? Where . . .?'

'The White Hart.'

'For dinner? But it's terribly expensive . . .'

'It's a credit-card world,' said Laura. 'You go upstairs and choose something to wear.'

'But the snow . . .'

'We can walk there. The roads are clear.'

'But, my dear . . .'

'No buts,' said Laura. 'We'll get there early, have a few drinks. Celebrate.'

'What do you think, Nigel? Do you want to go?'

'Dad's not coming,' said Laura slowly. 'He . . . he wants to hear something on the Third. Debussy, wasn't it, Dad?'

He looked at her, and nodded.

'Yes,' he said. 'Debussy.'

'But you must come, Nigel,' she said. 'The three of us. The family.'

'The two of us, today,' said Laura. She put her hands under those bowed shoulders, and lifted. 'Go on, go and get ready.'

'Well, if you say so. What will you have to eat, Nigel?'

'Let him cook his own for a change,' said Laura. 'You're capable of that, aren't you, *Dad*?'

He did not answer.

'Well, how . . . exciting,' said his wife. 'Going out.' She touched his sleeve. 'You have a sandwich, Nigel. In your room. You and your music.'

She went out of the kitchen and into the hall.

They waited until they heard a door close above them. And then he said:

'Will you tell her?'

'About what?' said Laura.

'What you know. The adoption.'

'I don't know. Probably. I don't like deception.' She stood in front of him. 'I'll go and get my bag. I'll stay at the Hart tonight, and go back to town tomorrow. Mother can stay with me over Christmas.'

'Oh?' he said. 'And what about me?'

'You'll have the whole house to yourself,' she said. 'Bring one back from Portsmouth. Live a little, Nigel.' She kissed him. 'Thank you for telling me. It cancels out the other. You're forgiven.' She moved away from him. 'Who was my real mother?'

'We don't know,' he said. 'Not even a name.'

'Good,' she said. 'Then I can choose my own.'

And she ran swiftly up the stairs.

Ambrose Calvin alias Jake Barnes

_____ 1 _____

The road in which he lived was rarely walked. For here were the big houses with acres of garden; with tennis-courts and swimming-pools; with wrought-iron gates and long drives and Mercedes and Rovers and Alfa Romeos in garages large enough to shelter any number of refugees. And so it was the cars that travelled the road: that took retired admirals and the directors of chain-stores and scrap-yards, and those with inherited wealth, to their companies or their reunions, or to the golf-course, or to shareholders' meetings.

Calvin was not of their number. He rented a small cottage, built for a gardener who, fired by the affluence of lesser men, had left to start a mower-repair business. The cottage stood halfway up the road, hemmed in by poplar trees, and on stormy nights it rode the wind like a lifeboat.

And so the road had not been cleared. Like Crusoe he trod a white, yet-unmarked shore: Friday fled away to a tax-haven. He ploughed on through complete silence; and at the end of every drive, huge Christmas-trees glittered.

Some attempt had been made to clear the small path to the cottage, but he had to force the gate into a thick shelf of snow before he could enter.

And then they were on him.

He had not yet accustomed himself to fatherhood. He was still profoundly astonished that he had helped to bring these two shouting, leaping, hair-flying beings into existence: into a world that, for all its inhumanity and despair and corruption, was still there to be won over, to be savoured and endured, and shaped. They launched themselves upon him – the boy aged seven and the girl aged five – and he had to acknowledge, with a smile, the Dickensian scene: the snow, the father home from town, the welcoming faces of the children, the mother standing in the doorway, behind her the sparkling, necessary tree.

'What have you got?' said Mark, punching Calvin's pockets. 'Where is it?'

'What have you brought us?' said Rosemary, attacking the briefcase.

He laughed, bundled them up in his arms, and carried them to the open door. They wriggled like fish, their voices sharp as knives in the cold air.

'What have you got for us?' they cried.

'Nothing,' he said. He kissed his wife, and lowered the children to the floor. He closed the door. 'Nothing at all.'

They looked up at him. Some of the light went from Mark's face, but Rosemary still believed in routine.

'You have, you have!' she cried.

'I did, but we used it on the train,' he said. 'And it's Sunday and nothing's open.'

'I've got some chocolate in the kitchen,' said Hilda Calvin, a once plump woman now made angular with childbearing and rearing, her hair a smooth black helmet about a face that was all eyes, which once were trusting.

'You said you didn't,' said Mark.

'I know,' she said. 'But I have. Share it between you. Second drawer. Go on.'

'You haven't got anything, *really*, Dad?' he said.

'No. Tomorrow.'

They raced off to the kitchen. The door slammed back, and Hilda winced.

'How was it?' she said, helping him off with his coat.

'Quite an experience,' he said. 'I could sleep for a week.'

Rosemary came running back.

'Mark's got more than me!' she said.

Hilda sighed.

'Mark . . .!' she called.

Calvin grinned and walked into the living-room. He was home.

He opened his eyes. Beside him, on a low table, was the coffee he had not touched. He stretched his arms, rubbed his sleeves, and reached for the poker. And then he saw the time.

'Hilda!' he called.

There was a pause, and then she answered from the kitchen. 'Coming!'

But he stood up and went to her. As he passed the bottom of the stairs a door opened above him.

'Is Daddy awake now?' called Rosemary. 'Can we come down?'

'No, I am not awake!' shouted Calvin. 'Stay where you are.'

He went into the kitchen.

209

'Is that steak?' he said. '*Fillet* steak?'

'Yes,' she said. 'I went and got it after you phoned from Waterloo. And mushrooms and broccoli and . . .'

'It's nearly one o'clock,' he said.

'I didn't want to wake you,' she said. 'I told the horrors to be quiet, on pain of death. God knows what they're doing up there.' She put her arms around his shoulders. 'Feel better?'

'I'm still half-asleep.'

'Hungry?'

'I could eat fillet steak,' he said: 'any time.'

'Good,' she said. She pressed against him and looked into his face. 'So you've made it. At last.'

'What?'

'You know what.' she said. 'How much?'

'Don't you want to know how I almost froze to death in that train?' he said. 'How I climbed through drifts to bring back the supplies? How I . . .'

'Not now,' she said. 'You're home, and you look relatively unharmed. How much?'

He knew it would come to this. It was what he had been dreading from the time of the rescue; the only thing that had filled his thoughts on the long walk from the station. He looked into the face of a woman he knew had waited too long, and was tired of waiting. Her lips stayed on a half-smile as she prepared herself for the ending of one life and the start of another.

'Well?' she said.

'There are snags,' he said.

He felt her body tense and grow hard. Her arms were still about his shoulders, but they no longer gripped. She took them away, and moved back.

'Potatoes in their jackets?' she said.

'There are snags, but nothing we can't discuss.'

'Shall I do jacket-potatoes?' she said.

'Yes.'

'Thank you.'

'Look, Hilda . . .'

She turned from the table and her voice was fierce.

'Is there any money, Ambrose?'

'There's some offered, but . . .'

'But there are snags.'

'Yes.'

'There always are, aren't there?'

'Don't you want to hear how it went?'

She folded her arms.

'You phoned from Waterloo, yes? You told me you had sold the film rights, yes? Has anything happened since then? Have they withdrawn the offer?'

'No.'

'How much was it?'

In the pause they heard something fall in the playroom, and Rosemary cried out.

'Forty thousand,' he said, and the figure sounded astronomical in the small, over-heated kitchen. But she still stayed hard and unyielding as rock.

'Dollars or pounds?' she said.

'Pounds.'

'They've offered you forty thousand pounds.' It was a statement, not a question.

'Yes.'

Rosemary was crying on the stairs.

'Hadn't we better see . . .?' he said, moving to the door.

'Leave her,' said Hilda.

'I'll just go and make certain she's . . .'

Rosemary had cut her finger. It was not deep, but there was enough blood to scare a child. He picked her up and took her into the kitchen.

'Get a plaster, will you?' he said.

She was coating the steak with flour.

'You know where they are,' she said.

He washed the cut and pressed home the plaster.

'All right now?' he said.

'It hurts,' she said.

'Not for long,' he said. 'Now, you go upstairs again. Mummy and I are talking.'

'I don't want to,' said Rosemary. 'I want to stay here with you.'

'You can't,' he said. 'Go and see if there's anything on television. There might be a cartoon.'

She went reluctantly. He put his hands on his wife's waist.

'Want to hear about it?'

She shook her head.

'I went out and bought the steak,' she said. 'And the broccoli. And some wine. Remember wine? I thought it was here, at last. You

211

sounded so . . . uplifted. I don't want to hear any more.'

'Look,' he said: 'I'll tell you exactly what happened . . .'

Rosemary came back.

'There's only a man talking,' she said. She swung herself on to a stool. 'I want to stay with you two. Mark made me cut my finger.'

Calvin rested his jaw on his wife's shoulder.

'Later?' he said. 'Tell you about it later?'

'You've been telling me about it for twelve years,' she said. She began to pound the steak with a wooden spoon.

'What's Mummy doing to that meat?' said Rosemary.

'Beating the hell out of it,' said Calvin.

_____ 2 _____

Later that day, in the evening, the children in bed an hour, they sat in separate armchairs, facing the fire which was the only light.

'Don't drink any more of that,' he said.

She stayed the bottle over the glass.

'Why?'

'You won't have enough for a toast.'

She poured some wine into the glass, and put the bottle back on the table. She settled back, still not looking at him.

'So tell me,' she said.

'A man died on the train,' he said. 'In our carriage.'

'I'm talking about money,' she said, and her voice was very calm. 'We'll talk about death later.'

'He was an art-teacher,' he said. 'Given his last lesson. Packing it in to paint full-time. Then he had a heart attack. Finished.'

'Other ships are lost at sea,' she said.

'You used to understand.'

Still looking into the fire, she said:

'Did I? Convince me.'

'I thought . . . what a waste. That he should go like that. I thought of myself. I thought about a kind of personal integrity. That sounds pretentious . . .'

'Tell me about the money,' she said.

'Christ!'

'The cheque for the coal has bounced,' she said. 'Tell me about art.'

212

'Bounced?'

'Forty thousand times,' she said.

'All right,' he said. 'I went there. We had lunch. They want to change the location to the States.'

She turned from her chair and looked at him.

'The location of the book?'

'Yes. From Northumberland to Georgia.'

'Could you do the script?'

'Are you listening to what I'm saying?' he said. 'Did it get through to you? Northumberland to *Georgia*.'

'So? You've always wanted to go to the States.'

'Look,' he said, patiently: 'you read the book, right? You checked the proofs, right? You know the atmosphere, what I was trying to say . . .'

'No,' she said.

He was appalled.

'What?'

'We're not on the same wavelength, Ambrose. I'm tired of atmosphere, tired of making do. I'm thirty-seven, and I haven't had a holiday since the honeymoon. If you can call it a honeymoon. Have you seen what I have to wear? We haven't a car . . .'

'You knew what I was when you married me.'

'I thought it would improve. Tell me: what are the snags?'

'You don't see Georgia as one?'

It was her turn to be appalled.

'You don't mean you'd turn down forty thousand pounds because the plot's shifted to the States? If you're telling me that . . .' She shook her head. '*Are* you?'

'Can you see it transposed to the American South?'

'What does it matter, Ambrose? What does it matter if it's shifted to *Ethiopia*? The book's still on the shelf in the library. Do you know what we could *do* with forty thousand pounds?'

'Can you see *War and Peace* transposed to Canada?'

'You're not Tolstoy,' she said. 'Although you have some of his less disarming features.'

'You've been reading the Sunday supplements again.'

She drank the wine and put the empty glass next to the bottle. She turned and faced him fully, and it was the face and the voice of a stranger.

'Was that the only snag?' she said.

'No. They had their own scriptwriter.'

'We expected that,' she said, dismissing it. 'And . . .?'

'They don't want Stanhope to break. They don't want him . . . carted off.'

'What do they want?'

'They want him to hand over the land to Frederick. They want him to depart, so help me, *a man of integrity*. Brady's own words. He's the producer . . .'

'You told me. It has its points. I was sorry that Stanhope *did* break in the end. He was too strong a man to go down that easily . . .'

Calvin was in despair.

'You, too?' he said.

'Have you signed anything?' she said.

'Not yet. I wanted to talk it over with you first. That's a laugh. I agreed to phone Weaver over the weekend.'

'To say what?'

'Yes or no.'

'You mean you think you have a choice?'

'We always have a choice. It's when we're dead that we haven't.'

'But we're not dead,' she said. 'And we're broke. I walked on air yesterday, even with you stuck in the snow. I thought: at last we can have a *real* Christmas. The kids . . .

'The cash wouldn't come that quickly,' he said.

'With forty thousand to come, the bank would be happy to increase the overdraft, and you know it, Ambrose.' She came off her chair, and rested her arms on his knees. She looked up at him, and she was still a stranger. She had changed, undetected, as he had written book after book. 'You know you haven't got a choice, don't you?'

'Have you *never* understood?' he said. 'Have you never been with me?'

'I've given you two children, I've cooked your meals, I've ironed your shirts, and I've watched you live in your own world,' she said. 'Now I want you to understand mine. I want mine . . . enlarged. Do you understand *that*? Forty thousand would be the beginning.'

'Or the end.'

'Oh, don't be so bloody *wet*!' she said, and sat back on her heels. 'I can't see how . . .'

The phone rang in the hall.

214

'That'll be for me,' she said. 'Louise promised to call about taking me to Guildford.'

'Good old two-car Louise,' he said.

'Don't knock what you can't supply,' she said, and went out of the room.

The fire shifted and a piece of coal fell burning into the grate. He put it back with the tongs.

She came back.

'It's for you,' she said.

'Who is it?'

'Weaver,' she said.

Calvin stood in the cold, shadowy hall and lifted the phone.

'Hallo, Mark,' he said.

'Hallo, old son!' The agent's voice was bright. 'How was your journey back?'

'You mean you didn't hear?'

'Hear what, old son?'

'I was stuck in the snow for nearly thirty hours.'

'In the train? You *weren't*! Where?'

'Between Milford and Witley.'

'I heard about some trains being held up. I thought you'd be home and dry before that. Thirty hours . . . *well*! How are you?'

'Fine. Tired.'

'You have a good rest. We can't afford to lose you, Ambrose.'

'No.'

'Have you talked it over with Hilda?'

'Doing so.'

'Why you had to do that, I don't know. I never ask Pam about anything.'

'Just as long as the fillet-steak's on the table, right?'

'Right. But you're your own man, Ambrose. Brady was quite taken with you, you know that? Could be a door opening there, old son.' He paused. 'Well, you're going ahead, of course . . .'

Calvin lifted his head and looked down the hall. Black night filled the glass panels of the front door, but, as he watched, a car passed smoothly by, headlamps blazing on the snow-thick poplars.

'Ambrose . . .?'

'Yes.'

'I said: you're going ahead, of course, aren't you?'

Silence.

'Ambrose . . .?'

Calvin stood, looking down the hall. The night had returned. In the living-room Hilda had switched on the radio. Calvin heard a snatch of music. He was still trying to recall the composer when Weaver spoke again:

'Ambrose, are you there?'

Anita Silverman

1

As the train drew slowly away from the platform, heading into a country suddenly and surprisingly lit by a white sun, she saw her son-in-law emerge from the booking-hall and walk quickly towards her. She put down the suitcase and stood still, and watched him come. He was not Jewish, but the world was never perfect, and he loved Carol – which, in the end, was all that mattered. He was casually but smartly-dressed, looking like something out of a skiing-brochure: the bright yellow windcheater vibrant against dull green paint and chalked notices still full of warning.

He came to her and kissed her. He stood back and looked beyond her.

'Where's Simon?' he said.

'Will you take the case?' she said, and walked with him. 'You have the car?'

'Of course,' he said. 'Nothing wrong, is there?'

'Apart from everything, you mean?' she said.

They walked through the warm breath of the hall, and into the cold forecourt where the snow was piled high. The car was very new: a long, tan station-wagon.

'Some people have the money,' she said.

He started the engine and a cassette began to play, too loudly.

'Sorry,' he said. The throbbing music ended.

'Thank you,' she said.

Resting his gloved hands on the steering-wheel he turned that dark face to her.

'Something happen to Simon?'

'You can drive away,' she said. 'I'll tell you as we go.'

The engine was a whisper as they took the small rise and turned to the left. She looked away from the full ash-tray.

'It reeks of cigarette-smoke already, Andrew,' she said. 'You'll have to stop, once the baby's here. It'd choke to death in here. How's Carol?'

'Looking forward to seeing you both,' he said. He waited. But she did not speak again until they were free of the High Street and heading north.

'Simon is dead,' she said.

She was not prepared for his reaction. The car veered sharply, caught a bank of snow, ploughed through it, and bounced back to the centre of the gritted road. He stopped a few yards further on, and turned the ignition-key. He shifted around in the seat, his good-looks muddied.

'What?' he said.

Saying the words had weighted the stone in her body. She pressed it down, but the effort strangled her voice. She coughed, clearing it.

'Simon had a heart-attack on the train. His body was taken off at Witley, and is going home. That's all I can say. At the moment.'

He went to put his arms around her.

'Don't,' she said. 'Please don't.'

He rested his hands on hers.

'I thought something was up,' he said softly. 'It's usually he that phones. And you were too . . . abrupt. Poor old you: stuck there all that time, and then that happening. When did it happen?'

'I don't want to talk about it, Andrew. Can you leave it . . . until later? I'm more concerned about Carol. Her reaction. How is she?'

'Fat as a capon,' he said. He pursed his lips, reached for a cigarette, but decided against it. 'This is going to shake her. Christ, it is.'

'That's what I mean,' she said. 'At this time.'

'Shall we tell her something else?' he said. 'Until the baby's here? Say he . . .'

'No,' she said. 'It can't harm the baby. She's a sensible girl.'

'She worships Simon. Worshipped.'

'I know. My mother used to say something always happens at Christmas.'

'But how are *you*?' he said.

'I don't know,' she said. 'Numb. That's all. It's the baby I'm thinking about. Simon's gone, and everything that was his. It's the baby.'

'Of course,' he said. 'Do you mind if I smoke?'

'I do,' she said. 'Find a little strength from somewhere, Andrew. We all use too many crutches.'

He re-started the car, pulled away from the bank of snow, and drove on, slowly. Another car passed in a whirl of white exhaust-smoke, dipping down towards black trees. He followed, and the smoke faded.

'It's due any time now, you know?' he said. 'Thank God we aren't far from the Cottage Hospital. They're all ready for her.'

'Good,' she said. She looked out at the far, white hills. 'It was summer, last time. When we were here. That hot day down near those stables. Remember? The brown horse that chewed Simon's sleeve? What a beautiful hot day that was.'

'I was only saying yesterday that winter was beautiful, too,' said her son-in-law. 'The frost on the spiders'-webs . . .'

'No,' she said. 'Summer is beautiful.' She nodded. 'More beautiful.'

He stopped again, a few hundred yards from the house, but kept the engine running.

'What do we do?' he said. His fingers beat a soft tattoo on the wheel. 'How do we . . .'

'We sit her down, and we tell her,' said Anita. 'We tell her . . . calmly, and with a great deal of love. And care. Times like these come. No one can dodge them. She's my daughter. She'll . . . accept it. Today she'll accept it. Later . . .' She shrugged. 'But we'll be around. Be there.'

He was scared; and now he was grateful.

'You'll stay?' he said. 'I mean – for as long as you can?'

'There's the funeral – eventually,' she said. 'There'll have to be that. But, yes, you can depend on me, Andrew. I'll stay as long as I can.'

He kissed her again.

'Thank you,' he said. 'If my own parents were around . . .'

'But they're not, Andrew,' she said; 'and we have to do the best we can.' She buttoned her coat and squeezed her arms around herself. 'Off you go now.'

Carol was enormous in a flowered robe that reached to pink slippers. She stood in the doorway of the new house in the new, carefully-planned estate, and looked over her mother's head to the empty path and the empty car. The smile left her round face, and she leaned, perhaps fell, against spotless gloss paint.

'I know,' she said. 'I knew.'

Her mother pushed her gently into the house. The heavy girl slumped against a fragile, thin-legged table, and tipped it forward. Anita steadied it. Carol's moon-face loomed towards her.

'There was a report . . . on the radio,' she said. 'About a man having died . . . on the train. They didn't give his name. Your voice was so strange on the phone. And I thought . . .' Her face began to crumple: air going from a balloon. 'It was Dad, wasn't it?'

'Yes,' said Anita. 'It was. Let's go in here, and sit down.'

Carol turned for the room; but instead of going in, paused, cried out, and fell towards the stairs. And, too heavy for her mother's restraining hands, struck the carpet, rolled over on her side, moaned, and drew her legs close to her swollen body.

2

Twenty minutes later, Anita and her son-in-law sat in the waiting-room of the Cottage Hospital. They sat close to each other, but did not speak. Somewhere in the small red-brick building Carol was giving birth, and her mother and her husband were alone in their own thoughts, while nurses passed the open door and smiled; or a far baby cried; or a young doctor shepherded a new mother and her share of immortality into a cold world and a waiting car.

Anita was remembering her own daughter's birth. It had been a Caesarean, and the baby, spared that forceful thrust into the light, had come smooth and pale and very beautiful to her bedside in that ward in Hammersmith. It was a perfect moment in an imperfect world, and Simon had sealed it, bending down and marvelling. Simon . . .

Andrew was dying for a cigarette. The need was so great, he could almost taste it on his tongue. When Carol had fallen, he had feared the baby might be harmed; but she was in capable hands. You could only trust . . .

'How long, do you think?' he said.

'Not long,' said his mother-in-law. 'She was almost having it in the car.'

'Was she?' he said. 'God, what would I have done?'

'Better than waiting hours,' she said. 'You men don't know you're alive. No periods, no giving birth.'

'Just the worry of providing,' he said.

'You don't look too bad on it.'

'I wish I had some of your strength,' he said. 'You've been through a lot.'

She was silent.

'Mind if I get a bit of fresh air?' he said.

'Say what you mean,' she said: 'you mean, do I mind if you go out there and smoke.'

'True,' he said.

'The last one before the baby comes,' she said. 'And I mean that.'

'Then I'll savour it,' he said. 'I'll take my time.'

'You won't,' she said. 'Have a few puffs, and come back. They might call us any minute.'

'Okay,' he said. He stood up and went out into the entrance-hall. It was full of flowers. He opened the front door, stepped out into the path fronting the winter garden, and closed the door behind him. He leaned against a tree and took out the pack and his lighter. He lit up, drawing that beautiful taste into his lungs. He looked at what remained: about eight. He considered them; then closed the packet and put it in his overcoat pocket.

He thought of his own parents, both dead of cancer within a year of each other. He thought particularly of his mother: how she would have loved a grandchild. He shook his head: life was a bastard, but it had to be lived – once here, you were stuck with it. He looked up at the windows of the first floor: was Carol there, or *there*? To have a son . . .

He finished the cigarette to the end, and tossed the stub into the snow. It fizzed for an instant, and turned black.

She was sitting in the same place, her head back against the wall, her eyes closed. A doctor was bending over her.

'Mrs Silverman?'

Her eyelids flickered.

'Is it time?' she said, half-standing.

'No,' he said. 'Would you like a cup of tea? Or coffee? What about you, Mr Morris?'

'Coffee would be fine,' said Andrew. 'Thanks.'

'Yes, coffee,' said Anita.

'Righto,' said the doctor, and went away.

Andrew sat down again.

'Better now?' said Anita.

'Yes.'

'I can smell it on you,' she said. 'Horrible habit. Did you not want to *be* with Carol, to see your child born?'

'Good God, no!' he said. 'I could never stand that. I'm not the type. I'd rather keep my illusions. I'm a romantic. I saw it once on TV. Or half-saw it, through my fingers. No, thanks. I'm trying to avoid thinking about nappies, too.'

'You'll learn,' she said, almost with satisfaction. 'We never had an unbroken night's sleep for the first two years with Carol.'

'That's right,' he said: 'cheer me up.'

She patted his hand.

'It's worth it all,' she said. 'All the worry and the little illnesses and the sleepless nights. To form another life. To point it the way it should go; to watch it develop . . .'

The coffee came, and it was hot and strong, and good. They had almost finished it, when another doctor entered. He was sweating slightly – there were dark patches on his shirt – but he was smiling.

'Congratulations,' he said. 'It's a fine boy.'

They were allowed into the ward. Other mothers slept or knitted or read magazines.

Carol lay in the third bed, her hair stuck to her forehead. She half-rose, but Andrew pushed her gently back. He kissed her, and then stood aside for Anita.

'You have a son,' said her mother. 'Aren't you clever?'

'I wish Dad . . .'

'Yes, but don't worry about that.'

'I saw him. The baby. They've taken him away to clean him up.' She looked at her husband. 'They said it was an easy birth, but it still felt like pushing out a football. You don't know how lucky you are.'

'So your mother says.'

Anita sat on the chair by the bed.

'Have you a name?' she said.

'Yes,' said Andrew, standing on the other side of the bed and holding his wife's hand. 'David.'

'David?' said Anita. 'Just *David*?'

'Yes,' he said.

'Did you agree to that, Carol?'

'Well, yes . . . It was Andrew's choice, and I . . .'

'Oh, not *David*,' said her mother. She took her daughter's other hand, and leaned closer to that pale, washed-out face. 'Could we have . . . Simon? After your father? Now that he's gone? Simon?'

Carol looked at Andrew.

'Couldn't we?'

'Well, I'd rather we . . .'

'You could have Simon David,' said Anita. 'Simon David Morris. How about that?'

Carol pressed her mother's hand.

'Yes. Yes, Andrew? Now that Dad's gone . . .'

He was unsure, but nodded.

'Yes, all right.'

'And I could be of such help to you both,' said Anita. 'There's nothing to keep me in London now.'

'Oh, you're to come and live with us, isn't she, Andrew? I mean, we have heaps of room, and . . .'

'For a time, yes,' he said. 'Certainly.'

'Oh, for always,' said Carol. 'Permanent baby-sitter and nanny.'

'Which I'd be happy to be,' said Anita. 'I . . .'

Andrew stood up.

'I think this might be him,' he said.

A smiling nurse was approaching the bed, carrying a white bundle edged with blue. Carol reached out her arms, and the baby was given to her. Anita and Andrew leaned over as Carol pulled the folds from beneath the boy's chin. To Andrew the child looked like raw meat, the open mouth too red, too embryo-like. A thin cry wavered, and all the heads of all the mothers turned. To Anita it was life instead of death, a beginning and not an end.

'May I have him?' she said.

Carol felt the baby taken from her arms.

Anita sat on the chair, and stroked the baby's face with one finger.

'Hallo, my love,' she said. 'We're going to make you the greatest painter in the world, aren't we? Yes, we are. That's what we're going to do, Simon. The greatest painter in the whole wide world.'

Sergeant Gordon Mason

1

There was a large mirror set into the snow-ridged wall of Petersfield station, embossed with golden curlicues which advertised a firm of local estate-agents. He glimpsed his own reflection, and that of the departing train, as he walked through the slush of the platform towards the exit. He went back to confirm what he had seen. The train had gone now, and the background was one of drowned allotment-sheds and frosty rigging. Standing before these was a dishevelled man with bleary eyes, dressed in a second-hand military uniform: a sergeant's greatcoat with dull buttons; stained trousers with torn yellow piping; scuffed shoes with grey ripples of damp. He sighed, straightened his cap, and moved on.

A porter was warming his hands on a radiator. Beyond him the town stretched away, humanless.

'Got a brush?' said Mason.

The porter took his hands off the radiator, and held them around his face.

'Brush?' he said. 'You mean a broom?'

'Clothes-brush,' said Mason.

'Don't think so,' said the porter. He shouted at the man behind the glass. 'We got a clothes-brush, Tom?'

The man behind the glass shook his head, not lifting his eyes from his spread newspaper.

'Sorry, mate,' said the porter. 'No brush.'

Mason put down his suitcase, and put his hand inside his coat for his diary. He knew the address by heart, but still checked. He turned the dog-eared pages: the last days of the year.

'Eston Avenue, Petersfield,' he said. 'Know it?'

The porter whistled.

'You've got a way to go,' he said. 'Way over, it is. Big council estate. I don't know how you're going to get there.'

'Bus; taxi?'

'Buses are off the road,' said the porter. 'Sunday, and all. You might try Jeff's . . .'

'Jeff's?'

224

'Think Jeff's'll be open, Tom?' shouted the porter.

'Anything to make a few quid,' said Tom, again not lifting his head.

'Taxi firm,' said the porter. 'Go down the hill, first turning on your left. Little office. He might be open.'

'How long to walk to Eston?' said Mason.

'You'd never make it,' said the porter. 'The wolves'd get you before then.'

'I'll just have to take that chance.'

'Ain't they got a car?' said the porter: 'the friends you're going to?'

Mason picked up his suitcase.

'They're not my friends,' he said.

*   *   *

Jeff's was a private house with a wooden shack to the side. Pinned to the planks were two posters edged with graffiti. *TAXI. 24-Hr Service. Airports – Weddings. Any Distance – Any Time.*

There was no sign of life. The house seemed withdrawn into itself: none of the rooms had curtains, and the dark interiors were as unmoving as the street littered with ditched cars. He cupped his hand against the window of the shack. There was a table and a chair, a telephone and a notepad.

He stepped back into the street and looked up at the house. Then he walked through the unmarked snow of the path, mounted the three steps, and used the black, lion's-head knocker.

Waiting there, the suitcase between his shoes, his hands deep in his pockets, he felt a cold wind come down the street. Ragged bushes either side of the steps clattered their frosty leaves. He turned up his collar and tightened it around his throat.

No one came to answer the door. He would simply have to walk. Or hitch a lift. But the town seemed dead.

He began to go back down the steps when a man came around the side of the house.

'Who'd you want?'

Mason looked into a stubbled face, into thick-lensed glasses that magnified the eyes. Looked at a shapeless body in a crumpled polo-necked sweater, baggy green corduroys and black, unlaced boots. One finger of a huge hand marked a place in a newspaper. All over Petersfield, men were reading the Sundays.

'Jeff's,' said Mason.

'You're looking at him,' said the man.

'I want a taxi.'

'What you want and what you get are two different things,' said Jeff. 'Taxi? In these conditions?'

'Okay,' said Mason, coming down the last of the steps. 'Forget it.'

'Where'd you want to go?' said Jeff.

'Eston Avenue.'

The man folded the paper and put it under his arm. He rubbed his chin.

'Deserter, are you?' he said.

Mason laughed.

'No.'

'You look it,' said Jeff. 'I was in the MPs, myself. I'd have taken you in on sight.'

'I was in one of the stranded trains,' said Mason. 'I have to get to Eston Avenue.'

'I'll do a favour for an Army man,' said Jeff. 'Cost you twelve quid.'

Mason did not argue.

'Okay,' he said.

Jeff felt in his trousers and took out some keys.

'Cortina, over there,' he said. 'Open it up. I'll go and get my coat.'

Mason took the keys. Jeff's hand was heavily tattooed: weighted with blue hearts and snakes.

'I'd like the cash now,' said Jeff. 'You don't look like you've got *two* quid, let alone twelve.'

Still holding the keys in his right hand, Mason took out his wallet.

'Three fives,' he said.

Jeff smiled, showing neglected teeth.

'Just cover the tip,' he said. 'All right?'

'I bet you were a great MP,' said Mason.

'The best,' said Jeff. 'It's a hard world.'

The car had been difficult to start. But at last it roared into life, shaking on its springs. Jeff moved the cigar to the corner of his mouth.

'That's my baby,' he said. 'Old faithful.'

The wheels bumped over the hard ruts and hit the grit of the

226

road. The interior began to warm up, the heated air man-made and tasting of metal. The town showed its desolation in street after street. Only the smoke from chimneys showed that some survived.

'What you doing over Eston Avenue?' said Jeff.

'People to see.'

'Staying over Christmas?'

'No.'

Jeff glanced at him.

'Want bringing back?'

'I don't know. It depends . . . I could phone you. I don't know . . .'

'Petersfield 2793,' said Jeff. 'Not if it's dark, though.'

Mason finished writing the number in his diary.

'It won't be dark,' he said. 'I won't be that long.'

'Always at your service,' said Jeff. 'For an Army man. Rain or shine.'

'For fifteen quid,' said Mason.

The ash fell from Jeff's nodding cigar.

'Right,' he said.

It was not a great distance, but the slow, careful progress of the car made it seem so. They were in a maze of identical streets: long, curving ropes of red-brick Council houses. Only the colours of the doors were different, but the winter and the snow had tamed even these: the tones subdued, waiting for Spring.

Jeff idled the engine on a corner.

'That's it,' he said. 'Eston Avenue. What number?'

'It doesn't matter about the number,' said Mason. 'I'll get out here.'

'It's a bloody long avenue,' said the taxi-driver.

But Mason had already opened the door.

'If I phone you,' he said, 'I'll meet you here. Right?'

Jeff leaned from the wheel, those strange, magnified eyes staring.

'I think you *are* a deserter, you know that?'

'I'll see you here,' said Mason. 'If I call.'

He slammed the door, stepped back on to the pavement, and watched the car reverse into a side street. It pulled away, and then there was a great silence.

Mason opened his suitcase, fitted the shells into the magazine, closed the suitcase; and set out for number forty-two.

227

2

Jeff had been right: it *was* a long avenue. And Mason had started at the wrong end. But the numbers fell back with every step, and as he neared what had filled his thoughts for the past ten days, his numbed, gloveless right hand burned on the hard handle of his suitcase. And with every step that sweet rage came back, needing no prompting or further fuelling – none but the constant memory of that shape under the sheet; and those bare, vulnerable, splayed feet.

He had not planned a killing: he had not seen beyond the house and the face of a stranger. He would wait upon his own rage, his own fire, the voice of his blood. Perhaps he had come only to terrify – but, if that were so, he would do it more than adequately. He found himself trembling, but not with cold. In truth, he was not aware now of snow or frost, or the now cloud-haunted sun. His eyes moved from fencepost to fencepost: the brass figures and the plastic figures that eventually declared four and six; four and four; and, at last . . . four and two.

He stopped and put his left hand on the gate. He looked carefully at the house – as if he saw it for the first or the last time. It was the same as every other house in the avenue. The same division of snow-covered garden, the same bricks; the same white, looping net-curtains. The door was painted blue, but appeared battered, as though kicked at, or attacked. Smoke rose slowly from a chimney, wavering to nothing.

He pushed open the gate.

Close to, the door appeared even more marked. There were deep dents, fringed with splinters, in the paintwork above the step. From inside the house there came a confusion of noise, fluctuating in volume, back and forth: shouts and cries and snatches of music and sudden heavy thuds that shook the glass panel above the letter-box.

He rang the bell. It was over-loud, as if designed to sound over a customary uproar. There was a lessening of the din behind the door; now only the music played – pounding out one of the week's Top Ten.

'Answer it, then!' a woman shouted.

A blurred figure appeared behind the glass, and the door opened.

Mason looked at a tall teenager in customary teenage uniform. The boy was tall and thin in a stained T-shirt which declared *Stones*

228

Rule OK? Behind him three other faces jostled to see who had come: younger children, two girls and a boy.

'Yeh?' said the youth.

The spicy smell of cooking was so strong that Mason stepped back, fearing suffocation.

'It's a soldier, Mum!' shouted one of the girls, and winked at Mason. 'Come in, Sarge.'

'What d'you want?' said the youth, barring the way.

'Jack Varley live here?' said Mason.

'What if he does?' said the boy.

A woman pushed to the front.

'Who is it?' she said, burdened with the season, the weather, the cooking, the noise of a house full of children. 'Letting all the cold in, you are.'

'It's a soldier, Mum,' said the smaller boy.

'I can see it is,' she said, wearily. Once she had been pretty in a blonde and brassy way, something to make the boys' heads turn, the wolf-whistles sounding, fingers itching to pinch that tight arse, find those melon breasts. But now the hair was tinted purple and the eyes were hooded by large, false lashes; and the breasts were girded and high, the red belt tight over a stomach gone to fat. 'What d'you want?' she said.

The faces craned around her.

'Asking after Dad, wasn't you, Sarge?' said the girl. 'I go for soldiers, don't I, Mum?'

'Oh, be quiet, Tracy,' said the woman. She pulled a shred of tobacco off her tongue, 'Jack's not here. Does he know you?'

'No. I was told to call. By a friend.'

'About a job?' she said. 'He's out on one now. He's full up till Christmas. This weather's made a difference.'

'It's urgent,' said Mason.

'They're all urgent,' said Mrs Varley. 'You can ask him, if you like. He's round his brothers'.'

'Where's that?'

'Ask him in for dinner,' said Tracy.

'Go inside, Trace,' said Mrs Varley. 'All of you – go inside. It's nothing to do with you.'

They did not move.

'He's round Derby Road,' said the woman. 'Number nine. Know Derby Road, do you?'

'No,' said Mason, dreading another long trudge.

Mrs Varley stepped out of the house, shivered, hugged her arms, and stepped back.

'Go down there,' she said, pointing to her left. 'Second turning. His van will be outside the house.'

'Thank you,' he said.

'That's all right,' she said. He sensed a stirring of interest in that puffy face. 'Anything to oblige.'

'Oh, Mum,' said Tracey: 'you are awful.'

There was a black van outside the third house in Derby Road. Its roof held a layer of snow, but the sides were clear, saying *JACK VARLEY LTD. Building Contractor. No job too small. The Complete Professional.*

A ladder rested against the wall of the house, and a man was perched at the top, hammering back a section of guttering. Below him, holding the ladder steady, was another, older man.

As Mason approached the van, the man at the top of the ladder ceased hammering. He tested the gutter.

'Got any more peg nails there, Brian? Need about three more.'

'You don't need any more,' said Brian. 'Christ alive! – you'll knock the sodding wall in.'

'All right,' said the other. 'It's your wall. Have it your way.'

By this time Mason was standing beside the van, and the man at the top of the ladder saw him. He looked at Mason silently and long. So silently and so long that Brian turned. They both looked at the soldier.

'Want something, friend?' said Brian. His breath hung in the air.

'Jack Varley,' said Mason.

Brian looked up.

'Man wants you, Jack.'

Varley did not move from the top of the ladder. He tucked the hammer into his jacket and rested against the struts.

'What can I do for you?'

'Can you come down?' said Mason. He lifted the suitcase and held it against his chest.

'What's it about?' said Varley. His black hair stirred in the wind. A gypsy face: attractive to women. To Barbara? To throw herself away for that? Mason forced his trembling body rigid.

'Come down, will you?' he said.

'Tell him what it's about,' said Brian. 'He can hear you. Doing a job, he is.'

230

Mason looked up and down the silent, empty road. He swiftly sprang the locks of his suitcase, reached inside, took up the gun and the magazine, dropped the case, and made the Sterling ready. He leaned against the side of the van and pointed the gun first at Varley, and then at Brian. Then back again, to the top of the ladder.

'Come down,' he said.

'Bloke's a nutter,' said Brian.

But Varley was very calm. He leaned his face against the ladder.

'Barbara's brother?' he said.

'Yes,' said Mason. 'Come down, quickly.'

'Been half-expecting you,' said Varley. He pushed himself off the ladder and started slowly down. 'It's all right, Brian.'

'All *right*?' said Brian. 'You know him?'

'Heard of him,' said Varley.

'You!' said Mason to Brian. 'Come and pick up this case, and close it.'

Brian looked at Varley, who was now almost on the trampled snow of the garden.

'Do what he says, Brian.'

Brian came down the path, crossed the pavement, picked up the suitcase and closed the lid. He was dark like Varley, but heavier.

'Anyone in the house?' said Mason.

'No,' said Varley, too quickly.

'Open the van,' said Mason.

'What?' said Brian.

'Open the back of the van,' said Mason. '*Move!*'

Brian opened it, and stood aside. Mason looked at the clutter of dust-sheets and buckets.

'Get in, Varley,' he said. 'And *you* – get in the cab, behind the wheel. Don't try anything.'

'Don't try anything, Brian,' said Varley, bending his head to enter the rear of the van. 'Do what Batman says.'

Brian went to the front of the van and opened the door of the cab. Mason, his back to the house, pushed at Varley.

'Hurry up!'

Satisfied, he began to carefully follow . . .

And something hard and heavy and brutal rocked his skull and shook his brain, and he fell into a bruise-coloured night that swiftly turned black.

3

His cheek was resting on ice. It ached through his face, deadening every bone, freezing the blood. He opened his eyes. The light was too bright. He closed them again. His head hurt. He tried to speak, but all that he heard was a faint croak. He opened his eyes again, slowly. Grassblades had borders of frost. Never so near. Earth.

He turned his body. The forest turned with him, and the black soaring trees steadied, pointing to a completely white sky. A face came into view. A strange face. Face of a stranger. Who smiled.

'Wakey wakey, Sarge.'

He tried to sit up, but something shifted in his head, and he groaned. But he forced himself upright, and pushed himself back against a tree. His hand went to his scalp. There was a deep cut, his fingers bloodied. He looked about him. He was surrounded by trees. And watching him were three men, who smoked and smiled: Varley, Brian, and the stranger. The dark triplets.

'Another brother,' he said, and his voice was not his own. He steadied it. 'From behind.'

'Correct,' said Varley. 'Meet Graham.'

The stranger nodded.

'Hi,' he said. Smoke and breath drifted over his face, was funnelled away through the trees. He tugged the fur collar of his bomber-jacket about his chin. 'Saw it all from the front room, didn't I?'

Mason touched his bloodied hair again.

'What did you use?'

'Spanner,' said Graham. 'Hurt, does it?'

'Where are we?' said Mason.

'You're up the creek,' said Graham: 'that's where you are.'

'Not far away from home,' said Varley. 'Just outside the town. Going to use it, were you?'

'I don't know,' said Mason. 'You deserve it, you bastard. You know she was pregnant?'

Varley grinned at his brothers, and back again.

'That's the trouble with me,' he said. 'I hit the bell every time.'

'Come on, Jack,' said Brian. He beat his arms around his body. 'Finish it, and let's go.'

'How'd you find me, Sarge?' said Varley.

'I had to go through her things . . .'

'Which one was this?' said Graham.

'Show him your thumb,' said Varley.

'What?' said Graham.

'The thumb you haven't got,' said Varley.

Graham pulled off his left glove and held out his lopped hand. The scar looked raw.

'Sliced it off at the sawmill,' said Varley. 'Had to rush him to hospital, didn't we, Brian?' He looked from the scar to Graham's face. 'Remember the nurse in Casualty . . .?'

'*That* one?' said Graham. 'You pull that one? Out of your class, I would've said, Jack.'

'No woman is out of my class,' said Varley, irritated. 'They're all the same under their clothes. I can be very persuasive, when I like. I'll give you a few lessons when you're grown up, Graham.'

Mason used the thin trunk of the tree to lift himself. He closed his eyes against the stabbing pain in his head. When he opened them again, Varley was standing very near. Cold narrowed his face, but it was still handsome: the skin clear, the eyes bright.

'And where d'you think *you're* going?'

Mason was silent.

Varley came even nearer.

'No one comes looking for me, or my brothers, friend,' he said. ''Specially with a gun. Two rounds, only? One for me and one for you?'

'Two for you,' said Mason.

And leapt.

He had his hands around Varley's throat before the brothers could move. But move they did; and it was soon over.

The silent, methodical beating took less than a minute. They left him in the snow at the base of the tree. Gasping, he heard the van cough into life, and bounce into the road. Seconds later there was no sound at all: from engines or from animals or from winter-thin birds.

He lay there for a further minute, and then clawed at the tree. Standing now, he watched his own blood spot the snow between his shoes. Groaning, he still acknowledged the beauty of the contrast.

He swayed forward, and the slope made him almost run towards the road. Floundering, he fell on the verge. He grabbed handfuls of snow and pressed it into his face. It fell away, stained.

He made his slow, swaying progress along the road. No one passed him in all that staggering mile and a half. Turning as the road turned, he saw ahead of him a crossroads, a single house with a smoking chimney; and a telephone-box on a triangle of white earth.

He gathered all his strength; and then he was there. There was a small square mirror set among local numbers. He did not look into it. He found the number in his diary, and dialled. Used the coin.

'Jeff's. Sorry, no taxis today.'

'This . . .' Mason cleared his clotted throat. 'This is the sergeant.'

'Oh. Finished your business?'

Mason lifted a hand and touched a loose tooth.

'Yes,' he said. 'Could . . . could you come and get me?'

'I suppose so. Same fare. Same place?'

'No. I'm at . . .' He looked at the words below the mirror. 'I'm at a place called Holt. In the telephone-box at the crossroads.'

'What the hell are you doing out there?'

'Tell you later. How . . . how long will you be?'

'Fifteen, twenty minutes. Cost you another five, on top of the other.'

Mason looked at the tooth in his fingers. His tongue probed the gap in his mouth.

'I thought it might,' he said. 'I'll be here.'

He put down the telephone; and then, suddenly drained of strength, allowed himself to slide to the floor. He drew up his legs, wrapped his arms around them, and rested his forehead on his knees. But the blood in his nose made breathing difficult, and he lifted his face. He carefully tipped back his head until he felt it touch the glass; and then he closed his eyes.

He became aware of a soft slither of sound. Still with his head tilted back, he opened his eyes. Snow was falling again, lightly at first, then steadily.

Watching it fill the windows, he heard another, surprising sound; and listened to it.

A bloody, battered man, in a soaked army-greatcoat, sitting on the floor of a snow-caught, isolated telephone-box, head back, he listened to the sound, the growing noise, of his own laughter.